STARGÅTE
SG·1™

TWO ROADS

GEONN CANNON

FANDEMONIUM BOOKS

An original publication of Fandemonium Ltd, produced under license from MGM Consumer Products.

Fandemonium Books
United Kingdom
Visit our website: www.stargatenovels.com

STARGATE SG·1

METRO-GOLDWYN-MAYER Presents
RICHARD DEAN ANDERSON
in
STARGATE SG-1™
AMANDA TAPPING   CHRISTOPHER JUDGE
and MICHAEL SHANKS as Daniel Jackson
Executive Producers ROBERT C. COOPER   BRAD WRIGHT
MICHAEL GREENBURG   RICHARD DEAN ANDERSON
Developed for Television by BRAD WRIGHT & JONATHAN GLASSNER

WWW.MGM.COM

Print ISBN: 978-1-905586-64-6   Ebook ISBN: 978-1-80070-031-4

PROLOGUE

THE HEAD of the Royal Palace Guard didn't know who would be in charge of his punishment if he should fail, and he wasn't particularly interested in finding out any time soon. The only way to avoid the loss of his reputation would be handling this crisis with a modicum of panic and with as little fallout as he could muster. His name was Ellum Shedri, the fifth in a long line of men with that name who had proudly worn the golden helm of Grand Protector to the royal family's home. Their legacy would not be destroyed on his watch. Unfortunately the current invader was not one he could fight or hold back no matter how strong his army.

The Queen was in labor and the midwife was nowhere to be found.

Shedri reminded himself to remain calm and keep a level head as he moved through the corridors with hands balled into fists at his sides, jaw set, eyes locked firmly on the door directly ahead of him. Since early that morning the room had been the nucleus of frenzied activity, and even now he could hear the shouting and clatter within. They had prepared for this moment, but it was all happening much too early.

He pushed open the doors to the royal chamber and was immediately shouted at from the bed. He winced and froze where he was, turning slowly until he faced the most beloved woman in the land. Queen Indell was recumbent amid a sea of wrinkled linens, her lower half draped with a sheet and the globe of her belly rising up like a pearl presented in an oyster shell. The Queen's gorgeous features, so recently immortalized on the three-diref coin piece, were fixed in a rictus of pain as she experienced another contraction. Her blonde hair was plastered to her sweat-glistened skin, and her brown eyes locked onto him as soon as they opened again.

"Where is she?" the Queen demanded to know.

Shedri tried to speak but his voice was caught somewhere between his chest and lips. He made a handful of inarticulate sounds before the Queen shouted her question at him again.

"I apologize, but she is out of the palace, Your Highness," Shedri said as he finally found his voice. "There was an emergency outside of the palace walls, you see, a breach birth that required expert care. All attempts to contact her have failed. Had we only known that you would require her services today, we would never —"

The Queen bellowed again, cutting off his apologies. When the latest contraction ended, she grabbed the empty red teacup from her bedside table and hurled it at him. Since it would be unseemly to cringe in front of his Queen, Shedri allowed the cup to hit him square on the forehead.

"I will not have the royal midwife seeing to some peasant while the prince is being born! Bring her back! Bring her here this instant!"

"As you desire." Shedri bowed and quickly fled the room. Once he was outside he finally reached up and rubbed the sore spot on his forehead where he'd been hit by the cup. It would almost certainly bruise. He walked swiftly down the hall in the direction he'd just come, hoping one of the riders he'd sent out with the message had returned with the errant midwife. So far it seemed as if the damned midwife had fallen off the face of the planet as soon as she left the palace walls, but doing the impossible was his job.

He should have admonished the chief physician for letting the midwife go, but in truth the man couldn't have known what a situation it would create. That morning there had been no reason to anticipate the Prince would choose to arrive on this day, far ahead of schedule. Queen Indell wasn't scheduled to give birth for another season yet. The prince was announced to be a Solstice ruler, a revelation that had caused great joy to spread throughout the kingdom. Solstice rulers often brought wealth and prosperity, as well as long stretches of peace. Now they would have to accept a king born during the Aphelion. There could be riots.

A sentry was posted next to the exterior door. The man was attempting to look professional but he looked as harried as anyone in the palace. Shedri inadvertently knocked off the man's red cap when he grabbed the collar of his tunic. "Any news from the riders?"

"None, sir. There's been no signal that they've even spotted the caravan."

Shedri restrained himself before growling in frustration. If he couldn't calm his Lady's ire with the midwife's return, he would have to try another tactic. "Find the palace maid and ask her to bring the Queen another herbal drink. Perhaps it will soothe her majesty's anguish."

"Yes, sir."

He released the sentry and stepped out into the courtyard. Another step would have taken him through the portico into the Agora, but he stayed back so he could harness his thoughts. He watched the people, the citizens his Queen was sworn to protect. It was bazaar day, and the clusters of canvas storefronts stretched through the winding streets of the palace city and left only a narrow dirt path between their markets and the stone edifice of the palace. Shedri squinted in the sun as he watched the people moving to and fro, selling their wares and gathering their purchases. Occasionally one would cast a glance at him or in the direction of the Queen's chambers. Obviously the sounds of her distress were audible even from out here, and the people were beginning to get nervous. The masses did not like it when their betters were in pain.

Shedri rubbed his hand along the lower half of his face, jutting out his chin as he stepped out of the hall and into the sun. He would have to be realistic about his chances of success. The midwife had left hours ago for a town at the edge of their realm. Even his fastest riders would take hours to close the distance, and if they found her while she was already with her serf patient, she wouldn't leave one mother in jeopardy simply to tend to another. Even if the other woman was the Queen. No, he was facing a wait of hours, if not days, before the midwife returned. He needed a different solution.

His first thought was nearly discarded simply because it was something that was never done. But desperate times required creative measures. The new prince could not be born alone so they required the presence of a midwife to prove without doubt the baby was properly and entirely of the lineage. The royal midwife, currently flitting about in the badlands beyond the walls, had been investigated before her employment began, and her reputation was unassailable. She would confirm the child was in fact the Queen's and settle any future doubt as to his rightful place on the throne. It was already a bad sign that the child was forcing his way into the world at the wrong time, but if no one was present to ease the minds of the doubtful, the future king could be usurped before he even came of age.

There was only one thing he could do. He would have to lie and then retroactively cover his trail.

Shedri stepped out of the castle's protective shadow and hurried down one crowded avenue of the bazaar. People instinctively moved out of his way, cowed by the sight of his uniform and the golden helmet that sloped low over his brow. He passed people who turned to whisper in his wake; first an unusual commotion from the palace and now the head of the Guard venturing out among the great unwashed masses? He knew that his presence would only serve to fan the flames of rumor, but it couldn't be helped. He had a mission.

Not far from the palace, he found a small nondescript shop tucked in the corner of a dead-end street. The windows were smeared and opaque, and scattered piles of trash blown by the wind accumulated against the side of the building. A wooden shingle over the door announced it as an apothecary's office and promised all manner of medical assistance. Shedri saw a list painted on the brick next to the door and scanned it to see if the physician offered midwifery before he burst inside.

He found himself in a dusty room with a continent of a table set in the middle of the space. Thick smoke wafted around the ceiling and he coughed at the pungent odors coming from a riser of small glass phials standing against the far wall. Shedri waved away the fug and bellowed, "Physician! I require your assistance at once!"

The physician came out of the back room wearing a brown apron over a dirty work shirt and brown trousers. Her black hair was tied back messily, leaving one shank with a streak of white hanging loose over glasses that comically magnified her eyes. She pushed the glasses higher up her nose and straightened her posture when she recognized his uniform, puffed out her cheeks, and squared her shoulders.

"I don't care if you are the Palace Guard, you will simply have to get in line! I have patients waiting, you know."

Her accent marked her as being from the Plains. He wanted to pass her off as someone who had been vetted for the job, so Lowlands would have been more believable. Still, even though it was less than ideal, he couldn't well afford to be picky. "The Queen requires your assistance. You are a loyal subject of Queen Indell and her family, are you not?"

The physician sighed and removed her headgear. "What could the Queen want with me?"

"She is in labor."

"I haven't trained to assist a woman in labor!"

"You know enough. All you have to do is catch the blasted thing and verify it belongs to the Queen. Hurry! We haven't much time."

The physician sighed and said, "Let me get my things!" She pulled open a drawer and withdrew a large black bag which looked big enough to conceal an infant. That thought gave him pause. "What could you possibly need with a bag that large?"

She turned away from him as she began filling it with things from the cubbyholes along her wall. "Would you rather I have to come back here to retrieve something I'll need in the event of an emergency, or shall I bring everything I might possibly require?"

"Fine, fine! Hurry!"

Once she had what she needed, he ushered her quickly outside. They weaved and elbowed their way through the crowd, Shedri forced to occasionally grab the physician's elbow to force her to match his pace as they ran through the bazaar. As they neared the palace the woman moved up closer to him and lowered her voice so she couldn't be heard as easily by the people around them.

"You said the Queen was in labor. I may not be a Royal Physician, but even I know that she isn't due until it becomes warmer."

"That was the plan," Shedri muttered without looking at her. They crossed the demarcation line between Agora and the palace grounds, and Shedri finally released her arm. He stopped and looked at her. "Take off the apron. Your hair... it needs to look neater. Fix it."

She did as she was told.

"If she inquires, tell her that you have been apprenticing with the midwife for... years. You have been studying to take her place when she retires. You are a student but more than qualified to stand in for your master during this auspicious occasion."

"But that's a lie! I'm no lowly apprentice, and I have never trained to be —"

He silenced her with a sideways swipe of his hand. She flinched as if he'd actually struck her, and for a moment he saw real fire in her eyes.

"You are trained enough to do what is necessary. You keep your patients breathing. This is just someone a bit younger than the patients you are accustomed to seeing. Now be silent if you value your health." He tossed her apron aside and led her to the royal chambers. The physician trotted behind him, rubbing her hands together anxiously as she followed him inside.

The maid, a slender brunette woman wearing the pale blue uniform of palace staff, had just refilled the Queen's red teacup when they entered. He waved a dismissive hand at her and the woman retreated to one side, remaining in the room but effectively rendering herself invisible. The Queen was still propped up against her pillows, hands clutching the sheets hard enough to tear them, face red and splotchy with white spots as she glared at him. Her eyes slid past him to the stranger trailing in his wake.

"Who is this? That is not my midwife!"

"This is… a-ah…"

The physician stepped in front of him. "My name is Shakatt, your highness. I'm here to help you give birth." She pointed at the maid. "You, what's your name?"

"Me?" The poor woman looked horrified. "Mayani."

"You can stay. I might need an extra pair of hands. Is that teacup full? Good." Shakatt put down her bag and began rolling up the sleeves of her shirt. She turned to Shedri. "You've done your part, my good man. You've gotten me here. Now you must leave me to my practice. The Queen and Prince both require a calm environment if they wish for this to be a success. Now go wait outside and make sure no one disturbs the birth."

Shedri nodded, grateful to be sent away. "Do you require anything else, milady?"

Shakatt answered. "If she does, I will send Mayani for it. Now leave!"

Shedri stepped out of the room, pulling the doors closed behind him as the Queen released another bellow of pain. He winced and shook his head. Someone else was now in charge of the Queen's comfort. He could take the opportunity to relax and catch his wind while they took care of the crisis. Of course just because the Queen now had an attendant didn't mean he could take the rest of the day off. He had to lay the foundation for the lie he had established about Shakatt's identity.

He assigned one of his underlings to watch the door of the Queen's chamber while he set about spreading the necessary facts to the right people. He spent close to an hour finding those who could help sell his lie, repeating his story over and over again while peppering the name "Shakatt" through his conversations. By the time he realized how much time had passed, more people in the palace knew Shakatt's name and profession than his.

Confident his lie wouldn't be discovered, Shedri returned to the Queen's chambers. The man he'd posted as guard was still standing tirelessly in front of the doors, his red cap tilted forward to the bridge of his nose and his eyes focused on a spot in the far distance. Shedri removed his helmet to wipe the sweat from his face as he approached. The chambers sounded blessedly silent, and he hoped that was a good sign.

"Has the birth made progress?"

"It must have. The room has been silent for quite a while, sir."

"Silent? It shouldn't be silent…" Even if the physician had eased the Queen's labor pains, there should be some commotion. No one entered this life peacefully.

Knowing full well he risked incurring the wrath of both the Queen and her new midwife, he stepped forward and rapped his knuckles on the thick wooden door. No answer came from within.

"Your Majesty? Does all go well?" He waited for a response and, when none was forthcoming, he braced himself and stepped inside. The Queen was still in her bed and slumbering peacefully, but the midwife and maid were nowhere to be seen. Shedri's heart leapt into his throat as he moved to the bedside and checked his Queen's pulse. She was alive, thank the gods, and in no distress. No distress at all, Shedri noticed, and his own vital signs spiked when he realized she was no longer in labor.

Shedri rose and called in the guard from the hallway. "The midwife and the maid. Where did they go?"

The guard glanced around the room. "They are not here…?"

Shedri ground his teeth at the man's idiocy. "I want this room barricaded! No one is to touch anything until we've examined it thoroughly. And gather the rest of the Guard. I want that midwife found posthaste!" The guard ran off, and Shedri turned to look around the room for more clues. He passed over the nightstand once before the red teacup caught his eye. He remembered the maid refilling it before he was shuffled out but now it was almost half-empty. He moved closer and picked it up to sniff the contents.

Ashroot.

In addition to a distinct fragrance even when dissolved in tea, the drug had a number of side effects. In high enough doses it could elevate body temperature, cause severe abdominal cramping, create shortness of breath… in short, it did everything except help someone manage their pain. It was generally used to create the appearance of false labor. He lowered the cup and glanced down at the Queen, spotting another clue to what had transpired in the room. The skin above the scooped-neck of the Queen's nightgown was bare when he should have seen a small brass key hanging from a heavy chain.

Shedri struggled to control his breathing as the cup dropped from his hands. "No," he whispered. He moved sluggishly toward the door as he realized the implications of the key's absence, only breaking into a run when he reached the wide expanse of the hallway. The guards he had summoned split to either side as he raced past them, muttering an endless litany of "No, no, no!" under his breath as he reached the treasury. Ordinarily he wouldn't have been able to get inside, but now he could see that the door was standing open and unsecured. He threw the door wide and stepped inside to have his greatest fears confirmed.

The room was empty.

Shedri dropped to his knees and roared with rage as he stared at the bare shelves. Hundreds of thousands of direfs, gone in a flash. Even if the thieves could only get a fraction of the coins' face value in exchange, they would still come out rich. For the past few months the royal family had been exchanging their old currency and stocking up on the new diref, a coin that wasn't even in circulation yet. The royal family had just become the poorest people in the entire realm.

When Shedri finally found the strength, he rose to his feet and turned to see the door barricaded by his men.

"We will find the people responsible," he declared, "and we shall make them pay! We must begin the search now, before they have a chance to escape!"

None of the men moved, save for a red cap who shouldered the others out of the way to join Shedri in the treasury. Shedri understood what was about to happen and felt his anger and dread giving way to reluctant bitter acceptance. He had failed the Queen and the entire royal line; he deserved his fate. He raised his hands and awaited the judgment for his failure. Whoever the midwife was, he hoped he would have a chance to repay her duplicity in the next life.

It had taken the maid nearly three weeks to discover the access corridor hidden within the Queen's chambers. It stood to reason it only existed so royalty had a way to move around the palace unseen in the event of an attack, so she knew it was there somewhere. But for the longest time its actual location had eluded her. She had been forced to actually clean the entire room several times before she discovered how it was triggered. She tracked it backward through the stone walls and created a comprehensive map of all its points of egress. The next step of the plan involved getting her hands on enough ashroot to achieve their goals, but not so much it would harm the mother or child. Finally, they had to get the midwife out of the palace on the necessary day so the Queen was forced to get help elsewhere.

Months of planning boiled down to less than an hour of frantic scrambling in the darkness. They had barely been able to carry their ill-gotten gains from the treasury to the tel'tak they had parked on one of the unfrequented turrets of the castle, but all her work scrubbing floors and lugging her cleaning supplies around the palace had left her strong enough to make it work.

Now at the controls of the ship, preparing their great escape, she struggled to remember her true self. She had spent so long as the maid that it was hard to shake off the identity, but now that she was in her own space she was starting to find the mask was dissolving with each passing moment. The engines hummed and she looked over her shoulder. Through the open door of the cargo hold, she could see her accomplice securing the last bag against the hull with stretchy rubber netting. "The esteemed physician Shakatt," as she would be remembered in the palace, but the maid knew her by a different name.

The physician exhaled, wiped her hands, and tucked her shock of white hair behind her ear as she strode forward. "Anything standing in our way?"

The maid looked at the readings that had just come to life. "Blue across the board. The royals might make a fuss about a search for thieves, but they won't be too eager to let people know just how serious this is. They don't want to tell people they're flat broke." She grinned. "Right now they're keeping it so low-key that no alerts or restrictions have been issued."

"Excellent!" The physician dropped into the navigator's seat and put her boots up on the console. "Let's get out of here before they decide justice is more important than saving face."

The engine hum increased in pitch until the hull shifted under their feet. The maid set a course with the practiced ease of someone who spent more time at the controls of a ship than on her hands and knees scrubbing tile, her face set in serious concentration at her task. They received a few radio signals that neither of them bothered listening to and, within moments, the view out the front of the ship faded from a winter afternoon blue to deep violet.

"And we're clear," the physician said.

The maid smiled. "Yes, we are." She linked her fingers and stretched both arms over her head as if she had just woken from a long nap. "Nice to be out of there. What's the next step?"

"We go straight to Lucia. I have a fence there who is trying to pad the treasury for that new alliance they're putting together. Coin is coin, doesn't really matter where it comes from so long as someone considers it legal tender. They'll only pay a fraction of what it's worth, but a fraction of a royal fortune will still buy us a few weeks of nice suppers. Maybe even some new clothes."

"It's good to be freelance. Well done, Shakatt."

"Ugh." The erstwhile physician stuck out her tongue. "No more of that. The job is done. We can be ourselves again."

"Right. That should be nice. I've missed myself."

Her partner smiled as she activated the hyperdrive to take them to their next port of call. She closed her eyes and linked her fingers behind her head to relax during the trip. She had gotten so accustomed to her cover identity that it would take a little effort to fall back into the habit of answering to her real name. But she was once again Tanis Reynard, and she would remain so for the foreseeable future. Plenty of time to get reacquainted with herself.

Mayani and Shakatt were dead. Until their next job required new identities, they could once again be Tanis Reynard and her partner in crime, Vala Mal Doran.

CHAPTER ONE

San Diego, California

SAM Carter remembered standing in this same spot when she was twelve years old, shaken and lost, trying to comprehend her mother's name on the headstone. It seemed unfair that the moment hadn't gotten any easier with time. Before she had been a frightened girl in her Sunday best, shivering in the shadow of someone in a crisp and beautiful air force uniform. At the time she took comfort in the uniform; someone that polished must have some idea how to handle something of this magnitude. So she had taken her father's hand so he could show her the right thing to do. Now she was the one in uniform and she realized it didn't give her magic answers. All she could do was try acting composed when she felt anything but.

The actual funeral had been over for a while, but she wanted to take a final moment to say goodbye to her father one last time. It truly was a goodbye this time; anything she had to say to the man had been said, and all the issues between them had been resolved during the past seven years. She smiled a little when she thought of their renewed relationship and the utterly bizarre way it had come about. Of everything the Stargate had given her, the wonders she'd seen because of her work, her resurrected relationship with her father was the biggest miracle she could have asked for.

He'd given his life not only in service to his country, but to save the entire galaxy from Anubis. The old soldier who had resigned himself to wasting away in a hospital bed was given a new and fantastic war to fight. He'd stood on the front lines and helped deliver the final, decisive blow. And even better, it had allowed him the chance to fight alongside his daughter. What was there to regret?

Well… maybe there was one thing.

She turned and smiled when she saw Mark watching her from a few yards away. She nodded that it was okay for him to come over, and he approached slowly with his hands in his pockets. She had been staying with him and his family since arriving in town. Their estrangement had caused her to miss a lot of time with her niece and nephew, but now she was more than making up for it. She had to admit that getting up to help make breakfast, helping them with their homework, and watching her brother and sister-in-law be parents had affected her. It was the same bond that had brought her closer to Cassandra Fraiser; sometimes she wanted to forget about being Colonel Carter so she could be Aunt Sam. Maybe now that the Goa'uld were no longer a threat she could take the time to figure out that 'life' thing General O'Neill kept telling her to get. She had sacrificed so much to get where she was. Maybe the time had come to start focusing on other achievements and possibilities.

Mark reached the grave and stood beside her. "I didn't want to disturb you. Just in case there was some kind of post-mortem alien telepathy thing going on that I don't have the clearance to hear."

She chuckled. "No, nothing that sci-fi. Just remembering." She looked at the graves, their mother and father together again after so long. "I'm sorry we didn't tell you earlier."

Mark sighed. "Me too. But I understand why you didn't. It's one thing to hear your father had a spontaneous remission and is off doing top-secret government work. It's something else entirely to know he was cured by an alien in his head and now he's fighting an intergalactic war. Oh, and that your sister is one of the frontline soldiers in that same war."

"Hallmark doesn't really make a card for that."

"No."

They stood in silence for a long time, but it was no longer the anxious and weighted silence they had grown so accustomed to. Now they were just adult children saying goodbye to their parents, two people with vastly different lives brought together by common tragedy.

"You know, Hallmark does make blank cards," Mark said. "So you could have dropped one of those in the mail to explain what exactly happened with Pete."

Sam bit back a groan. There weren't enough blank Hallmark cards in the world to explain everything that happened with Pete. A year earlier she'd experienced a hallucination of her father telling her that she needed to be happy. She took that advice to heart and started focusing on her private life as a new sort of experiment. When Mark called and told her he knew a great guy who lived in her area and just happened to be single, she jumped at the offer to be set up with him. In addition to saving her the trouble of going out to find someone for herself, it was another piece of the bridge between her and Mark. It was hard to make up for decades worth of bad feelings when she still had to lie to him about some very basic stuff in her life.

Pete came along at the perfect time in more ways than one, and it helped that he was sweet, funny, charming, and easy on the eyes. It made sense no matter how she looked at it, so she jumped in with both feet. He genuinely cared for her, and she found it so easy to trust him that she found herself telling him the truth about the Stargate rather than risk losing him because of lies. She had a man she cared about and they were happy together. That was what people were supposed to do. Marriage was obviously the next step, and saying yes when he proposed just made sense.

Saying yes was easy.

When Jacob died, he told her the same thing she'd heard in her earlier hallucination but with a slightly different phrasing. He told her, "Don't get in the way of your own happiness." She realized she was about to make an enormous mistake. When her father first revealed he had cancer, he surprised her with the news he'd gotten her into NASA. He'd been hurt when she refused, and rightfully so. On paper it made sense, and it was the absolute right thing to do. But there were things he didn't know, another path that was even more sensible, and she was already on that path. She'd broken her father's heart by refusing his offer because she'd known it was the only logical course of action.

She was doing the same thing with Pete. He looked perfect for her in theory, and the white picket fence was something everyone strove to achieve. Marrying Pete was NASA, and she was destined for something greater. Even if she couldn't say what that would be yet, she knew she couldn't use Pete as a placeholder until it came along. She loved him too much to destroy his life by walking away at some future point. So she had settled for breaking his heart now, when it still had a chance of recovering.

"I'm sorry, Mark. There are just some things I can't explain."

"Classified?"

She shook her head. "Just too complicated."

He nodded. "I understand. And thank you for finally spilling the beans about Dad and, uh… Uh…"

"Selmak."

"Right. Him."

"Her."

Mark shook his head. "Right. Anyway, it's good to finally know how Dad spent his last few years. And knowing everything he did for the planet. And us."

Sam smiled at her brother and nodded. "You deserved to know a long time ago. It was such a huge, closely-kept secret for so long. When Dad and Selmak first joined, there were soldiers stationed at the SGC married to people who didn't know the truth. We were so nervous about the secret getting out that we lied to the people we were closest to. And once things became a bit more relaxed, there was never really a good time for the 'Dad's got an alien snake in his head.'"

"Couldn't have slipped that in a Christmas letter?"

"I thought about doing a Candygram, but I couldn't find a

rhyme for 'symbiotic alien parasite'."

They chuckled together. Mark said, "Are you going to come back to the house? We could have some lunch before you head out…"

"Ah." She checked her watch and winced apologetically. "I should probably be getting back soon. The war might be over but there's still a lot of messes that need to be cleaned up."

"Right. It's an open invitation. Especially now that I know you can just, ah…" He gestured at the sky. "You know. With spaceships."

She turned and started walking with him back to the car. "Transporting people like that costs money, Mark."

"You can afford it. How much does World-Saving Ass-kicker pay these days?"

"Not as much as you might think."

He put an arm around her shoulder. "My big sister, saving the world for peanuts."

"No one gets into the world-saving business to get rich."

"Of course not," Mark said. "They do it for the glory and the recognition… Oh. Right."

Sam grinned and glanced back as Mark led her away, almost positive either he or his wife would eventually convince her to come back to the house for something to eat before she left. She didn't mind. It would give her one more chance to play Auntie Sam, a role she had missed out on far too much in the past. She was grateful to have Mark and his family in her life, and she owed their reconciliation to her father and the influence of the alien that had saved his life.

Goodbye, Dad. Goodbye, Selmak. Thank you both. For everything.

The work table in the middle of Daniel Jackson's lab was nearly invisible under the boxes and crates he'd placed there. He had a system, the fine points of which currently eluded him as he turned and searched for the crate of scrolls brought back from PX8-275. He spotted it under another box and put his pencil in his mouth and bit down on it to free his hands. As he excavated the box he wanted there was a knock on the open door of his office followed by a slow, quizzical, "Hello-oo…"

"Jack." The pencil fell from his mouth. "Want to give me a hand here?"

Jack O'Neill entered the room, saw what Daniel was doing, and took the box from him. He looked for a flat surface on which to place it, gave up, and bent down to put it on the floor at Daniel's feet. "There you go."

"Thanks," Daniel muttered. He took out one of the scrolls and skimmed it to make sure it had the information he needed before he took it to the worktable. "Did you need me for something?"

"No," Jack said, hands in his pockets as he looked over the clutter. They'd recently discovered that something he touched in Daniel's lab had telepathically connected him to a barber from Indiana. Since then he'd tried very hard not to touch anything he didn't recognize. "It's been eighteen hours since anyone on the base has seen you. I just wanted to make sure you hadn't gone all… glowfish on us again."

Daniel chuckled. "I don't have any plans to do that again, thank you."

"Yes, well. That's what you said last time. I figured if you were still among the non-Ascended beings, you might want to stick your head out for a little food. Cafeteria is serving… something. They claim it's meat. I'm not so sure."

"Sorry, Jack. I'm…" He gestured at the pile as if it made his case.

"Man cannot live by dust alone. You need to eat something."

Daniel sighed. "For the first time in, well, the history of the SGC, we actually have a little downtime. No imminent dangers on our doorstep, no Goa'uld running around threatening us, no missions on the docket. Teal'c is off with the Free Jaffa, Sam is in California, and I finally have the free time to go through the past eight years' worth of artifacts we've brought back with us through the gate. This is what I do for fun, Jack. It relaxes me."

"If you say so." Jack had already forgotten his ban on touching things and picked up an owl carved out of stone. "You ever thought about opening a booth in a craft mall? You could probably make a killing with some of this stuff."

Daniel snatched the figure away and returned it to the proper position in his chaotic system. "I appreciate what you're trying to do, honestly, but I'm fine. Clean bill of health, completely and totally descended in proper working order. I have a library of journals collecting dust in here with information I've collected on dozens upon dozens of worlds that I haven't had the time to go over properly." He rested his hand on top of a crate. "I'm not gun-shy, Jack. I'm not feeling anxious about yet another near-death experience. Frankly, I'm kind of used to them by now."

"You can see why someone might think otherwise. Locking yourself up down here..."

"This is relaxing to me! This, this, this..." He gestured at the room like a game show model. "This is... my lake in Minnesota with no fish in it. I'm an archaeologist. I study history, and for the past decade, I've had more history and more relics than I knew what to do with because somewhere along the line I had to become a soldier first and an explorer second. Do you want to know why no one's seen me in eighteen hours? I'm not hiding... I'm basking."

Jack didn't seem convinced, but he held his hands up in surrender. "All right, well... if you want to add a few more relics to your pile, SG-9 is scheduled to go off-world tomorrow. They have their own version of you, and according to what she saw on the MALP, it looks like the Stargate is located inside a temple dedicated to worshipping Kali. All our reports say she was one of the System Lords who backed Anubis' play in exchange for staying on his good side when he was establishing his new

Goa'uld order. Depending on how friendly they really were…"

"You're hoping he might have given her some lovely Ancient parting gifts in exchange for her loyalty. A ZPM, perhaps?"

"A man can dream," Jack said. "Anyway, the place is just sitting there gathering dust. SG-9 is confident that Kali skipped town after we wiped the floor with her buddy, so it should just be a walk in the park. And even if there aren't loads of goodies to dig through, there should be a lot of modern-day things scattered around if you want something to compare the old junk with."

Daniel perked up. "Wow. Yes, that would actually be incredibly helpful. Thank you."

"No problem. Just promise me you won't die on this one, huh? Every time you leave we have to sell your place, and then you get a new one when you come back, and I'm getting tired of updating my address book all the time."

"I'll do my best."

Jack nodded and started to back out of the room. "I wasn't kidding about that lunch, by the way. Genuine alleged government meat products. Mm-mm, good eating."

Daniel looked at the pile of work in front of him with the unsettling knowledge it was about to be made larger by whatever he found with SG-9. He put down his journal and said, "Yeah. I suppose I could eat, now that you mention it." He followed Jack out of the room and hoped there was an alternative to whatever purported meat product Jack was talking about.

Teal'c stepped away from the fire, walking until the din of conversation faded enough that he could be alone with his thoughts. They were in a wide clearing ringed by trees on an outcropping that overlooked the valley. Far below in the waning light, he could see the Stargate in its ring of stones. It seemed so very far away and, for the first time in recent memory, it was not a threatening sight. He knew that the shimmering blue surface wouldn't deliver his fellow Jaffa clad in armor and brandishing staff weapons. He had the security of knowing he would not have to fight his brothers for the greater good. It was an alien feeling, but one he expected would become more familiar over time.

He had stood on Dakara at the historic moment, saw with his own eyes the downfall of the Goa'uld oppressors. It was a moment of which he had often dreamed but to be there, to not only experience it but to have had a hand in bringing it to pass… His fellow Jaffa now looked upon him as an epic figure. He would have been called a "celebrity" in Tau'ri culture but he knew he had done nothing worthy of idolatry; he was merely one of the final soldiers in a long line of warriors who had striven toward their goal. He deserved no more praise than Bra'tac or the hundreds of Jaffa who had given their lives so that he could at last succeed.

In the past few weeks, he had seen just how far his people had come in only a few short years. While many warriors remained behind on Dakara to secure it for their own purposes, he and Bra'tac were acting as emissaries to spread the word to some of the more scattered settlements. For obvious reasons, many Free Jaffa villages were isolated and kept their heads low. Even if they heard rumors of the System Lords falling, they would not simply take the news at face value. They would need someone they trusted to assure them it was the truth before they risked coming out into the open. So far they had tracked down five different villages, and all of them insisted on having a celebratory bonfire in honor of the brothers and sisters they had lost to the cause.

Teal'c was grateful for the opportunity to share the news. It didn't matter how often he explained how it had come about or how many times he answered the same question, the words hit him with the same force every time: the System Lords had been defeated in a decisive victory. The Jaffa were free and had delivered the final crushing blow with their own hands. No Jaffa would ever again serve a false god. They would not only die free, they would have a chance to live free as well.

He heard the boy's furtive approach and smiled, giving no sign he had heard until he was within reaching distance. "Hello, Rya'c."

He could sense his son's disappointment and turned to look at him with a smile. The boy had grown into a respectable man, but he was still eager for his father's approval. These days, however, he showed off by trying to best the old man. The day hadn't come yet, but Teal'c knew that it was fast approaching. On that day he would proudly welcome his son to the ranks of adulthood, a maturity marked by the fact he would never have to bow before a false god even one day of his life.

"Ishta is looking for you," Rya'c said.

"And you elected to conduct a search for me rather than remaining by the fire with your wife?"

The boy — a young man now, though still a boy in Teal'c's eyes — smiled as he took a position next to his father. Teal'c could see his muscles through his shirt, the coiled strength in his arms. This was no longer the child who had been used as a pawn by Apophis. This was a fellow warrior.

"I can see her whenever I wish. It's far more difficult to see you."

Teal'c's smile faltered slightly. "For that, I can only apologize."

"You had greater responsibilities elsewhere. I understand that now, even if I haven't in the past."

He inclined his head in gratitude to the young man. "I hope things can change. Now that the Goa'uld have been defeated, my place is here among my own people. We have survived, but true victory remains to be achieved. There will be much to do in the future if we are to avoid collapsing under the weight of our own freedom."

Rya'c nodded. "And your friends? SG-1?"

He didn't have an easy answer for that. When he left Chulak to fight by their side, he had seen them only as a military unit he happened to fight alongside. Now they had become so much more, their meaning to him so much greater. They weren't just his unit, they were his family. It would be difficult to leave them, but he knew they would never be far away.

"When the time comes," he said slowly, "I will be forced to make a difficult decision. I will have to choose between my family… and those who have become my family. It will not be an easy choice to make." He rested his hand on Rya'c's shoulder and smiled at him. "But I have no doubt I will make the right choice when the time comes."

"Neither do I." He looked back toward the revelry. "I should probably return before Kar'yn sends someone to look for me as well."

"A wise decision."

Teal'c watched his son walk back through the trees. Once he was alone again, he looked down at the Stargate below. The choice to leave the Tau'ri and his friends at Stargate Command would be difficult, a bittersweet side effect of achieving his dream. But the man who attempted to live in two worlds was a true resident of neither. When the choice came, he had no doubt which he would choose, no matter how painful it might be in the short term.

CHAPTER TWO

THE ACTIVE Stargate provided enough light for them to see, but the first probe had revealed they would be in total darkness as soon as the event horizon shut down. Colonel Joseph Getty of SG-9 was the first person through the gate, taking a moment to confirm they were still alone in the dialing chamber before he moved toward the MALP. He turned on the lights and manually angled them to hit the far corners of the room as the rest of his team came through behind him. Their esteemed tag-along Dr. Daniel Jackson was the final person through the gate, and the shimmering pool disengaged with a quiet "chuff" behind him. Getty knew it was his imagination, but the shutdown of a Stargate always made him feel uneasy, as if an actual door had been closed. This time the concurrent loss of light exacerbated that feeling.

The room in which they found themselves was roughly the size of a hotel lobby, the walls decorated to show off the wonder and splendor of the resident goddess. Archways stood to either side, and Getty sent his team to clear the corridors. Lieutenants Huang and Shaffer went to the right, while Captain Frances Morello took the left by herself. Colonel Getty unhooked the flashlight from his vest and aimed it at the wall directly across from the Stargate. It had been adorned with a massive painting of Kali that looked similar to what he'd seen in history books: blue skin, long tongue, multiple arms, lots of swords. Definitely an imposing way to greet guests.

Daniel took out his own flashlight and got a closer look at the artist's work. Getty stepped out of the way without a word so he could get closer to the wall, and Daniel nodded his thanks. Eight years getting comfortable with SG-1 and now he was the odd man out once again. He was the outsider, the scientist who had to be reminded which end of the gun bullets went in. It felt oddly like coming home. He aimed the flashlight at the artwork and focused on trying to figure out its purpose.

The Goa'uld were narcissists who loved to terrorize, but the painting seemed extravagant even by their standards. Kali could intimidate with the Jaffa she would have had posted in front of the gate, or by using the darkness of the temple to unsettle anyone who came through. The portrait had to have some kind of deeper purpose. When he played the light against the stone he noticed a seam running vertically along the side of Kali's torso. There was another on the opposite side, and a horizontal one across her shoulders. It was almost as if it was meant to be opened, but there was no handhold to be seen.

"That's strange…"

Morello returned before Getty was forced to inquire further. "Place looks clear on this end, sir," she reported. "There were definitely skirmishes all up and down this corridor, leading back toward the throne room. The front of the building is pretty much decimated. If I was Kali, I would have hightailed it pretty quickly, too."

Getty said, "Sounds like the Jaffa aren't wasting any time turning the tables on their old rulers."

Daniel said, "It's not just the Jaffa rising up, at least not in this case. Now that Anubis is gone, everyone who stood with him is going to get it from all sides. They backed a losing horse and now they're paying the price. They have to face not only their Jaffa but the people they turned against in order to back the guy they expected to win everything."

"Can't say I feel too sorry for them," Getty said.

Huang and Shaffer returned. "All clear, sir."

"Is it this dark everywhere in the temple?"

Huang nodded. "Yes sir, not counting where the ceiling or walls have been knocked in. Doesn't seem to be set up much in the way of lighting."

Daniel said, "That makes sense."

Morello said, "Because of her animosity with Ra."

He looked at her and nodded, impressed. "Yes. Kali had a falling out with Ra a while back. A while back in this case meaning a few thousand years. Anyway, when you oppose the sun god, you don't really want his light entering your temple. So she designed her temples in such a way that Ra had no corners to hide in. And it didn't hurt that one of her names literally translates to 'black night.' Having her zealots worship in pitch darkness is just her living up to her reputation."

Morello aimed her light at a golden sconce high on the wall. "Those could be lit when Kali or her people actually needed to see what they were doing. It would be very dim, but it worked. Plus it was easily extinguished if one of their enemies showed up at the door."

Daniel said, "Nice catch."

"Thank you. I did a bit of research on Kali when I heard this mission would involve visiting one of her palaces."

Getty said, "Yeah, yeah, she likes to get all educated so she has pertinent information to save our asses when we cross some line or another. She only does it to make me look bad."

"Not true, sir. I do it so Huang and Shaffer look bad, too." She grinned and joined her flashlight beam to Daniel's. "Wow. I've heard of vanity, but this is a little much, huh?"

"I was just thinking the same thing," Daniel said.

"It's extremely aggressive," Morello said.

Huang said, "It's a Goa'uld. You expected something pacifistic?"

Daniel was aiming his light at the painting again. "No… no, she has a point."

Shaffer raised an eyebrow. "Correct me if I'm wrong, but that's par for the course when it comes to these guys. Right?"

"No, not… no," Daniel said. "Not Kali. She believed in treaties and peaceful accords when it came to dealing with her enemies, and once they had signed on a dotted line, she abided by the agreements."

"Oh," Shaffer said. "So she's one of the good bad guys."

"For lack of a better word," Daniel said.

Getty said, "All right, as much as I enjoy playing art critic, I think it's time we got this show on the road. Shaffer, get this room set up with lights so we're not squinting. I don't want to fumble with the DHD in the event someone else comes a-looting. Huang, you're with me on the perimeter. I want to make sure we're as alone here as we seem to be. Morello, you seem to be having a good time in the dust with Jackson. Let me know if you find anything ZPM-shaped."

She nodded. "Will do, sir."

"Check-in with the SGC is in ninety minutes. Let's get a move on so I have something to report."

As the team spread out, Daniel glanced at Morello. She was taller than she had seemed in the gate room, pretty even in the darkness with long black hair braided under her cap. He'd noticed on the ramp that she didn't seem to have any trouble with the weight of her gear, and he'd seen male soldiers grunt when they loaded on a pack. She had somehow managed to not only carry it through the gate, she'd done a quick recon and was now standing next to him looking not the least out of breath. She noticed his examination and looked at him, and he smiled apologetically.

"Sorry you got stuck with the babysitting duty."

"Actually, I requested it, Dr. Jackson. I told the colonel whatever grabbed your attention, that's where I wanted to be. I actually studied archaeology in college. You were a bit of an inspiration."

"Really?"

"Well, you and Indiana Jones."

Daniel smiled. "Ah, yes. Him. That guy lied to us all."

"But look at where he's led us."

Daniel nodded and examined the painting again. It had been damaged by multiple staff weapon hits that had chipped away at the stone and paint. He leaned in and tilted his head to the side.

"Some of these gaps go all the way through. I think this section of the wall is supposed to be removed." He tapped the butt of his flashlight against the stone. "Was there a chamber behind this wall?"

"Not that I saw," Morello said. A moment later, she added, "But there is space that isn't accounted for. I'd say enough room for a twelve-by-twelve room."

"How could you tell?" Daniel asked, then answered his own question. "You were looking for secret chambers."

Morello shrugged. "Are you going to lie and tell me you've never looked for one?"

"Are you kidding me? Half this job is looking for secret passages and stash rooms." He moved away from the wall and walked toward the exit. "Let's just hope her Jaffa didn't find it first."

"It seems kind of odd, doesn't it?" Morello asked. "You spend your entire life being told this person is a god, you dedicate your life to their service and their glory, and then one day someone says it's not true so you steal from her temple and try to kill her? I'm not saying the Jaffa are wrong, I'm just saying it seems a little strange they were so willing to believe the truth."

Daniel said, "Jaffa never worshipped the Goa'uld the way you or I might think of the word. Most of us think of, you know, going to church on Sunday and organized religion. The Goa'uld were revered as gods, but they weren't beloved. The Jaffa paid lip service because they had no other choice. People who followed the Goa'uld did so out of fear. They believed the truth that was presented to them: this person is infallible, this person gives you life, and it is through them that you survive. In their experience, that was demonstrably true. So they fell in line. Teal'c and Bra'tac didn't just disprove the Goa'uld divinity, they showed their people there was another way. That's why they took up arms so readily."

Outside they moved down the corridor with their lights trained on the wall. Daniel kept his eyes open for anything that looked like it might have been an access panel.

"Once word started spreading about what happened on Dakara, the System Lords became an endangered species. The ones who didn't leave had to stay and face the reality of a vast army who suddenly accepted they had a choice."

"Why would any of the System Lords elect to stay in that case? I mean, if it would only lead to their deaths…"

"Centuries and centuries of living the lie, lording it over the little people… a lot of the Goa'uld started believing the lie themselves. When the peasants revolted a lot of them figured the rebellion would be quashed without much effort. They were gods, after all. Must have been quite a shock to realize they weren't as all-powerful as they'd made themselves out to be."

"Must have been rough."

"No doubt."

"You know Colonel Getty better than I do. How long can we look at this stuff before he starts getting antsy?"

"We have some time. He's pretty into the whole history aspect of what we do. Don't tell him I told you this, but he's started taking night classes so he can learn some of the mythology."

Daniel whistled. "Wow, I'm jealous."

He paused and moved closer to what appeared to be a loose brick. He ran his fingers along the edges of it, displacing the dusty mortar until he could wiggle it free. When it cleared the slot, a narrow opening appeared in front of them. "Well. Not exactly 'open sesame,' but it'll do in a pinch." He used his flashlight to make sure there were no nasty surprises waiting for them inside before he stepped into the darkness. They crossed the beams of their lights and moved far enough apart that they could get the general idea of what they had found.

The majority of the room was filled by a golden table with various glyphs carved on the surface. One end of the table had a small control panel, and the opposite side had two crystalline uprights that reminded him of football goalposts. The uprights were positioned so they braced the panel between the hidden room and the main chamber. Daniel approached the table and Morello moved so that his shadow wasn't eclipsing her beam. He hardly noticed as he bent down and began reading the carvings. He brushed away the dust and ran the beam of his light across the whole inscription, getting the gist rather than the word-for-word message.

"Huh."

Morello said, "Is that a good huh or a bad huh?"

"It's a… huh." He furrowed his brow and raised his own light to the wall. He marked the shape of the panel. "This would slide out of the way, and then these uprights would basically be pointed directly at the Stargate."

"Sounds about right," Morello said.

Daniel looked back at the carvings. "Well, this… this is a warning written in Ancient."

"So it was either put here by Anubis or given to Kali by him."

"Yes," Daniel said softly.

Morello waited for him to translate or clarify. When he didn't, she prompted him. "Well? If it's a warning, what is it warning about?"

He took a moment to make sure his translation was correct before he spoke again. "Something very, very bad." He reached up for his radio. "Colonel Getty?"

"Find something interesting, Dr. Jackson?"

"Ah… more worrisome than interesting," he said. "We need to get back to the SGC as soon as possible. If I'm translating this right, then Anubis and Kali planned a retaliatory strike in the event of the Goa'uld being defeated."

"What kind of strike?"

"One that could kill every single Jaffa in the galaxy in one fell swoop."

Lucia didn't look like much from orbit, but Vala knew it was much less impressive from the ground. It was rare to find a monochromatic planet. Different cultures tended to thrive in their own little corner of the world, and each one was as unique and original as the next. Lucia was an exception to this practice. As near as Vala could tell, every person who had ever called Lucia home was a thief of one stripe or another. Pirates, fences, corporate raiders, confidence artists, grifters, mercenaries, and so forth all thrived in the planet's bustling business trade. The story went that if any child showed the least bit of compassion on the playground, they were immediately shipped off to a foster home in some lesser system. It was a fetid hellhole that one would have to be insane to risk visiting.

To Vala and Tanis, it was their home away from home.

Lucia was home to several of their contacts and, through them, they could easily spread whatever they had just stolen across the planet. One stop shopping for the instant destruction of their trail. Anyone trying to follow their tracks would hit Lucia and find themselves faced with a vast and untraceable mess. It was a lovely little quagmire from which they could shake off the strings of pursuit and set out on their next adventure without fear of being pursued by past victims.

Since the downfall of the Goa'uld, the planet's reputation had grown by leaps and bounds among the criminal element. The criminals who kept Lucia's economy thriving knew that none of them on their own were powerful enough to fill the universe's power vacuum, so they decided to join forces. Instead of trying to overtake and absorb each other's businesses, they combined forces and called themselves the Lucian Alliance. From what little Vala had seen, she was impressed with their infrastructure.

But a bureaucracy was still a bureaucracy, even if its sole clientele was made up of criminals. The Alliance would pay them a good exchange for the direfs in the cargo hold, but if they cut out the middle man and went straight to one of their men on the ground, they could haggle for a higher rate. Fortunately Vala knew one such individual that she was confident they could talk into seeing their way.

As with most places, the city that controlled the Stargate was the largest and most bustling. Tanis approached the city through a gauzy cloud cover and found an empty space among a row of rooftop landing sites. She settled their ship in among others that had made some not-so-clean getaways and a few paddock bashers that seemed to be on their last legs. Vala unlashed herself from the seat and went into the cargo hold as soon as the ship had settled.

"What's the name of this guy again?" Tanis asked.

"Siero. I've already told him what we're bringing and he's got it all arranged." She unfastened one of the boxes from its netting and dragged it to the center of the space with a grunt of effort. She flipped up the top and crouched in front of it to fill a small leather pouch with a sampling of what they had. "He's a good man. Trustworthy, as far as that goes in this environment." She held the pouch in her hand and juggled it in her palm. She added a few more pieces and stood up. "There we go. Should be enough to convince him we're on the level."

Tanis said, "Looks good to me."

"Excellent." She tossed the bag to Tanis, who caught it one-handed. "Siero usually hangs out at a club not far from the Stargate. He knows we've arrived so he should be waiting."

Tanis tossed the bag back to her. "Make sure he knows there's more where that came from."

Vala caught the bag and tossed it back. "One of us really should stay with the ship."

"I agree. Bad neighborhood." She tossed the bag to Vala.

Vala caught the bag and looked offended. "You don't trust me." She lobbed it back at Tanis, and it hit her in the chest hard enough to rock her back on her heels.

"Would you trust you?" She tossed the bag back, hard enough to hurt Vala's hand when she caught it. "Besides, you obviously don't trust me alone with the cargo, either."

Vala's jaw dropped, her eyebrows knitting together. "I am offended beyond belief! To think my own partner, the person whose hands I've placed my personal safety in more times than I can remember, thinks so little of me… well, it hurts. It hurts a lot, Tanis."

"Are you done?"

Vala sniffled.

"We'll meet Siero together. That way we don't have to worry about what the other one is getting up to with the rest of the loot. But if anything happens to my ship — "

"My ship!" Vala corrected.

"Our ship," Tanis allowed. "If anything happens to it while we're gone, I'm taking it out of your share. Understood?"

"Fine." Vala looped the top of the baggie around her belt and tied it tight, making sure it would stay put before she let go of it. She put on her long black coat to dissuade leatherwhips, the deft-fingered children who used stiletto blades to cut valuables away from people's clothing, and gestured for Tanis to lead the way out of the ship. Once outside Vala entered the triple-layer lock while Tanis draped a tarp across the ship's shell to make it less noticeable to casual passersby.

In truth, Vala wasn't offended by the other woman's lack of trust. She didn't trust Tanis either, when it came down to that. If anything it was a compliment; their mistrust came from a full knowledge of what the other person was capable of doing. Tanis was a Hebridan career criminal with multiple arrests to her name, but to date she'd never spent a single day behind bars. Every time she was captured and faced punishment for her deeds, she found some way to slip free of the shackles and carry on as before. Vala thought that escapism skill could prove useful. Vala could hold her own when it came to getting out of tough spots, but it never hurt to have an expert around. Vala knew Tanis could outwit her if she chose to, and Tanis knew the same about Vala. They were well-matched, and that made it volatile for them to be in confined quarters for very long. Vala knew that Tanis would do whatever was necessary to survive.

Over the year they had worked together, she'd picked up

the majority of Tanis' life. She was a natural-born Hebridian, which meant she was treated like a second-class citizen to the Serrakin people. She wanted to be a pilot from a very young age but couldn't get into any of the privileged classes. She ended up taking lessons from unlicensed border runners just to learn the ropes, and before she knew what was happening she had become one of them. Doing illicit runs was far more fun that shuttling Serrakin fat cats from their penthouses to vacation homes, so she decided to keep doing it.

From there she gained contacts of her own and earned a reputation as someone handy with machines. Serrakin tech was sufficiently advanced enough, and she was adept enough in it, that she could figure out most operating systems even if they came from other civilizations. That skill put her in high demand with some of the more dastardly criminal groups, and she was soon being recruited by reckless types who took on increasingly risky jobs. It was one of those jobs that led to her closest encounter with actual incarceration. Vala remembered Tanis telling her the whole story one night after they'd been celebrating a particularly successful heist.

"I got scooped up in a sting operation. I was on one of our off-world colonies running a long con in the form of a company store. Someone screwed up and my homeworld sent someone to pick me up along with a couple of other guys who were making problems on a neighboring colony. They sent a ship to bring us back home to lock us up, but we hit an asteroid field. We were forced to make an emergency landing on some barren rock. The ship was too damaged to take off again, so we were stuck."

Tanis and other prisoners managed to get free from their restraints and overpowered their Serrakin guards. And there they stayed, picking off their jailers one by one, struggling to stay alive on what little rations they had left.

"Trapped on a barren planet with two dark, handsome men?" Vala said the first time she heard the story. "I can think of worse fates."

Tanis had made a non-committal noise in her throat. "Different strokes."

"So? How did you finally get free? Fix the ship? Was there a Stargate on the planet?"

"There was, but back then we didn't even know what the damn thing was. Three years we wasted within walking distance of our ticket home. Anyway, I tried to fix that damn ship the whole time we were crashed there without ever making any real progress. It was starting to look like we were just fighting over which side would get to starve to death. But then a group of obnoxiously altruistic soldiers showed up. We conned them for a while, and they're the ones who told us what the Stargate was capable of, and almost got away scot-free. But they were just a bit too clever. They figured out the truth and helped our jailers recapture us."

Vala narrowed her eyes as a thought occurred to her. "Wait a minute. This altruistic third party that caused all the problems for you… it didn't happen to include a fellow named Daniel, did it?"

"I don't think so. I don't remember all their names, but I remember the man who tricked me into becoming a prisoner again. Jonas Quinn."

"Hm. I was thinking about an obnoxious do-gooder I ran into a few weeks back. Primitive technology, insisted on sticking his nose where it didn't belong. I thought maybe it was the same person."

Tanis had shaken her head. "The universe isn't *that* small."

"So? You obviously didn't spend very much time in prison."

"Not a day. We had a trial, of course, and my solicitor said that I had suffered cruel and unusual punishment being stranded on that rock for three years. I mean… sure, while I was stranded there I had killed a couple of the crewmen. But that wasn't my fault. I couldn't have killed them if they hadn't crashed in the first place."

Vala shrugged. "Seems like solid logic."

"Anyway, the argument wasn't going to win but it bought me some time and sympathy. I was moved to an area of the prison with lower security and managed to break out using an access panel in my cell. I hijacked an off-world transport and headed out to seek my riches elsewhere."

"And riches we shall find!" Vala had promised.

Now they were in one of the worst districts of the most rotten city on Lucia, called the Bellows because the bad element blew out from there to the rest of the planet. Vala had come prepared for the potential of thievery; she had three weapons hidden on her right side alone, and she could easily draw two more with her left hand if the need arose. She had little doubt that Tanis was probably equally armed. Despite that, they had been on the street less than a minute before she felt the tell-tale tug of pilfering fingers at her belt. She rocked back on the heel of her boot, into the pickpocket's reach, and forced his arms all the way around her waist. Once he'd been snared she gripped his wrist hard enough to bruise before spinning to look at him.

"Here now! What in blazes do you think you're doing? Thieving from a hardworking woman? Taking my mediocre earnings for yourself? Well? What have you to say for yourself? Are you mute?"

The would-be robber turned out to be a boy not yet old enough to shave. His eyes were so wide Vala thought they might pop out, his lower lip trembling as he scanned the area for the rest of his gang. He stuttered and stammered until Vala took mercy on him. She released his hand and waved him away dismissively.

"Go. You're not worth the effort of trying to find a constable."

The boy turned and fled. Vala adjusted her belt as she watched him go, surreptitiously making certain her pouch was still in her possession. Tanis, who had slipped into the shadows along the side of the street when the confrontation began, stepped forward to rejoin her. Vala glanced over and raised her eyebrows hopefully.

"Anything worthwhile?"

Tanis revealed a handful of coins and a few pieces of jewelry. "It's obvious he wasn't a very good thief, but I still expected a little more from him." She looked in the direction he'd fled. "Shame. If he goes back to his people empty-handed he'll be harshly punished."

"How else will he learn?" Vala had clear memories of her own trial by fire in the months after being separated from Qetesh. Being kind to the boy would have done him no favors; if he was meant to be a thief he would have to learn to deal with failure sooner or later. Vala gestured for Tanis to put away their mediocre spoils from the encounter and continued on. The little thief had driven home the fact that every person they passed was a potential thief, so they kept their wits about them as they moved through the crowd.

They turned down a wide alley that was crowded from either side with makeshift storefronts manned by people trying to sell things they'd most likely stolen earlier that day. Vala and Tanis ignored the desperate people who scrambled and pushed their merchandise, eyes always forward and refusing the more determined salesmen with terse shakes of their head. The alley ended in a red door guarded by two men who made no attempt to hide their weapons but also didn't move into defensive postures when Vala and Tanis arrived.

Vala smiled her best smile. "Hello, boys. Siero is waiting for us. I'm Mal Doran, this is Reynard."

"Don't know you, ladies," one of the men said. "Probably should turn around and go back the way you came."

Vala's smile collapsed. "Well, that was very rude. I don't feel very welcome. How about you, Tanis? Do you feel welcome?"

"Not even a little bit." She glared at the larger guard. "Mighty rude to turn away a couple of ladies who want to conduct business with your boss. You could be costing him a very nice payday."

The man met Tanis' gaze without changing his expression in the least. "Why don't you let us deal with Siero? Run along now, girls."

Vala and Tanis glanced at each other, shrugged, and then each grabbed the guard nearest to them. They both pulled and sent the men tumbling. As they fell, Tanis and Vala lashed out with their free hands to steal the weapons from the guard's holsters. When the men managed to get back onto their hands and knees, they looked up into the business ends of their own blasters. Vala's smile was back on display, while Tanis flipped her hair out of her face without taking her eyes off her target.

"Now, as much as I would love to continue this little display of emasculation, you boys are not our goal. We just want to go inside and speak to your boss. Conduct a little honest crime."

"Fine. Go in."

"Splendid." She flipped the gun and handed it back to him by the barrel. "We'll just let this little dust-up remain between friends." She winked at him and turned on her heel, flipping her coat in the guard's face as she went inside. Tanis held her gaze on them for another second before she followed.

Siero owned the club and currently he and his entourage made up the entire clientele. He operated from a booth at the back of the main room, a seat that was raised onto a dais so he could overlook everything that went on in front of him. He was surrounded by two advisors on either side, and their combined weight caused the platform to sag slightly in the middle. The money-launderer was a stubby block of an Oranian, his muscular body long since gone to fat due to sitting in a booth all day counting his chits. Even the tentacles hanging from the back of his equine face looked like pudgy little slugs.

Despite being closed, the kitchen was open in order to provide Siero and his men with plates full of something so pungent that Vala regretted not asking Siero to meet them at the ship. Siero saw them approach and laughed, waving them closer.

"My girls, my girls, my wily girls! You have come back. At

long last, we are together again." He sniffed and pushed his opticals up with the knuckle of one finger, gesturing to his guards. "Formalities, you understand, one can't be too careful in one's position, hm?"

Vala and Tanis held their arms out to either side so they could be patted down for weapons. She kept a mental count of what was taken from her, happy to see that their unnecessarily thorough search managed to miss two of her weapons. Still, the guard nodded to Siero that the ladies were unarmed and he pointed them to the seats in front of him. Vala sat down directly across from him while Tanis took a chair and sat a few paces away from the table so she had a better view of the room.

"Always a pleasure to see you, Vala. Mostly because it means more money for me! None of those greedy upper-ups getting their cuts."

"Hello to you as well, Siero. As much as it pained us to be away so long, I think you'll find our absence could be very lucrative to you." She leaned forward to drop the bag on the table. "Just a sampling of what we're offering."

Siero snatched it up, bounced the weight in his palm, and then untied the top. He peered inside and turned it one way and then the other to watch the coins within sliding over each other. "Oh, yes, yes, yes. This is quite lovely. Direfs, if I'm not mistaken. From the kingdom of Selos." He took out one of the coins and examined the profile etched onto it. "New issue currency at that. Hm, yes. And you have more? This is just a small sample?"

"Oh, just a fraction of the wealth we're offering."

"Excellent!" He grinned revealing a row of sharp reptilian teeth. "It just so happens we are in the need of funds. The Lucian Alliance is ready to start making its name known throughout the galaxy."

Tanis said, "Finally ready to try your hand in the big leagues, huh?"

"The wheels are in motion, my lovely. We're reaching out all over everywhere. People were so quick to boot the Goa'uld out, now they're starting to think… well, what's next? Now who is going to be in charge? I'll tell you who… us! The little guys, the ones who have been doing all the grunt work making this galaxy run smoothly while the snakebrains sat in their golden thrones and zipped around in their pyramids. They're gone and we're still around. So it's our turn to reap some of the benefits. So I think we can negotiate a fair price for your loot. Typical exchange rate?"

"Not this time, Siero," Vala said. "We're going to skip the laundering and get right to what we actually want. We're giving you this money in payment for naquadah. What would you say to ten direfs for eight ounces?"

Siero snorted. "I would say robbery!"

"You might want to think before you start throwing that word around, Siero. None of us here is a saint. But we can negotiate! That's what we're good at. What would you consider reasonable?"

"Fine, negotiation… instead of eight ounces for every ten direfs, you just give us everything you brought with you from Selos in exchange for walking from this building under your own power?"

Tanis glanced toward the door and saw the guards from outside had reappeared. This time they brought a couple of friends.

"Vala?"

"Mm-hmm." Vala kept her eyes locked on Siero, but there was no doubt she knew what was happening behind her. She crossed her arms over her chest and leaned forward. "I am very disappointed, Siero. I thought we had a good thing going here."

"Business! It's just business! I'm terribly sorry to do this to you ladies, really I am. But the Lucian Alliance needs money in its coffers if we're going to thrive, and we can't do that by paying for every little thing that crosses our table. But surely you must have expected this. You knew who you were dealing with when you walked in here."

"You have a point. But you also knew who you were dealing with. Tanis?"

Tanis reached into her jacket and withdrew four long silver bars. Siero's eyes widened at the sight of them, but she wasn't offering the bribe to him. She reached back without looking and waved the shesh'ta at the guards. "I don't know how much of a cut he's offering you," she said, "but I'd like to make a side offer. Will this buy your guns, gentlemen?"

The guards looked at each other, then at the money they were being offered. It was more than a years' wages for them both. After a long and tense moment, the guards took the deal. Tanis took their guns and handed one to Vala. They both trained their weapons on Siero as he tried to protect his face with his chubby arms.

"Wait! Don't! This… You don't understand! This was just business!"

"It was business," Vala said, "but then you made it personal."

Siero whimpered. "Do you have any idea how expensive it is to take the place of the System Lords in the universe? We are bleeding funds, Vala! I couldn't even come up with enough naquadah for what you have in that baggie, let alone an entire cargo hold full of it."

Vala was livid. "I wasted months on this job on the promise your little Alliance would make it worth my while in the end. And this is my repayment? You try to rob me, and when that fails, you stiff me?"

"A mo-moment of desperation and weakness, I assure you. Please! Please, show mercy to a poor and desperate man."

"Poor being the operative word," Tanis said. "We should kill him on principle."

Siero squeaked. "No! Wait! What if I did have something of use? Something of, of value in exchange? What if I could tell you about a job that would make you rich beyond your wildest imaginations?"

"Sounds like another desperate and weak moment to me," Tanis muttered.

"Might as well hear him out."

Siero swallowed the lump in his throat. "You can use the direfs to fund another job. It's a treasure hunt. It would make all your past jobs look like chicken feed."

Vala said, "Why aren't you going after it? Or one of your other Lucian Alliance cronies?"

"Who has the time? And like I said, if certain wheels have to be greased for information, the Alliance doesn't have the liquidity to make that happen. But you… if anyone can find it, you ladies can."

"Go on," Vala said.

"It's a treasure. A vast fortune just lying around waiting to be snatched up by the first person to get their hands on it. You don't have to worry about fencing what you steal because it belonged to a Goa'uld. All their stuff is a free for all right now. No one is asking for provenance on Goa'uld riches these days. All 'look the other way' and cash under the table. If you find it, it's yours. Every coin, every gem, every last piece. You could buy a planet with that wealth. I can tell you exactly where to start looking for it."

Vala looked at Tanis and saw she was intrigued by the prospect. "Which Goa'uld?"

"Does that matter?"

"Not all of them are entirely gone. You could be sending us into a trap."

"No, trust me, this lady isn't in any shape to come after you. The treasure belonged to Kali, all right?"

Vala's expression wavered. The wealth of a deposed female Goa'uld… it could be exactly the score she had been looking for.

Siero misread her internal debate for uncertainty. "She sided with Anubis when he came lumbering back, okay? Now that he's been defeated, even the other Go'aulds want nothing to do with her. You go after Kali's treasure, I promise you're gonna be the only ones looking."

CHAPTER THREE

JACK was waiting at the base of the ramp, arms folded casually over his chest, when SG-9 returned. They had radioed ahead to inform him of their findings, and his eyes locked onto Daniel as the Stargate disengaged. Jack raised his eyebrows at Colonel Getty. "I thought I told you not to let him touch anything."

"My apologies, sir. I turned my back for one minute, suddenly it's the end of the world."

"I won't judge you too harshly. I've been on the receiving end of that myself."

"Thank you, sir."

Jack glared at Daniel. "First mission after defeating the Goa'uld."

"I'm aware."

"A nice leisurely temple to explore, nothing to get excited about except a few dusty carvings."

"I know."

Jack thumped the back of his hand against Daniel's chest. "First time leaving your office in weeks, you go and find a doomsday weapon."

Daniel said, "Don't blame me. I was more than happy down in my office with my books and my journals. In the words of another SG team member: I retired. You wanted me back. Now that you're in charge, the shoe is on the other foot."

"Hm," Jack said. "Okay. Briefing room."

They handed off their gear to the SFs guarding the ramp. Daniel gave up his digital camera to an airman and instructed him to set it up so he could display the images during the briefing. As they climbed the stairs out of the control room, Daniel was distracted by thoughts of what he'd discovered. He was trying to figure out how to succinctly explain it all to Jack so that he could convey just how monumentally bad the situation really was.

As he entered the briefing room, movement from the corner of his eye caught his attention. The Replicator version of Samantha Carter turned toward him, eyes cold and dark, the overhead lights shining along the blade of her right hand. Daniel recoiled at the sight, tripping back a step and colliding with Jack. He brought his hands up in a defensive pose, already feeling ridiculous as the vision faded.

"Daniel?" Sam asked.

He relaxed and lowered his arms, anxiety giving way to embarrassment as he realized what he'd done. The person standing a few feet away was Sam, the real Sam, and the glint of light had reflected off the water carafe she was using to pour herself a drink. She had paused mid-pour, concern written across her face, and Daniel looked over his shoulder to see Jack watching him with the same concern. He coughed into his fist and straightened his jacket.

"Everything okay?" Jack said.

"Fine," Daniel said. "Sorry. I just… I didn't know you were already back."

Sam nodded, obviously still concerned. "I got in this morning. General O'Neill said you'd found something interesting and suggested I sit in on the briefing." She narrowed her eyes at him. "Are you sure you're okay? You look a little pale."

Jack seemed to sense Daniel wanted to drop it. "Oh, that's just from hiding down in his office all the live-long day. The poor boy hasn't seen the sun in weeks."

Daniel nodded and accepted the out. "Not to mention what we discovered on the planet." He put down his notebook and glanced at the airman, who nodded that the digital camera was set up. The rest of SG-9 took their seats at the table, leaving the two seats on either side of Jack's position empty for the members of his team. Daniel retrieved the clicker for the projection screen that had just been lowered over the window to Jack's office. The lights went down and Daniel clicked to the first image. It had been taken from the DHD and showed the painting of Kali that would have greeted every visitor to the planet.

"This is Kali, the Hindu goddess of death and darkness. This is a portrait that was painted on the wall facing the Stargate as you arrive in her temple."

"Heck of a welcome mat," Jack said.

"Yes, despite appearances, Kali was not an aggressive or violent Goa'uld. At first I thought this was meant simply as a warning, marking her territory so she wouldn't have to fight. Now, she was far from being a pacifist, but if there was a way to avoid all-out war she usually took it.

"Kali originally came to Earth as a follower of Shiva. She was one of the first Goa'uld to take a human host while others, including Shiva, were mostly still using the Unas. Now, the people they were attempting to rule didn't look at Unas and see 'god.' They saw Shiva as a demonic entity. Kali begged him to take a human host, but Shiva refused. He saw us as inferior in terms of longevity, strength, ah… well. He was losing control of his followers, and Kali went to Ra for help. She wanted Ra to convince Shiva to take a human host. Ra had other ideas. He ordered Kali to murder Shiva and take his place. After a bit of soul-searching, Kali did just that. She figured Ra would have him killed one way or another, so why not benefit from the murder?"

Colonel Getty said, "Sounds like snakehead politics as usual."

Daniel nodded. "Yes. Well, afterward, Kali obviously didn't want anyone hanging around who was still loyal to Shiva. According to the histories we've found, she managed to quickly and decisively kill anyone who refused to denounce their former god and accept her as his replacement. She wiped out all of Shiva's followers without harming those who had declared loyalty to her."

Jack said, "Neat trick."

"Yes, and for the most part no one's really bothered to worry about how exactly she pulled it off. That brings us to the device I discovered off-world."

He clicked a button to change the image to the table he and Morello had discovered.

"We found this in a hidden chamber off the Stargate room." He clicked another button to show a detailed picture of the carvings. "I was able to translate most of this. It definitely is as old as it looks, but I think it was moved here fairly recently. It seems to be a more modern marriage of Goa'uld and Ancient technologies. Using modern in a relative sense here, of course…"

"You think this was a perk of throwing her hat in the ring with old Anubis," Jack said.

"Yes. Now, the carving starts out with the typical Goa'uld puff and ruffle, but around the second paragraph it starts to get a little more specific. It speaks of a potential uprising of the Jaffa or, as they put it, a blasphemous rebellion of the lower castes but I think we can all read between the lines. It goes through the party lines… foolishness of their hubris, the consequences of incurring the wrath of their god. But here at the bottom is where things start getting more interesting." He stepped closer to the screen so he could point out the pertinent sections, even though he was the only one present who could read it. "'Those heretics who stand against their god Kali shall suffer grave consequences for their sin of blasphemy… cast into the pit…' so on and so on."

Sam said, "The Goa'uld are known for talking a big game. You said yourself the artwork was most likely meant as a deterrent rather than an actual threat."

"Right, but that was directly in front of the Stargate and impossible to miss. This was hidden in a secondary chamber that we would never have found if we hadn't been looking for it. Besides, while Kali may have been all about diplomacy, this device was given to her by Anubis."

Jack said, "And we know he wouldn't be above the whole 'weapons of mass destruction' route if it was available to him."

Morello said, "He already tried to eliminate the Jaffa once before, when he bred the Kull warriors. That could have been a precursor to using this device to kill them all. It would explain how Kali managed to kill all of Shiva's followers and leave all of her own alive. She just found a way to target the right people and flipped a switch. Anubis gave her a means to do it on a much larger scale."

Getty said, "Are we sure she actually pulled that off? I mean, 'worship me or I'll kill you' would go a long way toward making someone switch churches. Maybe they decided it was good enough to just pay lip service to the new boss."

"No. A Goa'uld would want to know," Jack said.

Daniel nodded. "Yes, and she had a way to make sure." He moved to the next photo. "This carving indicates that a failsafe device to ensure that even if Kali isn't around to make her followers pay, they'll still suffer for rising up. In the event of her Jaffa rising up against her, it would dial the Stargate and deliver a potent virus to a series of random addresses. And that's not the worst part. This, the device we found, doesn't have the apparatus necessary to set off a chain of events like the one it describes. This is just one domino in a much larger series. If the threat is credible, and we have to believe it is, I believe she has more of these devices on other planets in her realm."

Jack said, "Including Earth?"

Daniel shook his head. "No, Anubis would have only been able to give her the technology to go universal within the past few years. Long after she left Earth behind."

Getty said, "Seems like a long way to go just to get revenge."

Sam shrugged. "Maybe the inroads Teal'c and Bra'tac made the past few years scared her into taking drastic measures."

"Right," Daniel said. "It's been only recently that the Jaffa have even managed to gain a foothold against the Goa'uld. For the first time in history, Jaffa have been turning against their so-called gods in unprecedented numbers. It makes sense one of them would take measures like this."

Jack said, "Why do you think this is only a problem for Jaffa? How do we know this thing won't go off and kill everybody?"

"The engraving specifically mentions Jaffa, saying they will be struck down for their disloyalty. Now, it's not unheard of for the Goa'uld to take out their anger on innocent bystanders, but in this case I think only striking the Jaffa would be a more potent demonstration of their power. The Jaffa were genetically engineered to serve as the perfect hosts. It stands to reason that there's something specific about their DNA that can be targeted by these devices. The good news is that there seems to be a way to shut the devices off. Kali obviously had to have a way of deactivating it while her Jaffa were still behaving themselves. And if they did rise up against her, she couldn't guarantee she would be able to get to the machine in order to enable it."

Sam said, "A dead-man's switch."

"Right. It took me a while, but I found the shut-off switch on this device. This particular piece of the puzzle has been disabled. It's harmless."

"That's great," Sam said.

Jack held up a hand. "Wait. Every silver lining has a gray cloud around it. Daniel...?"

Daniel sighed. "We have no way of knowing how many of these devices Kali created. Taking this one out of the loop could also have disabled every device it was programmed to activate down the road. But we don't even know how many planets she had under her control. If even one device goes off, it could be devastating to the Jaffa."

"Wrath of a vengeful god apparently striking from beyond the grave?" Sam said. "They would lose all the progress they've gained since Dakara. They might never recover from that."

Jack said, "Okay, so what are the options? Go around checking all of Kali's summer homes, see if there are any of these devices lying around?"

Sam said, "We could ask the Tok'ra if they have any insights they'd be willing to share. There's a chance they won't want to talk to us at all given how they feel about us these days, but anything they give us would help. They could at least give us an idea of where to start instead of just going to every single one of Kali's planets and shutting off each individual device one at a time. There has to be some way to disable all of the devices at once."

"Why?" Jack said.

"Well, think about it, sir. Kali wouldn't take the time to manually shut off every single device in the circuit. She must have had some sort of…"

"Remote control?" Jack suggested.

"For lack of a better term."

Daniel said, "Sam's right. There has to be some way to shut them all off at once."

"Okay. So we find the remote control and shut down all the devices in one fell swoop," Jack said. "What's the time frame?"

"We don't know. I can't imagine it would be very long because she would want to punish them as swiftly as possible. Then again, she couldn't exactly devote every day to making sure the device didn't go off accidentally. Best guess is that every time she disabled the devices, they would remain dormant for at least a few months. It's been a few weeks since Dakara, so I have to imagine the clock is running out fast. I was going to suggest leaving SG-9 on the planet to investigate the temple further, maybe find out more about when and how this thing was installed. If there's anything left to be found, Morello will find it."

Jack looked at the woman, who seemed surprised by Daniel's suggestion. "You up for the challenge?"

She composed herself quickly and nodded. "I am, sir."

"Okay. We'll get in touch with the Tok'ra and see what they're willing to offer in terms of information. We should also reach out to the Jaffa and let them know what's going on."

Sam smiled. "Any Jaffa in particular you'd like to contact, sir?"

Jack returned her smile as he stood up. "Might be nice to

have the big guy back here again. Colonel, take your team back to the planet and continue the search. While you're there, use their gate to contact the Jaffa and ask Teal'c to hightail it back to the SGC."

Daniel frowned. "Why do you want to use a secondary gate?"

Jack hooked a thumb at the Stargate. "Have you seen the bill for turning that thing on? Might as well use someone else's phone if we're just going to send an RSVP."

"We should have killed him."

Vala clucked her tongue. They had just left Siero's bar and were strolling through the winding back alleys trying to decide their next step. At least Vala was thinking about the next step. Tanis seemed caught up on what she viewed as a missed opportunity.

"Now, Tanis. If we went around killing everyone who tried to scam us, we'd never get anything else done. Besides, it would set up an unfortunate eye-for-an-eye mentality that might come back and bite us if we ever scammed someone else. Not that we would ever stoop to something so low as a petty con."

"Perish the thought," Tanis said with a grin. "Fine. But we put in a lot of hours on that job. I had to clean that stupid place from top to bottom every day."

"You had a staff!"

Tanis stuffed her hands into her pockets and glowered down the street. "So you really think Kali has a treasure waiting to be found?"

"I'm positive of it. Siero is too cowardly to lie to me about something this large. He knows that if I don't find anything I'll come back here and have his tentacles on a platter." She hooked her arm around Tanis' and pulled her close. "It wasn't a total loss, after all. You got to keep that guard's gun."

"Hardly something worth bragging about. I paid for this with real money. Besides, this thing is an antique." She took it from the holster she had 'gently persuaded' the guard to hand over before they left. She turned it over in her hands and pursed her lips as she examined the clip. She'd always been a fan of the older projectile weapons, if she was entirely honest with herself. They had become hot commodities during the Replicator invasion. Even though the little scurrying buggers had been defeated, bullets were still being sold at a premium in markets like this all across the galaxy. She and Vala had made quite a tidy little sum selling bullets to desperate Jaffa just a few weeks earlier. Still, one gun was hardly a worthy reward for all the hard work she'd been forced to do. She shoved it back into her holster and sighed.

"Weeks of preparation, over a month of actual hard labor scrubbing floors, and all we have to show for it is a ship full of currency, a gun, and a promise from a criminal who has just proven he isn't trustworthy. Excuse me if I'm not exactly jumping for joy."

"You'll have plenty of reason to jump if this lead pans out."

"If," Tanis said. "He could have just told us some story to get us out of his hair."

Vala nodded. "True. He could have made it all up on the spot, plucked it out of whole cloth, and sent us on our merry way. But if that were the case, we wouldn't have been followed when we left his bar. The two hooded gentlemen on either side of the alley, and the young man on the rooftops tracking our progress. Don't look up, look down."

Tanis glanced at the mouth of the next alley. As they passed, a shadow flitted across the cobblestones from one building to the next.

"I believe they're planning to discover what Siero told us and hijack our ship. Lends some credence to his story, wouldn't you say?"

"Some. Not a lot. How do you want to play this?"

"We'll let them follow us to the ship, then we turn the tables and find out what they know about Kali's treasure. They might be able to give us an idea of where we should start looking."

Tanis accepted that plan with a slight nod of her head. They took their time moving through the marketplace, pausing occasionally just to make the men tailing them work a little harder. The men hid their faces with their hoods, but Vala could see weapons holstered on their waists when the cloaks flipped back. They had gotten their weapons back from Siero's guards when they left, but Vala felt the need for a little extra protection. She pocketed a small blade from one of the shop fronts they passed, and she knew Tanis had further armed herself as well.

By the time they reached their ship, the crowd had thinned out enough that their pursuers found it harder to remain concealed. Vala acted casually as she entered the ship's code and slipped out of her jacket as she stepped inside. Tanis followed her in and darted to one side of the door, slipping a long wooden staff from of her sleeve and grasping the padded end as she crouched down.

They heard rushed footsteps as their would-be assailants hurried to reach the door before it closed. Vala waited until the first man crossed the threshold before she whipped up her coat and let him run into the billowing material. She pulled it tight across his face, like catching a thrown boulder with a sack, and used his own momentum to swing him into the wall. Tanis swung out her staff and cracked the second man across the shins. The blow made him stop, and he turned toward her with his fist already flying. Tanis ducked to let his knuckles crack against the bulkhead, then slammed her shoulder into the soft bowl of his gut. He was thrown back, and Vala cracked him in the jaw with a well-placed elbow.

Tanis moved toward the door and peered outside, the sickly orange security lights shining down on her face as she looked for more attackers.

"Got any other friends out there?"

"It's just us," the first man groaned.

Vala thumped the man with her boot. "Be honest now. We saw the little bird you had tracking us all the way from Siero's bar. How many more are out there?"

The man Tanis had taken out grunted, "Don't tell them anything, Rewill…"

"That's a nice start," Vala said. "Rewill, was it? And what was your friend's name? Come on, he told us yours. Might as well even the score."

"His name is Cottim," Rewill grunted.

Vala grinned. "Wonderful! I'm Vala, and that's Tanis. Now that we're all acquainted with one another, perhaps you'd like to tell us why you were so interested in us."

Cottim said, "Well, you're both such lovely ladies…"

Tanis kicked him in a place that changed the pitch of his voice. "Try again."

Rewill grunted in sympathy for his companion and twisted across the floor so he wasn't in range of Vala's boots. "Siero's been sitting on that treasure trove line for weeks. He stiffed us on a job and tried using the information to pay us back. Only problem is, Cottim and I are in the same position as the Lucian Alliance. We just don't have the funds to go looking for it. So when you two show up with a ship full of goodies and you leave the pub empty-handed? I figured he made you the same deal but you have the means to go after it. So my pal and I thought we'd take it off your hands. Couple of ladies like you could get into all kinds of trouble."

Tanis smiled. "Trouble doesn't follow us anywhere," she said. "It just sort of starts happening once we arrive."

"I think we've proven we can handle ourselves," Vala said.

"Sure. We'll see how tough you are when you find the treasure and Siero's goons swoop in to take it away from you."

Vala raised an eyebrow. "Aha. I assumed he had something up his sleeve, but it's nice to have confirmation. Glad to hear it."

"Glad?" Tanis said.

"Well, of course, darling. If he's going to keep tabs on us so he can steal the treasure, then that means the information he gave us is good. He put us on the right track. So, Rewill, what exactly is in this treasure of Kali's?"

"Typical Goa'uld excess," Rewill said. "Gold, gems, jewelry, that sort of thing. Her palaces have been ransacked just like everybody else's, but no one cares about Kali or her realm. She chose the losing side and now she's paying for it. She went from being the queen bee of her corner of the galaxy to having everyone digging through her riches looking for something to sell."

"Any particular place it's being sold?"

"I've heard that most of the big stuff got funneled to a planet called Teunus. But you're not going to get very far on that track. Teunus has been annexed by the Jaffa and they're very stingy about who they let onto their planet. Couple of thieves like you would be turned away without a second glance."

Vala considered his answer for a moment before relaxing her gun arm. She gestured for Rewill to get up. "Thank you, gentlemen. You've been most helpful. Now run along before we decide to use you as an example for anyone Siero might choose to send after us."

Cottim roughly smoothed down his tunic as he stood up. "Can I have my weapon back?"

Tanis stared at him without saying a word. He waited, hand out, then grunted when it became clear she wasn't going to hand it over. He glared at Rewill before storming out of the ship. Vala stepped back and allowed Rewill to pass her, waving goodbye as cheekily as possible before she shut the door behind them. Once they were alone she looked at Tanis.

"See? Now you have two guns!"

"I'm well and truly blessed," Tanis said flatly.

"Oh, cheer up. Now we have confirmation that Siero was on the level, and we know why he was willing to part with such valuable information. All we have to do now is stay wary of anyone he has dogging our trail. There's treasure out there, Tanis, and it's just waiting to be plucked up."

Tanis grinned, her eyes glistening as she thought of the possibilities. "Then let's go get it."

CHAPTER FOUR

SAM AND Daniel tried to look inconspicuous as they stepped through the event horizon, leaving behind the comfortable environment of the SGC for the sights and scents of an alien bazaar. The Stargate was surrounded by a wooden corral with only one way out, and that exit was currently blocked by hucksters and shills trying to drum up business. As soon as they reached the base of the wooden steps they were bombarded by salesmen. A woman tried to sell Sam a string of polished stones, while Daniel was momentarily enticed by the promise of allegedly ancient books before Sam managed to pull him away.

"What are the odds the books will turn out to be authentic?"

"Oh, I have no doubt they're fake. But sometimes a fake can tell you just as much about a civilization as the real thing. Fiction tends to paint a much more honest picture of the world as it is."

"You're still trying to live down getting caught with Harry Potter books, aren't you?"

Daniel brushed past one of the salespeople. "So! Our contact said she would meet us near the Stargate, right? How do we know who to look for?"

Sam chuckled and let the matter drop. They managed to escape the corral without being forced to purchase anything and Sam looked around. "I figure she'll recognize us. But I'm sure the Tok'ra sent someone we know if anyone was available."

"I'm just grateful one of them agreed to show up, considering our relationship with them is hardly strong at the moment."

Sam nodded. The SGC had sent a coded message to the Tok'ra in the hopes one of them, any of them, would see fit to respond. They were surprised to get a response within two hours, a message from a Tok'ra operative who had not only worked with them before but knew where to start looking for items looted from Kali's palaces. Sam hadn't immediately recognized the Tok'ra's name, but she refreshed her memory by reading the mission reports in which she lent her services to the SGC. Sam was grateful that the woman was still willing to work with them despite everything that had happened recently.

The past year had been difficult for relations between the Tok'ra and the Tau'ri. Her father had done his best to try smoothing over any rough bits between the two governments, but he ended up putting the last nail in the coffin when he provided Earth with the method to track Ba'al's ships. The High Council had decided against sharing the technology, and by defying them Jacob had finally revealed where his true loyalties were.

As a result, he and Selmak had been on the verge of exile when they passed away. The Tok'ra held a memorial ceremony for him, but it was an extremely understated memorial for someone of Selmak's history. Sam found their response offensive given the fact that her father's actions had been instrumental in defeating both the Goa'uld and the Replicators, but hurt feelings didn't go away easily. She hoped that now things were starting to settle down both sides could let bygones be bygones.

And while she knew they couldn't exactly be picky about their meeting place, she wished they could have met up somewhere a little less fragrant. And as long as she was making fruitless wishes, she also would have preferred meeting somewhere they could have worn their regular off-world uniforms. The Tok'ra had warned them the planet was hostile and wouldn't be welcoming to a group of Tau'ri visitors, so they were forced to arrive in 'local garb.' Over the years, the SGC had accumulated a marvelously eclectic wardrobe culled from a myriad of worlds they had visited in the past. Sam was wearing a high-collared white blouse that, thankfully, wasn't cut low enough to be obscene. Daniel was in a sleeveless leather tunic that laced up the front and, to her delight, was actually much more revealing than what she wore.

Daniel seemed to be thinking along the same lines she was, as he adjusted the collar of his top and looked down to make sure it wasn't askew. "You know, I have a sneaking suspicion that no matter where you are in the universe, a large majority of fashion choices are based on a dare."

Sam smiled. "I'm sure aliens visiting Earth would say the same thing about high heels."

"Exactly." He glanced at one of the stalls they passed and adjusted his glasses. "So where are we supposed to meet this operative anyway? What was her name?"

"Sina. She was willing to share information with us when Anubis was first rising to power, so hopefully she'll help us out this time." She spotted a tall woman with red hair and cut through the crowd to intercept her. The woman saw them coming and gestured toward an alley, ducking in ahead of them once she was sure they'd spotted her. Sam and Daniel caught up with her, and she scanned the crowd over their shoulders before she spoke in the deep, dulcet tone of her symbiote.

"Colonel Carter, Dr. Jackson. Welcome to Lucia."

"Thank you for meeting us on such short notice."

Sina nodded. "I must admit your message was quite the cause for alarm. Several of our operatives spent time in Kali's inner circle and believe there is some merit to your fears."

Daniel said, "It's how she got rid of anyone still loyal to Shiva, right?"

"A similar method, yes. In the previous instance, she merely had to target a single world. This undertaking is quite a bit more extravagant, thanks to Anubis' influence, I have no doubt. The High Council has agreed to offer you our assistance in this matter. Hopefully this will serve as an example to both you and the Jaffa that your haphazard methods were perhaps not as successful as you originally believed. The System Lords may have been deposed, but the resulting chaos may prove disastrous for the galaxy as a whole."

Daniel said, "You're… welcome?"

"He means thank you," Sam said. "Thank you for your help, despite our recent problems."

Sina didn't acknowledge either of them. "It is in everyone's best interest that this device be deactivated as quickly as possible. If the Jaffa were victims of a genocide, it would throw the entire galaxy into even further chaos. We cannot allow devastation of that magnitude. That is why the High Council has agreed to help you on this matter, but after this we will part ways. I apologize if that sounds cold, but there are many other pressing matters which must be dealt with."

"We understand," Sam said, hoping to push the conversation back toward amicable diplomacy. "We appreciate you getting us this far."

Sina was obviously appeased. She looked out at the street again, motioned for them to follow, and stepped out into the flow of pedestrians again.

Sam lowered her voice and leaned toward him. "I think you've been hanging around General O'Neill too much."

Daniel sighed. "I just get a little sick of the holier-than-thou. But she is doing us a favor, so I'll try to control my inner O'Neill."

Sam grinned and moved through the crowd as it parted in Sina's wake. The Tok'ra only glanced back once to make sure they were following her. "We inquired to several of our operatives as soon as we received your warning, and we have begun to spread word to any Jaffa settlements we are in contact with. There are whispers among Bastet's people regarding the devices of which you speak."

Daniel said, "That makes sense. Kali and Bastet had a coalition, of sorts. Kali might have shared with her the means to stop the devices from activating."

"It is unlikely. Bastet merely allied herself with whichever System Lord would offer her the most protection from the others. Kali would not have entrusted her with anything quite so important. But because of her inferior status, Bastet sought favor wherever she could find it. Often she bought allegiance by trading secrets. The information she learned from Kali was shared with Bastet's lieutenants, who shared it with someone else, on down the line until it landed in the hands of a well-known thief named Siero. He's aware of a treasure trove stolen from Kali's palaces, and we have reason to believe the dead man's switch you seek is among the items he can point us toward."

"Let's hope," Sam said.

Sina led them down a short alley to the back door of a pub. Sam was sometimes amazed at how similar alien worlds could be to Earth. The languages and culture might be different, but wherever humanoid people gathered there were bound to be slums, red-light districts, and seedy bars. A man wearing a plastic bib moved to stop them as they passed through the kitchen, but Sina sketched out a quick hand signal that held him off.

"Friend of yours?"

"No. But he believes I am a friend of his."

In the main room of the restaurant they found Siero seated on a raised platform speaking angrily at two men who had apparently done something to irritate him. Sam was startled by his piscine appearance, the shoulders of his suit draped by twin tentacles that hung from the top of his head. She had gotten so used to encountering displaced humans from Earth that sometimes she forgot there were truly alien aliens out there in the galaxy.

Daniel tensed slightly as they approached. She looked at him and he leaned close to answer her unspoken question. "He's Oranian. A couple of them wanted to buy the *Prometheus* when it was stolen a few months ago."

As they approached, Sam heard one of the men complain, "She took my gun, Siero!" The other man started to say something as well, but Siero cut him off when he spotted the new arrivals.

"Who are you? What do you want?"

Sina responded in her human voice. "We wish to speak to you about Kali's treasure."

The men glanced at their boss, who waved them away. Once they were alone Siero gestured at the seats across from him. "Kali... Kali, yes, the name is familiar. The System Lord. Cast her lot with the losing team, and we all know how that turns out." His shoulders hunched as he laughed. "But treasure? Well, all Goa'uld have a treasure, but I'm certain I don't know anything about any specific treasure..."

Sina was suddenly on her feet, one arm extended across the table to grab Siero's right tentacle. The two men from earlier rushed to their employer's aid, but Sam and Daniel stood up to block them from getting close. Daniel held up his hands to prevent anyone from pulling any weapons.

"There's no need for violence," he said. "Right? Sina?"

The Tok'ra kept her grip on Siero's appendage. "That all depends on what this worm has to say. Kali's treasure."

"Okay! Yes, there are rumors of a treasure. Kali's palaces were wiped out after the Jaffa decided it was time for a change. What they didn't blow up, they stole. A lot of it has already been scattered through every inhabited world. Barter system is back in a big way these days. Passage from one planet to another, weapons, it's all getting paid for with thieved Goa'uld baubles. I get the impression you're looking for something specific? You're looking for a needle in a haystack, but hey, I'm not here to judge."

Daniel said, "Kali had devices in her temples that were set to be activated in the event of a Jaffa uprising. We're looking for a way to stop them from going off."

Siero's expression changed slightly. "Oh. You're looking for a way to stop the Purge. I always thought that was just a rumor."

"Believe me, we've seen the devices and they're primed to go."

Sam said, "Is there a way to disable the entire network?"

"Sure. Kali didn't want to spend all her time going around shutting the things off, and she didn't want to risk losing her army just because she happened to forget one. There was a device that she kept in her main chambers. All she had to do was input a code and the devices went to sleep."

Daniel said, "What did it look like?"

"I don't *know*, I'm not her architect. Everything I'm telling you is just what I know through rumor and second-hand knowledge. But I swear I'm telling you everything I know. Keep this *criniscao* away from me."

Daniel mentally translated the insult to something along the lines of 'tentacle-less,' but he had a feeling it was much more vulgar in the original tongue. "Okay, so you don't know what it looks like or where it ended up. Do you know anyone who might know?"

Siero sighed and Sino tightened her grip on his tentacle. He yelped and rose slightly from his seat before he whimpered and glared at her. "Yeah, yes, fine. The switch was installed in Kali's main palace so she would always have it handy. Understandably, that was one of the first places looted. Anything that was there has already been snatched up and tossed to the seven winds. But that was the really choice stuff. No one was using it for simple exchanges. You want to find something that big and that expensive, you should look on Teunus. They got the really choice pickings."

Sam said, "Do you have a gate address?"

Siero shook his head. "You're not setting foot on that planet, lady. It was neutral before the System Lords got the boot, but now it's been annexed by the Free Jaffa Nation. They're the ones gathering up the most expensive junk so they can auction it off. Trying to fund their freedom, you know. And you're not getting in the door unless you have a Jaffa to vouch for you."

Daniel looked at Sam. "Oh, I… I think we know someone who would lend a hand."

Vala couldn't help but think how easy it would be if they could just go straight to Teunus and start asking about Kali's treasure, but without a Jaffa to lead the way she doubted they would get far. She had worked with a few Jaffa in the past and tried to think of any that she could contact to get them in. Inago… no. Definitely not Inago. Better to leave that bridge burnt. But if the Jaffa were hoarding Kali's treasures in order to raise funds, it stood to reason they were selling things to people who weren't Jaffa. And where vast amounts of gold finery had to be moved, there was skimming. Vala had no doubt a good chunk of what she wanted was being moved out the back door under the table on the sly.

Tanis and Vala brainstormed about the possibilities. Teunus was in a relatively isolated part of space, and there was really only one person who operated in that area: a woman named Baleya. Neither of them had worked with her before, which was as beneficial as it was detrimental. They didn't have a personal relationship with her, but neither had they double-crossed her or stolen from her.

They had just left Lucia's solar system when Tanis picked up another ship on their sensors. "Looks like Siero's people have already slipped their leash around our necks."

Vala said, "Hm. Well, no sense in dragging them all over the galaxy just to prolong the inevitable. If we're going to send them in circles it would be kind to do it while they're still close to home." Earlier they had prepared two of the escape pods to use as a diversion once Siero's tagalongs made their presence known. She slowed the tel'tak just a bit to close the distance and then ejected the rigged pods on a trajectory that brought them back around to the other ship from behind. The pods could be manually controlled from her heads-up display panel, and she closed one eye to focus on the energy signature of their pursuers.

"Now," Tanis said.

"Not quite yet…"

Tanis checked her own display. "If you wait too long, it's going to be useless."

"Patience…"

Each escape pod held half of a malfunctioning generator.

tivated it, an electromagnetic pulse would pass
two and knock out the electronics of anything
he just had to wait until the pods were perfectly
ither side of their tail. She watched the little lights
n and, just when she feared they had passed the
eturn, flipped the switch. The blip representing
ickered and went out.

ed and clapped her hands together. "There we
nock out their systems for a few minutes, so we
e by the time they're back up and running. If
o kind as to set the course for Baleya's planet…"

She eyed the course and calculated the travel
a always said to grab all the sleep you can when
going to go catch a nap."

"Pleasant dreams," Vala said.

After Tanis was gone, Vala decided she had the right idea. She leaned back in her seat and placed her boots on the console. Might as well get some shut-eye while they were en route. Tanis had slung up a hammock in the cargo hold, but Vala preferred catching her sleep in the pilot's chair. If an alarm went off she could be awake and working on a solution within seconds. It also gave her the chance to watch the lights streaking past the ship as she fell asleep. That was one thing about traveling everywhere by Stargate; one never got the opportunity to just sit back and relax in the in-betweens.

Vala was still surprised by how quickly and easily she and Tanis got along. In the past, anyone Vala teamed up with was just an eventual patsy, a fall-guy she could cut loose to take the blame while she made a hasty getaway. She got the feeling Tanis treated her partners the same way. They met when they were both targeting a collector of rare art. Vala had a buyer and Tanis had the security codes. Rather than compete, they decided to join forces and split the reward. Afterward Vala recalled a few jobs she'd put on the backburner because they required a partner, and she suggested a temporary partnership in order to pull them off. Tanis was amenab[...] crime spree began.

Vala kept thinking the current job would be t[...] together, but something kept bringing them to[gether...] would part ways only to circle back around with a can't-miss score that required an extra set of hands or some skill the other possessed. As long as their relationship continued to be mutually beneficial, Vala saw no reason to cut Tanis loose.

Well... that wasn't exactly true. She didn't wholly approve of Tanis' approach to confrontation. Most of her tales about past jobs included off-hand mentions of "the surviving guards" and "while they were still dealing with the victims," indicating Tanis was a bit more violent than Vala was entirely comfortable with. Still, she was canny and clever, and Vala could rein in some of her bloodlust when they were working together. And just because her first instinct was to kill anyone who saw their faces didn't mean she was unreasonable. Still, Vala knew there might come a day when Tanis would go too far and she would have to cut ties with her. With any luck, that day would come after she helped Vala secure Kali's treasure but before they divvied it up.

At the moment she had a long trip and nothing to do but think. She came up with some of her best scams while en route from one place to another. Currently she had to think of the right approach to a fence neither she nor Tanis had met before. They needed a foolproof plan to gain the woman's confidence and convince her to hand over some very valuable information to complete strangers. She was confident she would come up with something brilliant.

She always did, after all.

Tanis climbed into her hammock, bumped the side of her foot off the hull to start herself swinging, and laced her fingers over her stomach as she settled in. There were pros and cons to working with a partner, and she had a tendency to focus on the cons. Splitting the take was a huge downside and more than enough for her to prefer working alone. But there was a reason she kept saying yes every time Vala showed up with another hair-brained scheme that required a shill or an inside woman. She didn't trust Vala any more than she trusted the majority of people she encountered but it was easy to tell when betrayal wasn't in her best interest. She doubted Vala would turn on her while they were in hyperspace en route to a meeting with a contact, so she let down her guard just a touch.

Trust. It was an odd feeling for Tanis, one she didn't claim to recognize when it first reared its unwelcome head. At first she thought she simply had a crush on the exciting, exotic pirate. Vala was indeed one of the most creative and successful confidence artists Tanis had ever come across. She respected someone who was good at their jobs. And Vala was beautiful. But after a while she realized it was something else. Tanis wasn't trying to find an angle… at least not always. She would feign independence and threaten to turn against Vala if the score was big enough, but in the end she knew that their partnership was worth more to her than almost any treasure. Getting on Vala's bad side would be as idiotic as trying to rob the central law enforcement evidence depository.

Her life was a string of betrayals, either by her or against her. She was taught by her school that the Serrakin were their saviors in lessons and histories that revealed that Hebridan was enslaved by the Goa'uld before the Serrakin arrived and saved them all. Her family taught her that their salvation came at a cost. The Serrakin needed a place to live, and Hebridan could hardly refuse. Thus begun their endless subjugation and their slow evolution into second-class citizens on their own home-world. As a little girl Tanis dreamed of flying, of being the pilot of her own ship, seeing the stars. Her parents had gently and sadly told her that she should give up that dream before her heart was broken. Flight schools were very exclusive, and an applicant without Serrakin blood would be refused outright.

Tanis did change her dreams, but not quite how her parents might have expected. She got her hands on flight manuals by less than legal means and spent time in junkyards learning the controls of salvaged vessels. She used simulators and games to hone her skills at the controls of a variety of ships before she started looking to get hired on the real thing. She couldn't offer her services to legitimate flight services without evidence of education so she went to the bad part of town and asked if anyone needed a pilot. When she finally strapped in to her first ship to take her first extra-system flight, she ironically knew more than most pedigreed pilots in the air.

In the end, she managed to get herself to the stars. The route didn't matter, and she didn't give a damn that her course had made her a criminal. Criminals had much more fun than anyone who followed the rules. She opened her eyes and looked toward the front of the ship where Vala was keeping them on course toward their promised treasure. Tanis knew she would tease and threaten to turn against her. She would pretend to have designs on making away with the whole thing, but she would never make good on those threats. Throwing away someone as valuable as Vala would be ridiculous.

Besides, crime was more fun when she had someone to share the spoils with. She smiled and closed her eyes, swinging the hammock again in the hopes of getting some refreshing sleep before they arrived at their destination.

CHAPTER FIVE

SAM AND Daniel left Sina outside of Siero's pub after she assured them she'd arranged for alternative methods of travel and didn't need the Stargate. They once again braved the gauntlet of shops to reach the DHD. Daniel hung back to look longingly at the display of books for sale before he followed her up the steps and through the event horizon. Occasionally Sam felt cheated by how quickly transport was between Stargates. They were travelling across galaxies and she didn't even get to feel the wind in her hair. Three-point-two seconds after leaving Lucia, her boot dropped down on the ramp. Sam took a moment to run a hand through her hair and noticed that Daniel stopped short so that he wouldn't advance ahead of her. She thought it was a bit odd, but didn't mention it as she continued forward.

General O'Neill came into the room and rubbed his hands together. "Tell me you have good news, kids."

Sam put Daniel's odd behavior out of her mind. "Hopeful news may be more accurate, sir. We have a promising lead on where to find Kali's treasure. We have the address, but we need a Jaffa to help us get through the door."

Jack raised an eyebrow and held back his smile. "Got one in mind?"

"Well, I suppose if Bra'tac isn't available..." She grinned. "How is the search going? Have we managed to track him down yet?"

SG-9 had been dispatched to Teal'c's last known location before Sam and Daniel left for Lucia, but she wasn't hopeful they'd made much progress. Judging from O'Neill's reaction she was right to be skeptical.

"Teal'c is definitely making the rounds on the victory circuit. By the time Colonel Getty's team got to the planet he was supposed to be visiting, the Jaffa there said he had already moved on. Same thing in the next two villages they checked. I'm starting to feel a little like a bill collector. But don't worry, we'll find him. It's only a matter of time."

"Hopefully we have that time, sir." She looked down at her outfit. "Permission to go change before the briefing?"

"Granted. Briefing is in ten; can't wait to hear the whole riveting tale."

"Yes, sir."

He went up into the control room while Sam and Daniel continued to the elevators. At one point Sam had to stop in order to let Siler pass, and she noticed Daniel stopped as well, even though he could have gone around the sergeant. When they reached the elevators he also stopped short and let her press the button. She debated whether to just chalk it up to coincidence or confront him and, as the doors opened, she decided on a quick test. She gestured for him to go first, but he smiled.

"Ladies first."

"Right." Sam stepped into the car and Daniel followed her. She pressed the button again, and Daniel took a position in the back corner. She turned to face him. "So are you going to explain this, or will I just have to figure it out myself?"

His face was the picture of innocence. "Explain what?"

"Why you're acting so weirdly around me. This morning you nearly jumped out of your skin when you saw me in the briefing room, and the entire time we were on the mission you made damn sure I was never behind you."

Daniel winced and adjusted his glasses. "Oh. I didn't think you'd noticed."

"I was willing to put it down to coincidence and nerves until just now. You practically tripped on your own feet walking down the hall. What's going on?"

He sighed and looked at the ground. The elevator opened on Level 19 and they stepped out into the hall. He looked to make sure they were alone before he spoke.

"You heard about what happened after the Replicators abducted me."

Sam nodded. "Vaguely. You were taken to their flagship where the Replicator version of me…"

"RepliCarter."

It was her turn to wince. "Oh, God. Who is calling her that?"

He shrugged. "It's not important. She held me hostage and tried to pry the secrets of the Ancients out of my head. She came damn close, Sam. You have to understand, I know it wasn't you. No matter what she looked like, there was nothing in her personality or in her eyes… there is no way I would ever mistake you for her or vice versa. But despite that, despite knowing that beyond a doubt, it was still your eyes I looked into when she was torturing me. It was your face behind the blade she shoved into my chest to kill me. I saw your face as I died, and it… was not a friendly face at that moment."

"Oh." Her voice was meek.

"I thought I was okay with it, but I obviously need a little time to get over the fact it was wearing your face and using your voice. I'm sorry."

"Don't be. I'm sure if I was in your situation I would feel the same way. Is there anything I can do to make you feel more at ease?"

"It's not your problem to fix. But thank you for offering. I'll do better to try and keep myself from reacting whenever you make a sudden movement."

Sam nodded. "And I'll try to keep any threatening movements to a minimum."

"That's all I ask."

She started toward the locker rooms, letting Daniel lag behind her out of deference to his recent confession. "So what do you think our chances are of tracking down Kali's device and stopping this 'Purge' thing from happening?"

"It depends on what we find at Teunus, I suppose. We're not even certain what we're supposed to be looking for. We may have to just hope SG-9 finds something in Kali's temple that can point us in the right direction."

Sam said, "Right. Maybe Kali left a directory and we can go around and disable them all without this treasure."

He nodded without confidence. "Yes. But we're dealing with a ticking clock and we have no idea how much time is left before it goes off. It would only take one device being active when the clock reaches zero."

"Yeah. Are we any closer to finding out when exactly that will happen?"

"I haven't had much time to work with the inscriptions, but I imagine it must be imminent. I'm positive the sequence has to be disabled manually. That said, Kali has had a lot on her mind this past year. What with Ba'al and the Replicators to worry about she wouldn't have time to slip away to take care of her fail-safe."

Sam said, "If she even would have bothered. The Jaffa rebellion was gaining footholds left and right, and destroying them completely would have given the Kull warriors a huge advantage. If the deadline had come up during the conflict, I don't doubt Anubis would have told her to just let it happen."

Daniel nodded. "We may not know exactly when it's going to happen, but all signs point to sooner rather than later."

"We'll find a way to stop it, Daniel. The Jaffa haven't made it this far just to be done in by some Hail-Mary time bomb. If push comes to shove and things start looking dire, we can tell them to hunker down and bury their Stargates until we've found a solution. I have faith that one way or another we will figure this out."

Daniel said, "That's actually a good idea. If Kali's device works through a series of gate connections, all we have to do to protect the Jaffa is get them away from their Stargates until we've found the solution. It's not a perfect or a long-term solution..."

Sam smiled and bumped his arm with her elbow. "See? We

don't always need General O'Neill to come up with the simplest solution."

"I guess not." Sam started to go into the women's locker room, but Daniel said, "Sam? You wanted to know what you could do to help me get over the Replicator situation?"

"Yeah. Anything I can do to make it easier for you."

He waved a finger between them. "This. More of this."

She chuckled and nodded. "I'll do what I can."

Baleya Pani hadn't survived as long as she had by making friends or taking risks. She dealt with extremely valuable items from across the galaxy and she traded with some of the most wretched scum ever to step off their planets to venture out into the stars. In the past few weeks, she had become the go-to for anyone looking to move anything Goa'uld related that had been looted from ransacked palaces and temples that were now standing abandoned. She knew well that she was a target, knew that anyone who succeeded in killing her would inherit one of the richest warehouses in seven systems, and so she had arranged for the best security ever devised to protect herself. It spanned most of the city she called home, turning what had once been an ordinary town into a stronghold dedicated to keeping her alive. Anyone who attempted to break the perimeter without being identified suffered greatly at the hands of her defenses.

When Vala and Tanis arrived at her planet, they found it surrounded by a cluster of other vessels waiting to be allowed permission to land. Vala kept her distance, using one of the planet's moons to obscure the ship's signature while she eavesdropped on the radio signals passing between the ships and the surface. Some of the petitioners were Jaffa seeking property that belonged to their former masters, while others were merely treasure hunters who had heard there was new stock and wanted to see what was available for purchase. Baleya granted some of them access while others were turned away seemingly at random.

Tanis had broken open their rations and was eating while she listened to some of the conversations. "Apparently she has some stuff from one of Lord Yu's strongholds. That could fetch a good price. People go crazy for all that ancient stuff."

"We don't want ancient stuff, we want Ancient stuff. Capital A. There's a reason Anubis crushed the other System Lords like mice. Some people pay for pretty, but everyone pays for power. We'll wait until we have clear confirmation that she's offering something from one of Kali's worlds."

Tanis finished her meal and tossed the empty container onto the console between them. "What's so special about Kali? There's gotta be an easier payday to go after. Not that I don't appreciate a good treasure hunt now and then. I'm just wondering what the point is."

"She was an impressive female System Lord. She didn't rely on men for her power or to gather her wealth for her. When she joined up with Anubis, she established a partnership rather than something subservient. I mean, sure, it hasn't exactly worked out for her in the long run, but I think it's impressive." She turned in her chair and laced her fingers on her stomach. "Besides, a lot of what was scavenged is bound to be of Ancient design. Fabulous toys, technology so advanced it will make our heads spin. The Jaffa out there might pay dearly for some dusty Goa'uld artifacts out of nostalgia or as a keepsake, but the things Anubis left behind? Oh, Tanis, darling, people will pay whatever price we ask for that."

"Junk is junk," Tanis sighed. "It just feels like a lot of work without a promise of a payoff."

"Patience," Vala urged.

They listened for a little longer before a message from the surface included the words they had been waiting to hear. "You're in luck. We just got a shipment from Teunus including items from the realms of Olokun, Amaterasu, Kali, and Ares."

Vala snapped her fingers. "That's our cue! Bring us around the moon and try to get us queued up for a hello."

Tanis brought the ship back to full power and sat up straighter in her seat as she swung them around to join the other ships. She opened a channel and, when she received the okay to transmit, spoke into the microphone hanging from her headset. "Two solicitors aboard an independent tel'tak requesting commerce with merchant Baleya. Please respond."

They had to wait close to half an hour before the receptionist on the surface got to their request. "Independent tel'tak, please state your interests."

"Am I speaking with Baleya herself?"

"Indeed you are."

Tanis glanced at Vala, who motioned for her to go ahead. There was a subtle art to negotiating this sort of thing. Vala was great at the long con, slowly gaining trust so that it lasted even after she had gotten away with the goods, but Tanis was extremely skilled at the quick sale. She didn't need the trust she built to last for weeks or even days, she just had to get them in the door. They needed her finesse with Baleya; they couldn't give away exactly what they wanted or else the price would rise but they couldn't be so circumspect that they were dismissed as window-shoppers. Vala trusted Tanis to strike the right balance between the two extremes.

Tanis straightened her shoulders and stared straight ahead, addressing Baleya as if the woman was in the ship with them.

"It's an honor to speak with someone of your reputation, Baleya. My name is Tanis Reynard, and I'm here with my associate, Vala Mal Doran. We're in the market for some treasures that have recently come under new ownership, and Siero of Lucia told us you were the woman to speak with. We're hoping to find something a bit more feminine, if you understand my meaning. Something ladylike to spruce up a few of our bolt holes and second homes." She tilted her head to the side and changed her voice slightly, making it just a bit more plaintive. "I don't suppose you might have anything like that? Some trappings from a female-hosted System Lord?"

"You might just be in luck. What do you offer as trade?"

"Riches pilfered from a kingdom preparing for an economic shift. Literally a king's ransom." She winked at Vala, who grinned brightly in response. "More than enough to pay for a few shiny doodads."

There was a pause as Baleya considered the offer. Finally there was an alarm indicating that their ship had been lassoed by the planet's security system.

"Your ship has been locked in," Baleya said. "Please use the rings to transport down to the planet so we can discuss an exchange."

"As you wish. We thank you for your acceptance."

When the signal went dark, Vala reached across the console and enthusiastically patted Tanis on the shoulder. "Well done, well done! Couldn't have done it any better myself." She stood up and walked into the cargo hold. She had hooked her jacket over the edge of the door and she plucked it down, swinging it on as she strode to the center of the rings. Tanis joined her after making sure she had a good selection of weapons concealed on her. She put on a short leather jacket that added a few more pockets where she could put anything small enough that caught her eye when they were on the planet.

"We would like to stay on this woman's good side," Vala reminded her. "Are you sure you want to risk that for petty larceny?"

Tanis said, "Depends on what the petty is."

Vala grinned and remotely activated the rings. The floor opened around them and they were blinded by a bright flash of white-gold light. When it faded and their eyes adjusted they had been transported to a circular antechamber. The door to the corridor was blocked by two men with guns, so the ladies held their arms out to either side and allowed themselves to be scanned for weapons.

"Heavily armed," one of the men reported.

Vala said, "Well of course! We would never insult a woman

of Baleya's stature by coming unarmed. We're smart enough to know when we're outmatched. We're just trying to level the playing field. Purely a matter of false security, I assure you. If weapons are required I have no doubt that the lady of the house will have us outmatched quite easily."

"You would be correct," the guard said. He lowered his scanner, and motioned them forward. "Miss Baleya is waiting for you in her offices."

They put their arms down and followed their guards-turned-escort out of the room. The corridor almost immediately branched out into a much larger warehouse, with sections separated by canvas walls that had been strung up with a metal framework. As Vala and Tanis were led through the maze, they used their periphery to scan some of the wealth they were passing. There were examples of alien technology, things that could either be weapons or energy converters, there were items Vala only recognized as headsets because they included goggles. Everything seemed to be stacked in a haphazard and sloppy manner, but Vala knew there had to be some kind of inventory to keep track of each and every bauble.

"Look at this place," Tanis muttered. "We could forget about Kali and just loot one room. We'd never have to work again."

"Settle down," Vala said. "You saw the security she has here, and that's just what she shows people to scare them away. I'm sure there are all kinds of hidden traps for someone foolish enough to try hitting this place."

"True… but if you hadn't lost my Kull warrior suit, we could have just strolled in here and taken whatever we wanted."

Vala rolled her eyes and raised her voice slightly. "Oh, God! Are you still harping about that?"

"Do you know what I had to do to get that suit? Not to mention cleaning it out so it wasn't a biohazard to put it on. Then I loan it to you for a simple shoot-and-snatch mission. But no, you had to go and leave it behind because a pretty boy flexed his muscles at you."

"It wasn't like that!"

"Sure it wasn't. Whatever happened, when we met up again and I asked for it back you were empty-handed."

"I was not empty-handed! I gave you seventy-five percent from our next score."

"Hardly a fair trade for potential lost," Tanis said.

Vala couldn't put up a very good argument because, to be honest, she had made a huge blunder losing that suit. It deflected most energy weapons, it was mostly impervious to projectile weapons, and the majority of people would simply turn and run when they saw it coming. Tanis had acquired the suit on one of her solo jobs, when her attempt to pilfer a few Ancient artifacts resulted in a foot chase with one of the beetle-like soldiers. The warrior moved slowly but with dedication, unwavering as she desperately tried to find a way out of the stronghold that had become her labyrinth. She spent close to an hour hiding from the thing only to have it suddenly and inexplicably fall over dead. It seemed like a trick at first, but the thing was too mindless to try anything clever.

Eventually she risked approaching it and discovered it had died. She didn't know what possessed her to even try moving the heavily-armored seven foot behemoth by herself, but somehow she managed to get it onto her ship. The hours and days afterward made her glad she wasn't squeamish. The thing inside the suit was barely humanoid but it was close enough to make her feel like she was touching a corpse as she extricated it from the suit.

Once it was thoroughly cleaned and sanitized, she put it on for a test run. She passed through force fields like they were water, she walked calmly past guards who were emptying their weapons on her, the energy blasts spreading harmlessly across the breastplate and helmet. When she got tired of being target practice, she could clear the room of security with a quick sweep of fire from her wrist-mounted guns. Then she could take her time clearing out their safes. It was the perfect accessory, and she thought it was going to change her life.

Then she got sick.

In retrospect it seemed like an obvious flaw. If she'd still had the energy she would have kicked herself for not seeing it earlier. Anubis had made the creature inside the suit to replace the Jaffa, and their genetic enhancements had been transferred to the golem. If she wanted to wear the suit for any length of time, she would need to be as strong, fast, and resilient as a Jaffa. Being a lowly human, the suit quickly sapped her of energy until she was too weak to even stand.

Fortunately Vala had found her and nursed her back to health. On their next job, Tanis figured out a way to disable most of the suit's features so that it took a much smaller toll on its wearer. It wasn't as indestructible as it once was, but they didn't need it to be. They just needed to deflect a few blasts from security guards and pass through the occasional force field. They would use the suit only in the most dreadful situations, when every other method failed. It would be their secret weapon.

Then Vala asked to borrow the suit for a solo job. It had been meticulously planned and carried out, but she hadn't anticipated Daniel Jackson's interference. She thought he'd been one of those vapid pretty boys, the kind that were occasionally allowed passage on ships in exchange for providing certain services. But no, he had to turn out to be a deceptively shrewd fighter. Just her luck. She had been fortunate to get off the ship at all, and she didn't have the luxury of gathering her things before she lit out. She thought Tanis would be happy that she was alive and overlook the minor quibble about losing the suit. And Tanis *was* glad Vala had escaped intact, but she had yet to forgive her for losing the suit. Vala doubted she would have been any more understanding if their roles were reversed.

She glanced at the stacks of items Baleya had lined the corridor with and wondered if she had a Kull warrior suit she would be willing to part with. She could purchase it as a present for Tanis, a peace offering and a worthy investment if it meant she would finally shut up about it.

They eventually reached a wooden staircase that ran along one wall to an elevated office. From that vantage point Baleya could look out over all her riches whenever she pleased. Vala was impressed; the fence was obviously a woman after her own heart. Their escort knocked on the door and stepped aside to let them enter.

Baleya Pani stood up as the door was closed behind them. Her red hair was tied back in a braid, and she wore a leather vest over a collarless blue blouse. She was younger than Vala expected considering the scope of her empire, but there was a hardness in her green eyes that revealed she wasn't one to be trifled with. A low-slung belt held a blaster against her right hip, a sheathed knife was visible strapped above her left knee, and Vala had no doubt there were multiple other weapons within easy reach. Baleya sized them up while they were doing the same to her and seemed satisfied with what she saw.

"Welcome to my world," she said.

"Thank you," Vala said. "I'm Vala Mal Doran, that's Tanis Reynard."

Tanis smiled flirtatiously. "Pleasure to meet you."

Vala turned and muttered, "Now's not the time."

"Jealous?"

Vala rolled her eyes and faced Baleya again.

Baleya said, "I've never heard of either of you before. Are you Tau'ri?"

"Nope. She's Hebridian, I'm —"

Baleya cut her off with a wave of her hand. "As long as you're not Tau'ri troublemakers, I don't care where you're from. So you claim to have a kingdom's worth of coin to trade with. I heard a minor fiefdom got cleaned out a few days ago. Whoever the thieves were, they managed to get away without a trace. Impressive work."

"That's why you've never heard of us," Tanis said. "In and

out, clean as a whistle."

"Commendable." She pursed her lips as she regarded Tanis for a moment longer, then looked out the window at her collection. "I came across a few items recently that originated with a female System Lord. I have a few relics from Amaterasu you might find interesting."

"Actually we're more interested in anything that came from Teunus."

Baleya looked at her. "The items from Kali's realm."

"Yes, exactly."

"Hm. A lot of that has been moved out already. A collector came through and picked some of it up, but there's still some left over. Care to take a look?"

Vala grinned. "I'm always up to do a little shopping!"

Baleya pushed off the desk and motioned for them to follow. Tanis eyed the woman as she passed, and Vala admonished her again.

"We don't have time for that."

"We never have time for that," Tanis said. "That's why I think we should make time whenever we can."

Vala took Tanis' elbow and dragged her out of the office and followed Baleya back down the stairs. They were led back through the narrow makeshift corridors, past rooms that were filled to the brim with other shining examples of Goa'uld excess. They were moving too quickly for Vala to identify everything, but she did catch glimpses of a few marks she recognized. Some of the collections were old enough to bear the symbol of Apophis and Heru'ur despite the fact both had met their doom years ago.

Baleya led them to a large open area that was so cluttered Vala assumed it had to be items that were waiting to be catalogued and moved to the appropriate section of the complex. Thrones were standing shoulder to shoulder, their seats filled with braziers that were overflowing with various jewelry and baubles. Wooden trunks that were too overstuffed to close entirely were set up to create pathways through the mess.

"How much of this is Kali's?" Vala asked.

"Unfortunately, just a very small amount. This is just where stuff gets dumped after people send it down to me. I try to keep things as organized as possible." She bent down to pick up a bejeweled necklace and turned it over in her hands before dumping it into a nearby chest.

"I thought you received the majority of Kali's treasure from Teunus."

"I did," Baleya said. "But I have regular clients who get first pick. One of them came in the day after I acquired Kali's things and bought up the vast majority of it all."

Vala let her mask of joviality slip. "Damn it!"

"What does it matter?" Baleya said. "Look around you. Just because it didn't belong to Kali doesn't affect the value of what's on offer."

"The deal was our money for Kali's treasure."

"I say again, what is so important about Kali's treasure?" Baleya nudged one of the trunks with her foot. "Olokun was just as egotistical, and he draped all of his throne rooms with golden veils. His servants wore so much gold and silver accessories that sometimes they couldn't even lift their arms."

Vala said, "I don't care about Olokun."

Tanis stepped closer to Vala and lowered her voice. "Vala, look at this place. With what we have in the cargo ship, we could make a killing here. Think about the trades just waiting to be made. A few coins in exchange for a golden bracelet, and then we can change that bracelet into a few dozen ounces of naquadah. This is a license to print our own money! Just look around you!"

"I'm looking." Vala wandered to one side and picked up a ribbon device. The pointed finger caps fell to the side as she held it, revealing the gem that would settle against the palm. The sight stirred a memory, one of the thousands she had tried so hard to suppress. She saw herself spreading her fingers wide, saw the frightened eyes of her victim as the gem glowed bright. She looked away from the weapon before the memory could unfold any further.

The room was filled with treasure and it would all trade the same no matter who it had belonged to. A throne from Cronus wasn't intrinsically more valuable that something from Ares' palace. The differences only mattered to her.

"Do you have anything from Qetesh?" Vala asked quietly.

Baleya furrowed her brow and looked around. "That's going back a few years. I think all of her stuff got scattered to the wilds a long time ago." She looked at Tanis. "First Kali and now Qetesh. You ladies looking for something specific?"

Vala ignored the question. "The client with a deep vault. The one who got all of Kali's things. What's his name?"

"I can't divulge that sort of information. My clients expect a high standard of anonymity and it is my duty to ensure they receive it. I offer you the same silence should anyone come looking for you."

Vala slipped the ribbon device onto her hand. She brought up her arm and spread her fingers. The part of Qetesh that had been left behind in her blood activated the gemstone and it glowed softly as she aimed it at Baleya's head.

Baleya stared in confusion. "But you're not Goa'uld…"

"Not anymore, no," Vala said. Her voice was calm, but her eyes were cold. Threatening someone, using the weapon again threw her back to the person she had been running away from for almost ten years. "I don't want to hurt you, but I want that information. I want Kali's treasure and I will do whatever is necessary to get it."

Tanis pulled her gun and aimed it at Baleya as well. "Vala, what are you doing? I'll back your play, but I need to know what's going on."

Vala said, "It's important to me."

"All right," Tanis said. "I guess that will have to do for now. But damn it, I want answers. Sorry, Baleya."

"And things were going so well," Baleya said. "Fine. The name of the man who acquired Kali's treasures is Dysmas Wyrrick."

Tanis said, "I've heard of him. He's an arms dealer. Tends to work both sides of a conflict in order to double his payday."

"He's more of a collector now," Baleya said. "The wars against the Goa'uld and the Replicators have calmed down, so he has time to focus on the finer things."

Tanis glanced over her shoulder to make sure they were still alone. "Vala, something's wrong."

"What?"

"She's being far too calm."

Baleya smiled darkly. "Clever girl. Pity. We could have been really good friends. But you had to come into my vault, my inner sanctum, and threaten me?"

"There's no reason this has to escalate any further," Tanis said. "You gave us what we wanted, so now we'll just be on our way."

"Oh, but it does. I didn't tell you Wyrrick's name because you were holding weapons on me. My security here is top-notch, Miss Reynard. You wouldn't have gotten that gun near me if I wasn't confident I'd have the upper hand. If you'd proven you were trustworthy I would have offered you a cup of tea, and in that tea would be a chemical that would counteract the gas in these corridors. You see, that's how I prevent theft. The atmosphere of this planet has a soporific effect on people who didn't grow up here. I take advantage of that to protect my investments."

Vala realized too late that her arm was quickly becoming too heavy to hold up. She turned her head to see if Tanis was feeling the same effects, and the motion made her so disoriented that she nearly fell over. The hand device powered down as she grabbed for a shelf to keep herself upright. Tanis wavered as well, bumping her shoulder into a shelf before falling gracelessly to the floor. Vala looked up at Baleya, who seemed to be looming over her like a monolith. Gravity finally won out and Vala slumped face forward onto the floor.

Baleya walked forward, her boots echoing like percussion instruments with every step.

"If you survive, you will eventually come to regret threatening me in my own home, Mal Doran. But in the meantime, let us see what regrets you already have."

Anything else she might have said was lost to the increasingly thick haze closing in on Vala's vision, until there was nothing to do but surrender to the darkness.

CHAPTER SIX

THE NEWS reached the village just after dawn, a warning passed through several messengers before it finally reached Teal'c. He was already awake when the young man burst into his tent. Teal'c had thanked the boy before sending him to share what he had learned with the others. He was preparing to leave when Rak'nor found him. "You have heard the news?"

Teal'c nodded. "Indeed I have. Stargate Command has requested my assistance in stopping this atrocity from occurring. I trust you will serve as my proxy until I return."

"Of course." Rak'nor paused and looked at the ground for a moment, obviously grasping for words he found difficult to say. "I am always willing to be here in your stead, brother, but perhaps you should begin thinking about how often you are asking me to take your place."

"Am I infringing on your time?"

"That is not the issue, Teal'c. We all truly appreciate the time you have given us these past few weeks and months, but we cannot help but wonder when it will end. Many believe the day is fast approaching when you will bid us farewell and return to your Tau'ri friends. Many are beginning to express their concern about your long-term dedication to our people."

Teal'c tightened his jaw and straightened his shoulders. "I see. I was not aware I had become the subject of such idle gossip."

"Perhaps not so idle these past few days. No one doubts your dedication to our cause or the sacrifices you've made to get us to this place. But now that we have achieved victory, your attention seems divided between us and the Tau'ri. They call and you run to their aid."

"We are seeking to prevent an unspeakable attack from devastating our people."

"In this instance, yes. But what about the next?" He sighed.

"Everyone understands you owe them a debt, Teal'c. Perhaps soon it would be best if you choose to remain with them until that debt is repaid rather than trying to divide your time between two worlds."

Teal'c cinched his bag shut and slung the strap over his head. He turned to Rak'nor and extended his arm, and Rak'nor clasped it in the center of his forearm. "Thank you for speaking so frankly with me, and for your candid advice. I will consider it while I am away."

Rak'nor nodded and stepped aside so Teal'c could precede him out of the tent. "I hear your friends are due to arrive at any moment."

"Indeed. They have been trying to find me for several days, but my movement has been sporadic at best. I am fortunate their message found me as quickly as it did."

"I'm torn between warning people of this threat or keeping it quiet in the interest of maintaining calm. This is a very fragile time for many of us. There have been so many changes lately, and it would be easy to believe it was only temporary. This threat could convince many that they have made a mistake in turning against their gods."

"Alternatively, our success in preventing such an attack would serve to cement our resolve. This crisis may be just the catalyst we need to sway those who are still uncertain."

Rak'nor stopped at a turn in the road. Teal'c would continue ahead through the woods to the Stargate, while Rak'nor had to go north to the council chambers.

"I wish you luck, Teal'c. And I look forward to your return."

"Thank you. I hope to send word soon."

They parted ways, and Teal'c was left alone with his thoughts. He appreciated Rak'nor coming to him with his concerns. If he was feeling uneasy about Teal'c's divided loyalties, then certainly there were others who felt the same way but didn't feel comfortable confronting him. He would have to make an effort to assure anyone who doubted him upon his return.

Though he could never fully repay the Tau'ri for what they had done for the Jaffa, he still felt obligated to them. He believed he would always respond if they needed him, and he would not want it any other way.

He passed into the clearing just as the chevrons lit with an incoming wormhole. Despite the dire circumstances of their visit, he couldn't help but smile as Samantha Carter and Daniel Jackson stepped through the event horizon. It had been far too long since he visited the SGC and he had missed them greatly. Colonel Carter obviously felt the same way based on the width and brilliance of her smile as they met up at the DHD. He smiled and inclined his head in greeting to them.

"My friends."

"Hello, Teal'c," she said. "It's good to see you again. I wish it was more of a social call."

He nodded. "I have sent word to as many settlements as possible so they are aware of the danger. The suggestion to bury their Stargates until the matter has been resolved was met with some resistance."

"Well, that's understandable," Daniel Jackson said. "After fighting for so long to escape the Goa'uld, suddenly they're encroaching on your lives again. You finally achieved victory and burying your Stargate would make it feel like you're hiding."

"We wouldn't have suggested it if we didn't think it was absolutely necessary. They aren't cloistering themselves, they're just buying a little time and keeping themselves safe until we can defuse the threat."

"Your intentions have never been in doubt, Colonel Carter. Relations between our people have been fragile at times, but the majority of us believe the Tau'ri are true friends to the Jaffa. I have done my part to spread that belief. Your efforts to prevent Kali's scheme will reinforce that message." He gestured at the DHD. "I am prepared to depart for Teunus immediately."

Daniel said, "Oh! You don't need to pack or anything?"

Teal'c patted his bag. "I have everything I require. Rak'nor has agreed to take my place on the council until my return."

Sam said, "No staff weapon?"

Teal'c's expression wavered. "No. Many among the Jaffa have decided against continuing to carry the weapon that was so often used to strike down our brothers. I personally have had strong misgivings about carrying it since one was used in the death of Janet Fraiser. In her honor, and in her memory, I have vowed that I will use the weapon only when it is unavoidable."

"She would have been honored," Sam said softly.

Their reflective moment ended when a group of Jaffa appeared at the edge of the clearing. Teal'c noted their arrival. "They have volunteered to bury the Stargate upon our departure. I have assured them it will not have to be buried for long. In the meantime, any travel from one community to the next will have to be done via transport ships. We will not be crippled, only inconvenienced." Teal'c stepped in front of the DHD and began dialing Teunus.

"We'll do our best to make sure that inconvenience is as temporary as possible," Daniel said. "The bright side is that we're dealing with a pre-programmed event instead of an army. Hopefully preventing this attack can be done with a minimum of violence or bloodshed."

"We are attempting to do more than prevent this attack, Daniel Jackson. A Goa'uld making such a decisive blow from beyond the grave would be seen as a sign that they have the power of the gods. Stopping Kali's machinations will do much to shore up our burgeoning nation. Our actions on Dakara brought the Goa'uld to their knees and opened the door for a final, decisive victory. With luck, this will be the moment that proves once and for all that the Goa'uld are fallible."

"Well then," Daniel said. "What are we waiting for? Next stop, Teunus."

Vala startled awake, choking on a gasp of fear and confusion. Her arms were tense, fingers curling into fists as she fought the instinct to lash out. She only remembered being in some sort of peril before she passed out, but the details were too hazy for her to lock onto. She was dressed in a flimsy golden gown threaded with stripes of silver, cut low at the collar to show off her décolletage. She was lying on a massive bed in the center of an oval room, the sides of the mattress draped with curtains suspended from the ceiling to create a privacy screen.

"No. This can't be real." She slid to the edge of the bed and dropped her feet to the floor. There were slippers waiting for her, but she ignored them. She recognized this room, understood what it meant, and the knowledge terrified her. She stood up and ran to the door, waiting a moment before she crossed the threshold into the corridor. The halls were empty, as she remembered, but she knew that wouldn't last long. She could already hear voices being raised outside, the angry crowd closing in on the palace. The gown flew out behind her like streamers as she ran, choosing left instead of right as she had so many years earlier.

She entered her throne room and came up short in front of her throne. The back had been broken in two places and the ornate carving at the top was shattered on the ground. Tapestries that had flanked her elevated platform were shredded as well. She felt her panic and nausea rising as she moved closer. A few days ago the people of the village approached her palace en masse. Her Jaffa tried to stop their approach but they were quickly outnumbered. Staff weapons were deflected by rough-hewn clubs, while thrown rocks opened cuts in the Jaffa's foreheads so they were blinded by their own blood.

In the past, in reality, she had tried escaping through the secret side entrance only to find a mob waiting for her there. She had been captured, tortured, and beaten until the Tok'ra who incited the violence in the first place took pity on her and saved her life. This time she wouldn't take her chances. There was a tel'tak in the courtyard. She could use it to escape.

But if she wasn't rescued by the Tok'ra, she would never

get Qetesh out of her head. Did she have to suffer such violence and degradation simply to live as herself? No. No, she would find another way to get the Goa'uld out of her head. She couldn't bear to go through that ordeal again. She stared at the throne and thought of all the horrible things she had witnessed from that seat. Witnessed… that was a kind way of putting it. She had caused pain and death, ordered torture, and she had watched it gleefully. Tears burned her eyes as she remembered the horrors Qetesh had wrought with her hands.

You enjoyed it, an evil, familiar voice echoed in her head. *Vengeance on your enemies, on those who had laughed at you and ignored you. Finally you were the powerful one and you enjoyed every moment of your triumph.*

"Lies!" Vala's voice shuddered but she refused to let herself cry. She couldn't let the Goa'uld get to her, not after being free of it for so long.

Somewhere a door shattered. She realized she had lingered far too long in her reverie and looked for an exit, some way to avoid what she knew was coming next, but the room filled quickly with people she had once called friends. She retreated back toward her throne, wishing she had a weapon but knowing she couldn't have wielded one even if it appeared. She had already caused these people too much pain. She deserved what they were going to do, but that didn't make it any easier to bear.

"Please… I'm sorry… it wasn't me!"

The first stone hit her in the arm. She cried out more from surprise than pain. She held the sore spot, knowing a bruise would bloom soon enough. If history repeated itself she would soon be covered by welts and cuts. Someone shouted that she was a false god, his voice echoing off the high stone walls, and soon others joined him. Their cries were deafening as they closed in on her. More stones were tossed and her name was cursed. Vala covered her head when they descended, beating her with fists and various weapons. It wasn't long before she was thrown off balance and curled into a ball to protect her stomach.

Part of her knew the moment couldn't be real, knew it was all just a remnant of her distant past. She knew she had survived this ordeal relatively intact. Another part of her thought maybe the past decade had been a hallucination created by her cracked mind to free her, however temporarily, from this hell. Maybe she had just created her life as a thief and smuggler, maybe she had created Tanis from whole cloth, as a way to deal with the fact the villagers — her friends and neighbors before they were Qetesh's unwilling worshippers — were slowly beating her to death.

She had lived in the village before Qetesh came. She had a life, a future, and then she was chosen. Her people didn't understand that she and the Goa'uld were different creatures. She begged them to stop, but they ignored her cries until she was certain that this time they meant to kill her. They had been at it for days, but this time she knew they would go too far.

"Stop! Leave her be."

Vala collapsed to the ground, bloody and battered, and cringed away when someone hooked their hands under her arms.

"It's all right," he said. "I'm here to help you."

It was the Tok'ra. She remembered him now, although she knew this was the first time he'd actually come to her aid. There was something wrong with her mind. She was reliving this moment, but how? Why? She'd worked so hard to suppress the memories of this time, embellishing them and adding whatever elements were required to fit her current lie, and all of her stories had helped diminish the painful truth of what had really happened. And now she was back again. It seemed like a cruel twist of memory.

The Tok'ra was named Nol'ka, and he half-carried her back to the room where she had been found. He sat her on the edge of the bed where she'd awoken. This time she noticed a door that hadn't been there in real life; it didn't match the rest of the décor, and there was a peculiar cyclone symbol etched into it.

The Tok'ra opened his bag and slipped a healing device over his hand. Vala barely had time to register it before he started using it. She cringed away at first, but then her pain was replaced by relief and a tingling coolness. Vala let him heal the freshest wounds, the blood drying on her skin as he mended fractures and caused bruises to fade.

When the worst of the pain had receded, she opened her eyes. Behind him, leaning against the open door, she saw Baleya watching them.

"You!" Vala suddenly remembered the storeroom on the smuggler's planet, the gas that had knocked them out. She pushed Nol'ka out of the way, her head clearing enough that she knew that the situation wasn't real. Her anguish gave way to fury as she realized the entire thing had been created by Baleya to punish her.

"What did you do to me?"

"Relax," Baleya said. "You're still on my planet, and you're completely safe. For the most part." She looked at Vala's gown, still stained with blood from the violent uprising, arms crossed and face passive. "You were a Goa'uld."

Vala took a few steadying breaths, struggling to regain her composure now that she knew she was being manipulated. She smoothed the wrinkles out of her clothes and noticed that she was trembling. She squeezed her hands into fists and held them at her sides before she answered.

"I was host to Qetesh for a time." She tossed her hair over her shoulder and felt herself slip into the casual nonchalance she usually affected when talking about this dark time. "A Tok'ra incited a rebellion. He was horrified by what happened when the palace was raided, so he took pity on me. He saved my life and the symbiote was successfully removed. I survived, but I was… I was no longer welcome among my people. I had to give up everything I had ever known and ventured out with nothing but the clothes on my back."

Baleya said, "That's why Kali's treasures are so important to you. You want a reminder of a time when you were a Goa'uld and surrounded yourself with gold and jewels."

Vala wrinkled her nose. "No. Don't be ridiculous. The fewer reminders I have of that time the better. I want Kali's treasures because I lost everything I had when I was Qetesh." She touched the gown again. "All this glorious, beautiful gold and the trinkets…" She sighed. "By the time the Tok'ra healed me I just wanted to get away from the planet as quickly as possible. I left without taking anything. A fortune, left to rot in a palace. After everything I'd gone through, the horrible things I was forced to witness myself doing, I couldn't even profit from selling off Qetesh's things. I lost absolutely everything. Afterward I had to make my way begging, stealing, learning how to survive with the most meager rations imaginable. Meanwhile the people I'd called my friends and family were doing just fine profiting off things they had looted from my palace. They beat me to within an inch of my life and then stole from me. Acquiring the treasure of another female System Lord and then selling it for a tidy profit would be a way for me to make amends for that."

Baleya stared at her for a moment as she considered the argument. Finally she made her decision and pointed at the peculiar door. "Walk through there and you'll be out."

"Out?"

"Just go through the door, Mal Doran. All this will go away. I'll see you on the other side."

Vala frowned, but she was willing to do anything to escape this nightmare. She looked back at Nol'ka, who had been watching the exchange with a look of confused neutrality. Vala crossed to him and cupped his cheek. "Thank you, Nol'ka. I don't think I bothered saying it back then, and I know it hardly counts now. But thank you for freeing me, and thank you for coming to my aid when those people tried to kill me."

"I'm not sure what's going on here…"

Vala smiled. "Makes two of us, darling. I hope you're well,

wherever you really are."

She left him behind and went to the door. She hesitated only briefly before she put her hand against the symbol and pushed. At first she thought it was simply very bright on the other side, and she squinted as she stepped into the glow. Then she realized that she was propped up against something, her arms strapped to her sides, and there was something sticky pressing against her temples. She tried to tug her hands free but the restraints were too strong.

The world slowly swam into focus. She was in a chamber on Baleya's planet, in a cramped room where the walls were lined with tall black clamshell beds. She was strapped into one of the beds, held upright by surprisingly sturdy pipes. She felt groggy, as if she had been drugged and was hungover at the same time, but she forced herself to remain focused. Tanis was just coming to as well, her head hanging forward so that her face was covered by her hair.

"Tanis? Are you awake?"

"I don't know." After a moment she lifted her head a little further. "Vala? Is that you?"

"It's me. I take it Baleya played with one of your deepest, darkest memories as well?"

Tanis suddenly growled and thrashed against her restraints. "Baleya! That bitch!"

"Watch the language, my dear Miss Reynard." Baleya entered the room and Vala tugged at the pipes holding her arms against her chest.

"Baleya! Let me out of this contraption or so help me…"

"You're hardly in a position to make threats. But you can relax. You wouldn't be awake if I didn't intend to free you."

Baleya touched a console next to the door, and the pipes retreated into the wall. Vala stumbled as they were withdrawn but she managed to find her footing before she fell. Tanis wasn't quite so coordinated and careened slightly to the left. Vala caught her before she hit the ground, and Tanis recoiled violently from her touch. She drew one arm across her chest and lashed out with the other, nearly clipping Vala's chin with her knuckles.

"Easy! Relax, Tanis. It's just me."

Tanis flipped her hair out of her face and squeezed her eyes shut. "Vala. Right."

"Sometimes there's a bit of a recovery period," Baleya said. "The man who created this technology only used it on a handful of people for a very, very long time. Sometimes there are echoes and lingering auras. They should fade in a couple of minutes."

Vala looped an arm around Tanis to keep her upright. "Why? Why would you subject us to that?"

"You're the ones who came here under false pretenses and threatened me! You asked me to divulge privileged information about my clients. I didn't get to where I am by having loose lips and betraying confidences. But I figured there was something behind your actions, so I decided to push you to your limits so I could see what kind of people I'm dealing with. Mal Doran, you're trying to right a wrong. I can respect that." She looked at Tanis. "As for you…"

"I'm with her," Tanis said. "I'm doing this for her, not for myself. So whatever you saw in there, it's not valid."

Baleya kept her eyes on Tanis for a long moment before she gave a slow nod. "All right. Package deal." She pushed back her coat and reached into her back pocket. Vala tensed, still half-expecting her to pull a weapon, but she instead produced a small tablet. "I already told you my client's name is Dysmas Wyrrick. What I neglected to add was the fact he's a bit of a grandstander. And by 'a bit,' I mean he makes the Goa'uld look restrained and humble by comparison. He's having a masquerade party, ostensibly to celebrate the downfall of the System Lords. He actually just wants to show off all his cool new toys. If something got looted from Kali's realm, you're going to find it there. He gave me an invitation when we finished our transaction."

"And you're giving it to us because…?"

"I'm selling it to you," Baleya corrected. "As for why I'm offering it to you despite the fact it's not for sale… well, consider it an apology for what I put you through. The man who made these things called himself a Gamekeeper, but his people apparently had a weird definition of the word 'game.' Selling you the invitation is the least I can do."

Tanis shook her head. When she spoke, her voice was rough. "I don't get it. You attack us, strap us into these… these…"

"Virtual entertainment pods. At least, that's what the technical name is."

"Whatever. You subject us to all that, and now you're fine with helping us? What changed?"

Baleya looked at Vala. "Someone I loved was taken as a host. What I saw in your recreation? It hit home. And not in a very nice way. Let's just say you're not the only one who wants to symbolically atone for something you did in the past. Maybe this will make up for some sins I've been running from."

Vala took the tablet. "Thank you, Baleya. We weren't lying about the money we have on the ship. I'm sure we can work out fair compensation."

"Oh, I'm well aware of how much you have. While you were in the pods, I had my men search your ship. I took what I determined to be a fair price for the tablet."

Vala pursed her lips. "Ah. I suppose it saves us a tedious negotiation. Does this make us square? We threatened you, you emotionally scarred us… no need for anyone to retaliate down the line?"

"For the time being. But I wouldn't expect any favors the next time we run into each other." She looked at Tanis. "Hopefully there will be a next time, though. No need for a bad first impression to affect a potentially lucrative relationship."

"Right. Square one. Could be worse, I suppose."

Baleya nodded. "The rings are out the door, to the right, and then the third left. I trust you can find your own way without taking any detours. Your ship is waiting for you just where you left it. Maybe riding a little lighter, but none the worse for wear." She crossed her arms. "Despite everything, I am glad I met you. It's rare to meet women in this line of work, let alone women who match my deviousness."

"Likewise."

"Until next time, Mal Doran. Tanis."

Vala couldn't help but notice she'd said Tanis' name a little softer than hers. She helped Tanis out into the hall, but after a few steps she'd gotten back enough strength to push away from Vala's side. Vala reached up and rubbed her temples with two fingers, grimacing at the sticky residue the virtual device had left behind. She looked at Tanis and saw her doing the same thing.

"So what did you see?"

Tanis averted her gaze.

"Right. So… never speaking of it again?"

"Sounds like a plan to me. Come on. Let's go see how much of our loot we have left."

Vala looped an arm around Tanis' waist and pulled her close. Tanis tensed but didn't pull away. Vala decided that forgetting would be achieved easier with a bright attitude, so she put on a smile and lightened her voice. "Yes, let's! Hopefully she left us enough to buy some new outfits. Apparently we have a party to attend."

CHAPTER SEVEN

JACK O'Neill glanced out into the gate room as he came down the stairs. The Stargate was active, its shimmering surface reflecting off the control room's windows. He kept waiting to become desensitized to the sight, waited for the day when he could walk past without giving it his attention, but it didn't seem likely to happen very soon. Despite that, with the responsibilities of his new position, he couldn't help but feel a twinge at the sight of an active and seemingly unused event horizon. Bureaucracy had turned him into the grumpy old man who complained about running the air-conditioner when the door was standing wide open.

He pushed aside thoughts of their budget and approached his favorite technician. "Am I about to be relieved or disgruntled, Walter?"

"I would say relieved."

Jack sighed. "Well, that would certainly be a change of pace." The screens receiving the video signal were active, showing a dark stone passageway and the back of Captain Morello's head as she spoke to someone standing behind her. "Ahoy-hoy," he said loud enough to get her attention. She turned around fast, eyes wide as she leaned close to the camera lens. Jack winced; he used to do the same thing, and never realized what an annoyingly distorted picture it sent back.

"Hello, General…"

"Captain, why don't you just… lean back about five inches?"

She immediately retreated to a more comfortable location. "Sorry, sir. I wanted to touch base in regards to the device Dr. Jackson found here, and… if I could be so bold, offer an alternative mission."

"All right. Start with the update."

"Colonel Getty and the rest of the team have done an extensive sweep of the room and the rest of the palace, but there doesn't seem to be any sort of map or guidepost indicating how many of these things there are. I did find a subspace receiver inside the shell of the device which would support the theory that each one sends a signal to the next one in the sequence until they've all been activated. It would also serve as a receiver so that Kali could disable them all from a single location through an active Stargate. All she'd have to do is press one button and they all go cold."

"All good news," Jack said, "assuming we can actually find that one button."

"Yes, sir. Like a needle in a haystack, I understand. But I was thinking that if Kali was still around, we could just ask her."

Jack raised an eyebrow. "*If* being the operative word. Is there any indication she's still alive following her Jaffa rising up?"

"No, sir. In fact, there haven't been any reports of Kali anywhere in the galaxy for the past few months. It's like she just vanished into thin air."

"And you just happen to know that?"

She smiled sheepishly. "Of course not. Once I learned we were going to be investigating one of Kali's strongholds, I dug through some recent mission reports. There are sightings of other Goa'uld on the run, but so far nothing on Kali. The Tok'ra also haven't heard anything about her."

"Nice. You did your homework."

"It's kind of my thing." She grinned. "Uh, anyway, it makes sense that she would have gone further underground than anyone else. She not only lost her Jaffa, she lost her allies among the other System Lords because she was affiliated with Anubis. Right now she's persona non grata. It would be extremely difficult for her to find safe harbor."

"All the more reason to assume she's dead," Jack said.

"I don't think so. Goa'uld don't die quietly."

"Do they do anything quietly?"

Morello smiled. "I think she managed to find that safe

haven, sir. She couldn't rely on her former allies, since they all had problems of their own to deal with. Anyone who fell in line with Anubis would be fighting for their own survival."

Jack glanced at the Stargate again, the ticker in his head clicking over another digit. "Uh-huh."

"Sir, Bastet was killed a few months before Dakara happened."

The apparent change in topic was too much for him. "What does that have to do with anything?"

"Kali and Bastet were long-time allies, sir. If Kali needed to escape the rebelling Jaffa and the other System Lords, Bastet's worlds would be the perfect hiding place. Custom-made for a Goa'uld of Kali's stature but no one would be looking there because Bastet was dead before all this began. Her Jaffa moved on before the uprising and anything that could have been looted was already long gone. It would make sense for Kali to lie low on one of her planets. If she was found, she could be compelled to tell us what we need to know to disable these devices. At the very least she could tell us how much time we have before they go off."

Jack considered the strategy. "Is there anything else you can do with the device?"

"Not really, sir."

"Then tell Colonel Getty to get your team back here. You're going on a snake hunt."

Morello grinned brightly. "Yes, sir. Looking forward to it, sir."

Jack nodded and had Walter close the Stargate. It would have to be reopened in due course to bring his people home. *Forget heating the whole neighborhood*, he thought. *I'm holding open a revolving door to the whole damn galaxy.* He sighed and patted Walter's shoulder before turning to go back to his office. In the end it didn't really matter how much it cost; it was just the price of doing business.

The Stargate on Teunus was located in the bottleneck of a valley that widened just enough to enclose a small village within its walls. On the opposite side of the valley was a squat pyramid that, according to Teal'c, had once been home to Amaterasu. She was one of the many Goa'uld who had been kicked out either by their Jaffa or by locals who had come to understand their ruler wasn't actually a god. There was evidence of violence all around the Stargate, from staff weapon blasts on stones, to destroyed carts that had yet to be cleared away. Sam noticed that the debris, while seemingly random, had been placed in strategic positions to limit the movement of anyone coming through the Stargate.

When the event horizon collapsed, a strong voice said, "Declare any weapons you have brought with you!"

The team turned slowly to see a group of five Jaffa standing behind the Stargate. Sam and Daniel slowly lifted their hands, but Teal'c stepped forward and lifted his hand to appease the guards.

"Friends! I am Teal'c, of Chulak. I am here under the banner of peace and mean you no harm."

Their demeanor completely changed as soon as they heard his name, and the weapons were lowered as they gathered around him.

Daniel and Sam kept a respectable distance so Teal'c could serve as their emissary. Approaching one of the carts which had been moved to create the barrier around the Stargate, Daniel said "You know, it's a shame we don't have more time to really talk to some of these people in a more relaxed capacity. The Jaffa we know have all been part of the resistance for years. Teal'c and Bra'tac stopped believing the Goa'uld were gods years ago, but so many of them were still proudly serving and worshipping when the curtain was raised. It's amazing they've been able to function at all, let alone start building the foundation of an entirely new nation."

"Well, they are Jaffa." Sam looked at the men speaking to Teal'c. Three of them bore the mark of Moloc, while the other two had elaborate bird-like marks that she couldn't immediately identify. "Their entire life consists of fighting the armies of other gods. When one was defeated they would shift allegiances. I think deep down most of them knew this day was coming."

Daniel said, "It's one thing to know a day like this is coming. Actually living through it and trying to survive in such a vastly different world is something completely different."

Teal'c finished speaking to the guards and returned to them. "They have agreed to allow us entrance to their village. Word of Kali's plan had not reached them yet, and they were grateful for the warning. They will disable the Stargate while we meet with the leader of this place, and open it only when we depart."

Sam lifted her hand in thanks to the men. "Hopefully that will be enough to keep them safe. Did you ask about the items from Kali's temple?"

Teal'c nodded and led them toward the village. "One of them confirmed they received a great many things originally owned by Kali, but there is no guarantee it remains. There have been several transactions, both authorized and illicit, since Kali's treasure arrived and much of what came may have already changed hands. If it is still here, we will find it at the base of the pyramid. A bazaar has been set up to spread the wealth of the Goa'uld among other Jaffa settlements. Those who require funds to establish their new homes may find items to sell or barter here."

Daniel said, "Hopefully if they do have the means to stop Kali's devices from activating, they'll see the benefit in sharing the information with us for free. It's not like we have anything to trade."

"On the contrary, Daniel Jackson. When I revealed we were en route to Teunus, the Council provided me with several ounces of naquadah with which we can negotiate a trade."

"That was nice of them."

Teal'c said, "They are most grateful for the Tau'ri's assistance in this matter, Colonel Carter. Seeing as it has become dangerous for us to travel between worlds, there existed the possibility that we would not have the means to combat this threat."

Sam said, "Of course we're helping. Why wouldn't we?"

"Tau'ri and Jaffa have long been enemies, despite your assistance with our struggle to be free. Now that we have achieved our goal, many believe you no longer have an incentive to help us. There is also the fact that you are outsiders who cannot begin to understand the struggles we have been through. This plague that we endeavor to prevent only affects Jaffa. Many would question why you would expend the effort and risk your own lives on this quest."

"Because it's the right thing to do," Daniel said. "I mean, my God. We're talking about genocide. If we just stood by and let that happen, we'd be no better than the Goa'uld."

"Not to mention all the times our asses have been saved by the Jaffa in the past," Sam said. "Yes, many SGC missions involved fighting Jaffa, and yes, several of those missions involved fatalities. But we're not going to discount all the times you guys saved our asses, too. If you hadn't been a member of SG-1, Daniel and I would both be dead a dozen times over. Hell, we wouldn't even have gotten off Chulak on our first mission if it hadn't been for you." She furrowed her brow and glanced sideways at him. "Did we ever actually say thank you for that?"

"Many times and in many different ways, Colonel Carter." He smiled at her and inclined his head. "And you are most welcome."

She returned his smile.

"Do not take their wariness as antagonistic. They are simply being… cautious. For the first time in our history we have the opportunity to draw our own path. We would not wish to allow outside influence during these nascent stages."

"No, we totally understand that," Daniel said. "The Jaffa need to figure out who they are as a free people. Government, culture… you need to work out what works for you, and you can only do that yourselves. That being said, there's nothing wrong with seeking advice from people who have gone through this sort of rebirth as well."

"I thank you, Daniel Jackson. When the time comes, we would greatly appreciate your assistance. But for now the work must be our own."

They passed other Jaffa on the road to the pyramid, and Sam couldn't help but think of how recently her reaction to seeing them would have been to grab her gun and take cover. She and Daniel remained behind Teal'c, letting him take the lead so there was no doubt he was their escort. A few of the men and women offered polite head nods or paused to briefly greet Teal'c, but for the most part the groups moved on without saying a word.

Soon they arrived at the town which had grown up in the area around the pyramid's base. Everything looked new and freshly built, but there were already signs of life in every corner; toys that had been left in the street, laundry flapping on strings that stretched between two buildings, and the smell of something delicious that wafted through narrow alleys. The majority of people Sam saw bore the mark of one System Lord or another, but she also saw a handful of people whose foreheads were bare.

"Siero said this planet was neutral before the Jaffa annexed it. Are these the people who lived here before this place was set up?"

"Indeed," Teal'c said. "This is a rare planet in which the Goa'uld were not responsible for their woes. There is a quarry on the other side of these hills where the men extract stone used in construction on a nearby world. Raiders and thieves from other worlds took advantage of the lack of men protecting the village and began attacking while they were at work or off-world selling their stone. Their reign of terror ended when a group from the Hak'tyl Resistance arrived seeking to set up trade and saw the dilemma. They offered to remain in order to protect the residents from further attacks, and in return the citizens of Teunus offered to provide shelter to the Hak'tyl."

Daniel said, "Sounds like a beneficial arrangement for both sides."

"Indeed. The Hak'tyl taught the women of the village to defend themselves, while the villagers taught the Hak'tyl valuable lessons in farming, building shelter…"

Sam said, "Probably even simple things, like setting a household budget."

Teal'c nodded. "When it became necessary to create a safe haven that was restricted only to our people, the people of Teunus were more than happy to oblige."

Daniel said, "And the woman we're meeting…"

"Nicia."

"Right. She was one of the first to use tretonin after Ishta's group."

Teal'c said, "And that is one of the reasons she has agreed to meet with us today. She credits the Tau'ri with the creation of the drug."

Sam said, "It's nice to know some people in the galaxy still see us as the good guys."

Teal'c smiled at her. "The ground is still shaking beneath our feet, Colonel Carter, but it will eventually grow still. When that day comes, the Tau'ri will be given the credit they so richly deserve. I shall make certain of it."

They walked on until they reached a pair of open-air cabins connected by a covered porch. A breezeway ran between the two buildings, and the space was filled with people crouching, sitting, or leaning against the wall. As they stepped onto the porch a dark-skinned woman in a sleeveless V-neck tunic came out of the cabin on the right. She carried a bag so heavy it made the muscles of her arms bulge as she crouched to set it down next to the nearest person, a weary-looking woman with tears in her eyes.

"This will pay the merchants and get you the grain you require. There should be enough left over for you to build your savings back up. Don't let them cheat you on the price."

The woman nodded, barely containing her tears as she pushed herself up. "Thank you, Nicia." She wrapped her arms around Nicia's shoulders. "Thank you so much."

"That is unnecessary, Phera. Now, do you need someone to help you carry this home? I'm certain we can find some trustworthy men who are willing to help you." She looked at Teal'c and Daniel. "Why, here are two such men now. Sirs? Would you help this woman take the bag back to her home?"

Daniel stammered and looked at Sam, who cut off any denial he might have made. "They'd be happy to, Nicia. In the meantime, perhaps you and I could speak inside?"

Nicia agreed with a silent nod of her head. As Daniel and Teal'c gathered the bag and helped the woman past the crowd, Nicia assured those who were waiting that she would be as quick as possible. Sam smiled apologetically as she skipped the line, waved goodbye to Daniel as he hauled away the sacks of whatever bartering material Nicia had given to the woman. She stepped into the cabin and was surprised by how hot it was. The temperature on Teunus was a good twenty degrees warmer than what they'd left behind in Colorado Springs, and this particular room had to have another thirty degrees on that. She felt a film of sweat on her forehead by the time Nicia had crossed the room and bent over an open ledger.

Sam waited until Nicia had marked the transaction before she spoke. "I'm Colonel Samantha Carter of SG-1. Thank you for agreeing to meet with us."

"I am Nicia. You and your team are well known among the Jaffa, Colonel Carter, if not always well-regarded."

"We've had some differences of opinion," Sam admitted warily.

Nicia smiled reassuringly. "I am among those who believe we would not have our freedom were it not for your efforts. We owe the Tau'ri a great debt, and if what you fear is true, then I am willing to do whatever I can to assist you in your endeavor. This Purge could be the end of us all."

Sam blinked in surprise. "Wow, word travels fast. Teal'c said the people at the gate hadn't even heard about the situation."

Nicia smiled and nodded her head. "On a world such as this, information is key. Thankfully we have ways to communicate with the men we have stationed at the chappa'ai." She picked up a small radio off the table, and Sam recognized it as a slightly out-of-date SGC issue. "Scavenged, of course, but they still work very well."

"I'm afraid to ask where you got that."

Nicia said, "And where do your soldiers gather the zat'nik'tels they carry?"

"Point taken," Sam said. "That radio looks pretty beaten up, though. We can see about getting you some newer models."

"I thank you. But before we begin discussing trades, I must regretfully inform you that what you seek is no longer here."

Sam's shoulders sagged. "Everything from Kali's realm has already been moved out?"

"Everything we received from her palaces was in excellent condition, and I was able to get good exchanges for what I had. There is also the matter of inventory loss."

Sam said, "Which means?"

"The current atmosphere allows for an unfortunate amount of illicit activity. I am sorry to say that much of what we recovered has been moved onto the black market. I understand that the need is great, and the theft is far too small in the grand scheme to take the time to investigate. We must operate in the knowledge that certain things will go missing under the table. Larger and more valuable items were either stolen very quickly, used to pay for the treasure's transit, or were given to those in the most need as soon as it arrived. All we have left are baubles and trinkets, nothing that could possibly be used for the purpose of which you speak. I apologize, Colonel Carter, but the simple truth is that whatever you're looking for has already been given away."

Sam tried not to sound too disappointed. "It's surprising it could be moved so quickly."

"Not really," Nicia said. "In my work here, speedy turnaround often means the difference between helping someone out of a bind and sending them away empty-handed. Kali had many items that could have easily been sold or exchanged for a high price. They would have been the first out the door. Had I but known what I had…"

"No, it's not your fault. You couldn't have known how important it was — and we don't even know what it looks like."

Nicia said, "Perhaps all is not lost. You know only that you're seeking the mechanism through which Kali could prevent the Purge?"

"That's right. We've found a device on one of her planets, and we were able to shut it off. But its construction proves that it's just one piece in a larger network."

Nicia thought for a moment. "There was an item among the spoils that may be what you seek." She motioned Sam closer and began flipping through her book. "It was a large faceted pedestal with a control panel built into one side. There was a pad with Stargate symbols that she could use to dial, and a set of alphanumeric keys with which she could enter a code." She put her finger on one line and nodded slowly. "Does that sound similar to the device you have seen?"

"It does. I don't suppose you marked down who has it?"

Nicia smiled. "I am a businesswoman, am I not?" She looked again. "It appears it was one of the items that was given away illicitly. But just because it was stolen does not mean the trail goes cold." She grinned. "The last person authorized to handle the pedestal was Imeda. She does most of her trade with a fence named Baleya Pani." She drummed her fingers on the paper and narrowed her eyes as she thought. "And Baleya Pani would not keep something that valuable for very long. The question is who would have the funds to buy it. Someone she has an existing relationship with." She smiled. "Dysmas Wyrrick. He made his fortune running arms for the

Goa'uld and now he's reaping the benefits of his hoarding. Baleya was one of his sources, and I believe she would go to him to move something this large. He is one of the few people who could afford to buy it. She would definitely contact him as soon as possible."

"Do you have any reason to believe he actually bought it? What if she showed him the items and he decided not to buy?"

Nicia shook her head. "It is possible, but Wyrrick is hosting a party soon. He's using it as an excuse to show off all the beautiful items he's acquired over the years. I doubt he would pass on the opportunity to increase his collection."

Sam said, "Would he be open to trading with us?"

"No. Even if you approached him honestly about your intentions, he would be unmoved by the plight of the Jaffa. And any Tau'ri who set foot on his planet will be imprisoned until he can think of an amusing way to execute them."

"Sounds like a fun guy."

"These are difficult days, Colonel Carter. We do not have the privilege of choosing the people we must do business with. But you are correct, Wyrrick has few friends, only those who do business with him because they have no other choice."

Sam nodded. "I understand. Desperate times call for desperate measures. But that does leave the question of how we can get the pedestal. It's not like we can just sneak in and rob the place."

"On the contrary. I mentioned that he is holding a party in the next few days to show off his collection of finery from across the galaxy. If he did purchase Kali's items from Baleya, they will be among the items he's displaying. And the party will be a masquerade."

Sam raised an eyebrow. "You think we could get inside just by wearing a mask?"

"Yes, I do. As long as you had the proper invitations. Before you ask, yes, I happen to know where you can get a couple."

Sam recognized a shrewd negotiator when she saw one,

and she crossed her arms over her chest. "And what exactly would that information cost?"

Nicia matched Sam's pose and smiled. "That depends, Colonel Carter. What do the Tau'ri have to offer?"

CHAPTER EIGHT

AFTER fleeing Baleya's stronghold, and confirming the woman had indeed taken a reasonably unreasonable price for the information she'd stolen, Vala and Tanis agreed to find a quiet little backwater planet to recuperate. Neither of them were willing to talk about what they had seen in the pods, but Vala could tell from Tanis' silence and the haunted look in her eyes that she'd seen something as bad, or even worse, than Vala's experience. They spent the trip avoiding each other as much as possible in the cramped quarters of the ship, taking turns at the controls so the other one could retreat into the cargo hold for some alone time.

Vala wasn't too concerned about taking time off from their search. If Kali's treasure was indeed going on display at Wyrrick's party, they had more than a week to kill before they could get close. That was plenty of time to allow them some rest and relaxation, even if they were forced to travel by ship. Tanis was still wary of Stargate travel, partly because it was so advanced that even she was unable to grasp how it worked but mostly because she saw it as a tactical disadvantage.

She had explained it once when Vala asked about her aversion. "Picture this. You get a Stargate address and you dial it on the platform. Stargate opens and you think you're going one place, but instead you wind up standing in a concrete box with a whole damn army aiming their weapons at your head. Not to mention the fact that you could walk through the thing, and when the shimmer drops, you have an armed response team standing behind the gate with their weapons aimed at your back."

"Good lord. Did that happen to you?"

"Not to me," Tanis admitted, "but I heard there were Jaffa who had started doing it to protect their new settlements.

Traveling by ship may take longer, and it may have its own inherent risks, but at least you're in control."

Vala couldn't find any fault in her argument and, when they worked together, she yielded to her partner's preferences. She found she quite enjoyed it. Traveling by Stargate could get them wherever they needed to be in a matter of seconds, but going the slow way opened up a world of possibilities. She had encountered at least a dozen different spacefaring civilizations cluttering up the sky, and all of them had been ripe for the plucking. The extra funds they gathered from their occasional side work as highwaymen more than made up for the delay in getting to their destination.

Thirty-six hours after departing Baleya's planet, they arrived at the nearest planet Vala knew of that had the sort of night-life they required. It was a crowded and cluttered world called Qacha Teq, a jumble of clashing enclaves. The rich had their city centers, and the poor had sprawling ghettos that clung to the affluent areas like carbuncles. The atmosphere was so polluted that it seemed to scrape across the screens of the ship as Vala descended. Finally breaking through the cloud cover, she set her course for one of the largest of the shanty towns. Any and every method of distraction was available for the person with enough funds to buy it, and Vala thought it was a worthy expense before heading off on the next step in their journey.

Vala had been to the city before and she easily found a place to leave the ship. Tanis was out the door almost as soon as the engines died down, and Vala knew better than to follow her. They'd had this kind of layover before and she'd found it was best to leave Tanis to her own devices. Odds were good that she was going in search of a willing local or two for a night of debauchery to forget whatever she'd seen. Vala's intentions were slightly different; she wanted to numb the memory and push it back from the forefront of her mind, but she didn't want to forget. She never wanted to forget those harrowing days.

With Tanis gone, securing the ship was up to Vala. She took

a handful of credits, more than she would need but not so much it would harm them too terribly if she was mugged, and folded them into the inside pocket of her vest. Once she was satisfied that their ship wouldn't be robbed in their absence, she put her hair up and tugged a floppy-brimmed hat down over her eyes before heading out to find the nearest pub.

The best part about being in a slum was that one never had to venture far to find alcoholic content. The people forced to live in this sort of environment were always eager to spend their meager paycheck on cups of liquid amnesia. The wealth of options gave her the freedom to skip some of the more crowded venues, and she avoided the sleazier dives where the drinks were more water than intoxicant, wandering through the dark and winding streets until she found a perfect medium in a little rathskeller in a dead-end spur. She assessed the clientele from the door and saw a mixture of Jaffa, human, Oranian, Enkarans, and a few others she couldn't identify. She had a feeling she would fit in well among them.

A woman on the stage was gesticulating wildly as she sang, hunching her shoulders and throwing her upper body back to indicate the passion in what she was singing. She swung to and fro, the green and black curls of her hair whipping against the side of her face as she contorted her lips around each word, fingers stretched out in desperation. Most of the patrons paid no attention to the theatrics but the band was too loud to ignore. Vala welcomed the clatter; it kept her from spending too much time inside her head.

Vala moved to the bar and rested her elbows on the rail until she could get the bartender's attention, eyeing the other customers as she waited. There were certain possibilities if she wished to take Tanis' methods as her own. She had often used sex as a weapon and a distraction, not to mention it was a fantastic way to take the edge off when she was bored. Normally she preferred seduction to actually going through with the act, but sometimes it was unavoidable. She tried not to deploy her seduction method on anyone she wasn't actually willing to bed, so it was rarely unpleasant. Then again, she had very little to gain by seducing anyone in the bar, and after reliving her experiences in Qetesh's palace, however, she was feeling decidedly unsexual.

After several minutes of waiting patiently for the bartender to notice her, she was finally able to place her drink order. The haggard man behind the bar handed her the glass and took her money with one fluid motion before turning to the next customer. Vala blew the head off the drink and brought it to her lips for that first wonderful sip.

"Vala… Mal… Doran!"

The shout echoed off the rafters, even cutting through the shriek of the band. Vala's eyes widened and she slowly turned, feeling the bubbles of her drink on her upper lip. She licked it away as she watched the man barreling toward her and tried to identify him. He was a few inches shorter than her, his face almost obscured by a beard and the too-long curls of his hair. His hands were balled into fists and he held his arms out so that they bracketed his stone-shaped body. Images of past victims shuttered through her mind in quick succession until she found a match, and she put on her widest and most innocent smile as she put her back to the bar. Only when she mentally erased the beard and pulled his hair back in a braid did she realize who it was.

"Jocia! What a pleasant surprise! How long has it been?"

"Three years," he growled when he was standing in front of her. Vala leaned back and chuckled nervously. The men on either side of her scooted away to avoid being caught up in whatever was about to happen. "It has been three years since you last darkened my door, since you filled my head with your lies! I was held responsible for your theft!"

Vala couldn't help but think that was only fair. After all, if he hadn't been so moon-eyed over her, she wouldn't have been able to steal his access codes. She never would have gotten into the vault and the hangar locks certainly would have been impossible to break. He'd been a completely invaluable accomplice. Of course she understood how he might not agree with her on that mark.

"Jocia, Ocie, darling! How could you possibly think I would do such a horrible thing to you? No, no, I was a victim as well. These horrible men burst in when you weren't home and demanded —"

He cut her off by aiming a stubby finger in her face. "Save it! Thermal registers revealed you acted alone."

Vala dropped the smile and rolled her eyes. "Well, it was worth a try." She swung her arm around and smashed her mug against the side of his head. The glass shattered and his head was drenched with the alcohol she'd sadly not had a chance to sample. She pushed herself up to sit on the bar and placed her boot in the center of his chest. She kicked him backward, stood up, and high-stepped over the glasses of the bar's other patrons. No one seemed more than mildly perturbed by the distraction, giving her the impression it was a normal occurrence.

"Stop her!" Jocia shouted, still struggling to see through his soaked bangs.

Vala reached the end of the bar and leapt for the staircase stretching overhead. She grabbed the banister and, after a bit of kicking and swinging, managed to pull herself up. She slithered between the posts, got onto her hands and knees, and stood up as she ascended the steps to the second floor landing. She could hear Jocia shoving his way through the crowd in pursuit of her, his rough tactics turning the initially impartial crowd against him. They held him back long enough for Vala to push through a curtain separating the main corridor from the more private areas.

She could hear Jocia on the stairs as she reached the window at the end of the hall. She gave the glass a quick shove and, when it opened, she squirmed out onto the small landing that encircled the building. She took the time and risk to push the window back down, scooted sideways along the precarious ledge so that she wouldn't be seen, and flattened herself against the building's clay brick façade. Though she knew it didn't make a difference, she closed her eyes and held her breath.

Inside she heard Jocia in the hallway. There were six private rooms, and Jocia began pounding on one of the doors. "Come out of there, Vala!"

The door was opened violently. "You are interrupting our transaction!"

"I'm looking for the woman who ruined me! Stand aside! I'll search every one of these rooms if I must." There were sounds of a scuffle, followed by Jocia grunting as he forced his way into the room. Vala rolled her eyes; six rooms carefully searched? Odds were good that she would be trapped out on the ledge for a good long time. She hoped Tanis was having a more relaxing evening than she was. She looked around for an alternative escape route. Across the alley was another building with darkened windows, but it was much too far to jump. The roof was a good ten feet away, which might as well have been a hundred feet.

Below her, there was a wooden cart stacked high with wooden boxes. She didn't know if the boxes would bear her weight, or if what was inside would hurt her if they shattered, but beggars couldn't be choosers. She said a silent prayer and jumped. The boxes held, and Vala rolled off the side of the cart. She hissed and rotated her shoulder, massaging the point where it met her neck as she got back on her feet. She tossed her hair, looked up to see if anyone had heard her, and hurried out of the alley to the safe anonymity of the street.

"The things one has to do in order to get a drink in this town," she muttered as she adjusted her vest and slipped her hands into her pockets. She had only gone a few blocks before she passed another bar and, though she hadn't planned to enter, two Jaffa cut her off on their way inside. She would have ignored the rudeness if she hadn't overheard a snippet of their conversation. "…truly supposed to be afraid of someone like Kali?"

She changed direction and followed the men inside. They were dressed casually and she could see weapons dangling from sheaths on their hips. Both of them had burned away their tattoos but the shape indicated they had once fought in the service of Ba'al. One was several inches taller than the other, with thin salt-and-pepper hair. The other was shorter, balding, and wore a thick mustache that obscured his lips. The taller man was the skeptic, while the shorter seemed to be the one sharing the gossip.

"Kali has been known to employ methods such as this in the past. It would not be outside the realm of possibility to believe she's doing it again to punish her Jaffa for turning on her."

The taller Jaffa shook his head. "You heard wrong. The message was too short."

"The length of the message does not change its meaning. They had time to prepare the message before activating the Stargate to send it through, so I know I can take it at face value." He signaled for a bartender and rapped his knuckles on the bar. He snorted, which made his mustache twitch. "I understand why they must bury the Stargate, but after everything we have accomplished… cutting off all communications until further notice makes it look like we're running and hiding."

"Yes, but it's to protect you! From the plague of the gods that will descend upon us for our hubris. This is all just a bunch of religious zealots harping on the end of days in a world without gods. Their altars have been shattered and they have nothing left. They're grasping at straws and all it will do is serve to make us look foolish in the eyes of every other race out here."

"It would be simpler if you were right. Cowards and alarmists afraid of what freedom would mean. I would much prefer that to the alternative." He sighed and slapped the taller Jaffa in the side. "If he returns before I do, order me something alcoholic."

As he made his way through the crowd, Vala sidled up next to the tall Jaffa. "Well, hello. Tall, dark, and muscles. Quite a combination."

He smiled at her. "I am Miri'k."

She extended her hand. "Vala. A bright spot in the darkness."

"You certainly are."

She arched an eyebrow and pressed closer to him. "I hate to intrude, but I couldn't help overhear part of your conversation with your friend. Some sort of plague threatening the Jaffa? I think I heard you mention, uh… Kali? Was it Kali?"

"That's the rumor. Baq'rel doesn't believe it's worthy of concern."

Vala said, "Then he's a fool! The Goa'uld are petty creatures. I've no doubt one of them would go to devious lengths to respond in the event of a Jaffa uprising."

Miri'k nodded. "That is my fear. Perhaps if the rumor were less vague, or if it named a different System Lord. Kali is notorious for disposing of her enemies in this manner. The message warned that a sickness, a plague, would soon be sent through the galaxy via the chappa'ai. Every Jaffa exposed will fall ill and die. It is very similar to the way she eradicated the followers of Shiva after taking over his realm."

Vala pursed her lips. "Goodness. After all this, forced to hide… well. If you have need of alternative transportation to see friends and loved ones on a now-inaccessible planet, I'm certain ferry services could be arranged for the right price."

He smiled at her. "A very kind offer."

Vala winked and returned his smile. "How long are you expected to hide away from the threat of this plague which may or may not be coming?" She was trying to calculate how many trips she could book with him and his friends.

"I do not know. But perhaps it will not be long. A member of the new Jaffa government is said to be working with several humans in an attempt to stop the virus from being released. If they are successful we can raise our chappa'ai within the next few days."

Vala's attention shifted again. "Stop the virus… how?"

Miri'k shrugged. "There is said to be a device in Kali's treasures that will deactivate the delivery system. Their intention is to recover anything that originated in her realm until they find something which can prevent the plague. But why are we dwelling on such matters?" He slid his hand onto her thigh under the bar. "Perhaps there are better things we can discuss to pass the time."

Baq'rel returned at that moment, saving Vala from manufacturing an excuse to extricate herself. He grumbled when he saw her but directed his comment to Miri'k.

"We must leave."

"Really?" Vala feigned a pout. "But we were just getting better acquainted. We were going to run a transportation business together."

Baq'rel said, "This does not concern you! Miri'k, I received word from Jocia. Apparently a grafter he's been hunting down for years finally showed her craven face, but she slipped away before he could get hold of her. We're gathering a group to seek her out." He looked past his friend at Vala. "I suppose if you wish to join us, we would welcome the extra set of eyes."

"Oh, I couldn't possibly impose. It sounds like 'man-business.' And I just remembered that I need to speak with a friend of mine if we're going to start flying Jaffa all over the sky." She patted Miri'k on the chest and slipped away from him. "But we will definitely reconnect just as soon as possible. You can be my inaugural passengers! Ta for now, boys!"

She turned and fled from the bar before he could protest or any of Jocia's friends could get a closer look at her. Once she was outside, her smile faded as quickly as her memory of Miri'k. A woman she passed had a multi-colored scarf draped over her shoulder, and Vala plucked it away so deftly that the woman wasn't aware of what happened. She wrapped it loosely around her face, lifted it up over her nose, and hunched her shoulders to keep from drawing attention to herself.

There was nothing she could do to find Tanis; she could be warming far too many potential beds for Vala to even hope of tracking her down. Her only option was returning to the tel'tak, keeping everything shut down so she didn't register on any scans, and trying to think of her next step. She didn't like the idea of waiting until morning to leave but she also couldn't risk staying on the streets if Jocia and his goon squad were scouring every dive and pub for her. There was no doubt she could extricate herself from whatever they had planned. Jocia was no murderer and torture was outside of his vocabulary. At best any vengeance he wished to serve would involve a lot of yelling and futile attempts to shame her. But she couldn't spare the time. If what Miri'k and Baq'rel said was true, she and Tanis needed to act as quickly as possible to prevent a potential catastrophe.

Somebody was trying to steal their treasure.

"Medical supplies?" Jack squinted at Sam and Daniel for a moment, trying to gauge if they were setting him up for irritation. They had just entered his office, Teal'c at their shoulder, and it was all he could do not to join them on the other side of the desk. He reluctantly took the seat of power and laced his hands on the blotter in front of him. "That's really all she wants in exchange for this information?"

Sam said, "Yes, sir."

"This isn't like when we were going to trade water for weapons, right? There's no such thing as heavy medical supplies."

"Well, some of them can be quite heavy. But no, sir. She's asking for the basics: bandages, sutures, tools. Her patients are Jaffa so most of their needs are met by either a symbiote or tretonin, but physical wounds require a little bit of help. Nicia has been doing a great job up to this point trying to keep up with demand, but there's only so much that can be traded and so much time in the day. If we provided a few necessary supplies it would give them a nice cushion to work with."

Daniel said, "And they're asking for the sort of things I would hope we'd be giving them even without the promise of getting something in return."

Jack nodded slowly. "Okay... and the invitation to this party

Wyrrick is throwing… she can get that for us?"

Daniel hesitated before speaking. "Not… exactly. She doesn't have one. Like we said, she's entirely focused on taking care of the villagers right now. She isn't trading for anything she can't use to heal or ease pain."

"So she doesn't have any invitations to give us."

"Not as such. No."

"But she can tell us how to get some."

"Yes."

Jack rolled his eyes and leaned back in his chair. "Gotta tell ya, it's starting to feel a lot like you kids are just running around the neighborhood stacking up favors."

Teal'c, who had remained otherwise silent, finally spoke, "But the cause is just."

Jack looked at his old friend. "Indeed. Look, I'm not complaining about why we're doing it, I'm just starting to wonder if it's not all just a wild goose chase. Treasures and masquerade parties and borrowing from here to bribe there to get information from that. How do we know there's a real solution at the end of all this? How do we know we're not just spinning our wheels while this clock keeps ticking?"

Daniel said, "I think it's a risk we'll have to take, Jack. For the sake of the Jaffa, we can't just ignore the potential solution until we've confirmed its validity. You have SG-9 looking for Kali in Bastet's strongholds, so you're not putting all your eggs in one basket. I think this is the best shot."

Jack drummed two fingers on his desk and glanced toward the briefing room. Another team was due back in forty-five minutes. If he agreed to exchange medical supplies for information, it would take time to put the package together. After that, the next available time for SG-1 to take it back to the planet would be the next day at oh-eight-fifteen. If he didn't decide the mission was a wash. So far they'd only come up with information, slowly moving one step at a time closer to a hopeful solution. What if they got to Wyrrick's shindig and discovered he had given the pedestal away to a friend? How long could they afford to chase this wild goose across the galaxy?

"I've spoken with the infirmary," Daniel prodded. "They have enough of a surplus that they could begin preparing a shipment immediately. They just need your say-so."

Jack made his decision. He could spend a few hours debating the pros and cons, weighing the potential costs, but he knew where he would end up. Why waste the time? "They have it. Tell them to put together everything Nicia asked for, and whatever they can think of that she didn't. You leave tomorrow morning if the supplies are ready."

Sam said, "Thank you, sir."

"Thanks, Jack."

He gestured at the door with his pen. "Now get out of here. Rest up. You've been running around the galaxy for thirty-six hours by my count. You've earned a break."

They left with little argument, a testament to just how tired they must have been, but Teal'c lingered until they had gone. He stepped closer to the desk. "Uneasy lies the head that wears the crown. William Shakespeare."

"I'll have to take your word on that. The author, not the quote. Trust me, I buy the quote." He sighed heavily and rubbed his face. "General Hammond made this look so easy."

"Indeed, he was truly a great leader."

"And I'm not?"

Teal'c refused to take the bait and only smiled. "General Hammond had a great many years in which to hone his skills as a leader, and yet he still questioned himself. It was those questions that led to him making the right decisions, which is what leads you to deem him a great leader. It will take time, but I have no doubt you will one day be as respected and revered as your predecessor."

"Yeah. Well…" He looked down at his desk and sighed. "Right now I'm regretting the decision to let Dr. Weir go ahead to Atlantis. How about you, T? I'm not the only one struggling with the yoke of leadership. You've been hornswoggled into a pioneer role yourself with the new Jaffa nation."

Teal'c took a slow breath, which for him was the same as a heavy sigh. "It is a burden. However I admit I was naïve to think I could simply help my people achieve freedom and afterward step back into anonymity. I believe the reverence they feel toward me was better earned by Bra'tac."

"You're the one who got them to Dakara. You're the one who took a chance on a snarky, unarmed soldier because he had a cool wristwatch. You were the one who took the steps necessary to get your people to this point."

"You are correct, General O'Neill. And you are also the one who has taken the steps to get your people to this point. Your decisions as commander of SG-1, and as the leader of this base, have earned your seat behind this desk. Do not question your wisdom, O'Neill, for it has served you thus far."

Jack raised an eyebrow. "Didn't know I was signing up for a therapy session. But fair point." He drummed his knuckles on the edge of the desk and a slow smile began to form. "It's good to have you back here at the SGC."

"My return to the base is only temporary, O'Neill."

"Sure. I understand. Doesn't make it any less nice to see you back."

Teal'c looked out toward the briefing room. "It has been a very long time since I had a home to miss, but I often find myself nostalgic for these halls."

"Yeah. I know what you mean. This whole place kind of looks different when you're on this side of the desk. But you don't have to worry about that. Any time you want to come back… I mean, it costs an arm and a leg just to light this place, and that Stargate out there is a bitch to turn on. But for you? The door is always open."

"I will not forget, O'Neill."

CHAPTER NINE

TWIN obsidian spires rose on either side of the courtyard, reaching high enough to be seen above the temple's walls. Morello and Huang crouched next to the entrance with their P90s at the ready, waiting as Getty and Shaffer proceeded to the next doorway. Morello took the opportunity to examine the wall carvings, her keen eye and scholar's mind cutting through the overgrowth and desolation to see the palace for the beautiful place it had once been. The alabaster walls were cool to the touch even through the sleeve of her uniform jacket. Straight ahead was a reflecting pool that was half-full of unclean water, but she could imagine it brimming with fresh water brought in from the nearby stream.

Getty and Shaffer cleared the next section of the temple, so Morello was forced to give up her appreciation of design and be a soldier for another thirty seconds. She and Huang advanced with their heads low, brushing past their teammates to enter the secondary ring of the temple. Here there were unlit braziers high on the wall flanked by carvings of regally-posed cats or lions. According to her reading, there would be a third inner room, and beyond that was Bastet's personal sanctum sanctorum. It was protected by a thick door it would take three of them to move if it had been closed. She shone her light through and saw, to her relief, it was open just enough for them to enter.

They had sent MALPs to five different planets in Bastet's domain, using out-of-date Tok'ra intelligence to determine which ones were most likely to be abandoned. The information was from a time when Bastet was still alive, so details were sketchy at best. The first three planets, along with the fifth, all showed signs of vast devastation. Apparently the people Bastet had ruled wasted no time in leaving after she was killed, and her Jaffa showed no regard for the trappings of their former goddess. The fourth planet, however, looked promising enough to justify sending them to check it out in person. Equal amounts of destruction, the same outwardly abandoned appearance, but some of the clutter had been moved out of the way to clear a path away from the Stargate.

After arriving on the planet they found more signs of recent activity: storefronts in the village were ransacked and doors on certain buildings had been forced open. There wasn't enough damage to indicate a full-scale looting incident, so Morello was growing more confident of her theory that Kali was hiding out somewhere on the planet. They had searched the village and found nothing, so she was hoping they would find the missing System Lord hiding in her former ally's throne room. Outside it was bordering on a hundred degrees and she was very aware of the sweat gathering on her skin. She couldn't easily wipe her face without removing her goggles, and she didn't want to risk sand-blinding herself in the process, so she simply let it drip down onto the collar of her jacket.

Her palms were also sweaty against the grip of her gun and she again felt a moment of lightheaded shock at the route her life had taken. She'd wanted to explore ancient cultures, unlock the mysteries of the past. One day someone had shown up with an unbelievable opportunity to follow those goals, but there was just one catch: training and military service and aiming guns at dark doorways in case bad guys were lurking around the corner. She pushed back the feeling of disconnect and focused on the task as her commanding officer approached and crouched down to her left. She had shot at people, possibly even killed them, but they had been in the process of trying to kill her at the time. Dr. Jackson proved it was possible to live in both worlds, but she was still straining to find that balance.

Getty checked to make sure his team was in position before he spoke, raising his voice so that it echoed off the stone walls around them. "Hello, in there. I'm Colonel Getty of SG-9. We're from Earth and we're only here to have a nice, civilized chat.

We're going to come in with our weapons drawn, but it's up to you whether we fire them or not. I figure you went to all this trouble to stay alive. Wouldn't want to throw all that away now, would we?"

There was only silence from within, not even the scrape of shoe against stone as their prey changed position. Getty held up his hand for a silent five-count, then motioned for Shaffer to lead the way. He stepped to the door, slid sideways through the gap, and swung his weapon to the left.

"We have one hostile, sir. She's not making any aggressive moves."

Huang and Getty went next, leaving Morello to bring up the rear. By the time she was in the room, the rest of her team had taken up positions with their weapons triangulated on a spot near the opposite wall. In the middle of the room was an altar, the scuttles once used to gather blood of sacrifices repurposed to hold food. Behind the throne was a giant black statue of a woman with the head of a cat, her arms stretched out to either side as if bidding them entrance.

Standing at the base of the throne, dressed in a dirty chambray shirt and a ratty floral skirt was a dark-skinned woman, her hair an unwashed rat's-nest of curls and tangles. A ratty piece of lace was wrapped around the lower half of her face, but the veil was short enough that Morello could see the woman's jaw moving when she spoke. She scanned the four of them with disinterest bordering on irritation, her arms held slightly away from her body in a posture of surrender.

"Stargate Command. You said your number is…"

"Nine," Getty said. "Nice to meet you."

She nodded slowly. "You are here to execute me."

"Actually, lady, it's your lucky day. We're here so that you can help us."

Kali raised an eyebrow. "You suggest we ally ourselves? To what end?"

"According to Captain Morello here, you're not above the occasional alliance. Figured we'd give it a shot now that you're not so high and mighty."

Kali looked at Morello, and she had to remind herself that the woman wasn't actually a god. It was easy to see how people could be fooled; Kali definitely had a deep well of power even standing in the middle of a devastated throne room and dressed in rags.

"You know of me."

Morello swallowed the lump in her throat. She refused to be intimidated. "I've read a few things. Did a little research when I knew we'd be dealing with you."

"And how can I assist the mighty Tau'ri?"

Morello glanced at Getty, who gave her the go-ahead with a slight dip of his chin. She faced Kali again and spoke with a bit more strength in her voice. "You left a failsafe behind in case you were ever overthrown. It's going to kill the Jaffa if we don't stop it."

"Ah. That." The skin under her eyes rose, indicating a smile. She brought her arms up and crossed them over her chest. "Your people have achieved your victory. The System Lords have been exiled and the Goa'uld are no longer feared. We are forced to hide like rats. Congratulations. But battles cannot be won without bloodshed. You will pay for your victory with the blood of your allies. This war will end only when the Jaffa have paid for their betrayal in death."

Getty said, "You sure you want to draw the line there? The only other option here doesn't bode well for your continued survival, you know."

Kali spread her arms further apart. "Then strike me down, knowing that my legacy will continue once every *shol'va* in this galaxy dies at my hand."

"Easy there, sport," Getty said. "We might not have anything to talk about, but I know General O'Neill would like to have a chat with you. Lieutenant Huang, kindly secure the prisoner. Captain Morello, contact SGC and let them know we'll be bringing a guest back with us."

The manor was built into the side of a promontory so that it jutted out over the sea which crashed against the rocks below. Vala stood before the curved glass wall that made up one side of the parlor, hands on her hips to hold back the tails of her jacket as she looked out over the choppy waters. It was absolutely freezing in front of the window, and she wondered who could possibly live in such a place. The moon hung just above the horizon, reminding her that it was night.

She and Tanis had been moving nonstop since leaving Qacha Teq, operating on little to no sleep trying to keep ahead of the Jaffa forces who seemed to be on the same trail they were. A few well-placed inquiries revealed that the rumors Vala overheard were true: a Jaffa along with another man and a woman were searching for Kali's treasure. They sent a message back to Lucia to threaten Siero, but he swore on the graves of several family members that he hadn't shared his information with anyone else. Tanis didn't believe him, but Vala knew it didn't matter either way. The information was out there, and suddenly they had competition.

They had the invitation to the party, but now Vala wasn't sure that would be enough of an advantage to achieve their goals. Hence their side trip here, to the home of Anton Bellee. The System Lords gathered all the gaudiest, tackiest items they could find in their conquests, then they hired Bellee to find the perfect balance between gloating and intimidation. He'd earned a reputation for his work among some of the most flamboyant Goa'uld, which was saying something, so Vala knew someone like Wyrrick wouldn't have gone to anyone else when it came to decorating his own mansion.

Bellee had been asleep when they arrived, and Tanis had taken great pleasure in waking him. At the moment she was keeping an eye on him while he changed out of his pajamas and freshened up. When he finally came out into the main room, prodded from behind by Tanis' blaster in his ribs, Vala didn't know why he had bothered to change clothes. His sleepwear had been replaced by a long lime-green kurta with a white silk stole trailing him like a cape. He walked with his heavy jaw thrust forward in irritation, his beetled brow knit in consternation. He twisted and glared back at Tanis and spoke with a resonant Goa'uld inflection.

"You don't have to keep poking me with that. I'm walking, aren't I?"

"Yeah. But it's fun." She poked him again just to prove she could. "Meet my friend."

He stopped in the middle of the room and glared at Vala as she turned to face him. "I hope you and your friend enjoy prison. Once my security arrives, you will find yourselves very extremely under their restraints. They will not be kind because of your gender!"

"Oh, dear, Tanis. Security? Were you aware he had security?"

"If he had security, I think they would have stopped those morons we found walking the perimeter of this place. It looked like they were casing the joint, Mr. Bellee."

Vala grinned. "Don't worry. We took care of them for you."

Bellee worked his jaw back and forth, his fists balled at his sides.

"So, either way, it seems as if we have a bit of time to kill. Why not chat? Have a seat. My associate and I don't want to hurt you, and we don't intend to rob you. And you can give up that ridiculous Goa'uld rumble. The Goa'uld chose the finest specimens for their hosts and, well, no offense…"

Bellee glared at her, then reached under the collar of his kurta and removed a small device.

Vala said, "We just want a little information about one of your clients."

He walked to the largest armchair and threw himself down like a petulant child. His Goa'uld timbre was gone when he spoke again, leaving behind a vaguely piercing voice. "I don't discuss my clients. And anyway, ninety percent of them are gone. If you want to rip off a design, I'm sure no one is going to come looking for you."

"If they're all gone, who is going to come after you if you tell us what we want to know?"

"I have my principles! I have business… acumen."

Vala tossed a small burlap sack onto the floor in front of him. When it landed, it made a distinct sound of coins clinking together. He pursed his lips and tilted his head to the side as he considered the size of the bag and how many coins it could conceivably hold.

"Ninety percent of your client base is gone?" Vala said. "Sounds like you're not going to be getting much repeat business in the coming months. And years. In fact, your entire career may have gone up in smoke along with the System Lords. I hope you managed to save some of your earnings and didn't throw it away on frivolous things." She let her eyes drift across the room at the various indulgences that surrounded them. "Seems the Goa'uld aren't the only ones with expensive tastes."

Bellee shifted in his seat. "Well… a man must eat, yes? Which client are you looking for?"

"Dysmas Wyrrick."

Bellee laughed. "Dys? One of the few people who still has the means to hire me, not to mention sending his goons after me if he finds out I betrayed his secrets. No deal."

"We just want to know the layout of his home. Apparently he's holding a party there soon. Tanis and I have an invitation, but we'd like to know our way around so we can …"

"Mingle," Tanis said.

Vala smiled. "Yes. We need to strategically mingle."

"Right." Bellee chuckled. "You just want the floor plan so you can gossip better… at the party where Wyrrick just happens to be showing off some of his newest treasures. Why would that ever be a problem? Look, you're obviously planning to rip him off, and when you do, who is he going to come looking for? He's going to come after me, the only person who could possibly have handed over that information. No, I think I'll just sit here and wait for my security. You might have taken care of the men outside, but they work for a company. I sent a signal from the panic button next to my bed the moment you came in and started roughing me up. They're going to be here any second."

"I'm sure they will be," Tanis said without concern.

Bellee glared at her. "You're not going to bluff me. The signal is hard-wired. It can't be disabled."

Vala said, "If it has electronics, Tanis can disable it."

Tanis said, "Oh, no. He's right. Whoever set it up was kind of a genius. Even the sloppiest disable technique would still send a signal to the company just in case. Technically it is impossible to stop the signal from getting out."

Bellee smiled smugly.

"Of course... just because the signal has to go out doesn't mean it has to take the most direct route. I managed to make sure it passed through our ship first. I have a couple of relay programs set up that shot the signal off the atmosphere. It's taking a few laps around the planet before it finally goes where it's supposed to go. Once it gets done touring the nine continents, your security forces will be alerted to what's going on here." She checked the timepiece on the inside of her wrist and nodded. "Yeah. We have time."

Bellee looked at her for signs she was bluffing, but she gave nothing away. He huffed and blew out his lips. "So... what? Either I give you what you want or you kill me?"

"Nothing so crass," Vala said.

Tanis said, "Aw."

"Hush. If you don't give us the blueprints, we'll simply bring you with us. We'll leave you behind at Wyrrick's party when we're done with you."

Bellee's face changed shades and he pushed up from his seat.

"Sure. Let him do the dirty work. Fine. Out of my way, pokey."

Tanis stepped away from a large painting and Bellee hooked his fingers under the frame to swing it out. Behind it was a recessed panel with a safe. Once his back was turned, Tanis caught Vala's eye and tapped her ear with two fingers. She glanced toward the front of the house. Vala signaled to ask how long they had and Tanis swept her hand in an undercutting arc. Not long. Vala walked to the window and looked outside, craning her neck so she could see along the land's edge. Lights were sweeping across Bellee's side lawns as his security surrounded the structure. She didn't betray her anxiety as she moved closer to the wall, out of sight from the window.

"Having problems remembering your passcode?"

"It's a little dark in here, okay?" He sighed and finally got the door open. He shuffled through a rack of crystals, lifting them at random in order to read the small identifying glyphs written on the surface. Finally he found one and withdrew it, turning to hold the disc out to Vala.

"That has everything you'll need to know. It's the blueprint to the house where he's holding the party. The treasure rooms, the armory, the main ballroom, it's all there. Even the grotto is there."

"Grotto?" Vala said. "Sounds positively divine. Hope we get a chance to partake while we're there. Thank you, Anton. You've been an absolute peach. Shame we're going to part ways soon. Unless you plan to attend the party."

He laughed. "With you two there? I think I'll keep a few planets between us if it's all the same to you. But you know what? If you're going to wreck the place, try to spare those tapestries on the wall in the main room. I had to go to eight different agoras to find those damn things."

"No promises, but we'll do our best. And it goes without saying that Wyrrick doesn't find out about our little visit."

Bellee barked a laugh. "Why would I go to Wyrrick and tell him what you did when it would be so much easier and cleaner to just commit ritual suicide right here in my home?"

"You might get the idea that he would forgive you for handing over the information if you give him a chance to change his defenses before we arrive, or let him set a trap for us." Vala stepped closer. "But that would be a very bad idea, Mr. Bellee. You see my friend here? Tanis? She gets arrested quite a lot… but she always gets out."

"And I always remember the people who set me up."

Bellee swallowed a lump in his throat. "Look, just get out of here and…"

"Sire Bellee?" The person speaking pounded on the front door. "Are you well, master?"

Bellee forgot his submissive act and turned to face the front of the house. "They're still here! Get in here and arrest them, you scissorbills!"

Tanis rushed to stand beside Vala, who backed up closer to the window. "Tanis, I believe that's our cue. Hold on tight, dear." She pushed up the sleeve of her jacket and used three fingers to activate the device strapped to her wrist. Their tel'tac rose from the waves below the cliff, the water cascading from its curves as it surged into the sky. Vala used her thumb to activate the small charges she'd placed in the window caulking while Tanis was retrieving Bellee. The explosives shattered the floor-to-ceiling window's center pane. Cold wind blew in from the ocean and filled the room with its frost, knocking Bellee to the ground with surprise as Tanis turned and fired her blaster at the ship. The wind tried to catch the grapple, but it had a homing signal that carried it directly to the ship's underside.

Security officers flooded into Bellee's house and he shrieked orders at them as Vala and Tanis leapt out into the frigid night. The tel'tak changed course just before impacting the house and Tanis' rope was pulled taut. She and Vala swung like hooked salmon underneath the vessel. Vala tilted her head up and, when their position was right, she hit the final button on the wrist control. The aperture on the bottom of the ship blossomed to drop the transport rings around them as they dangled.

Both women tumbled when they arrived inside the ship, the centrifugal force of their swing to freedom causing them to fly in opposite directions. Vala hit the ground and skidded, looking up to see Tanis hit the far wall and tumble down. Vala coughed as she got to her feet, dizzy from the sudden switch from spinning in mid-air to standing on solid ground. She used the wall to brace herself as she moved into the cockpit, found her seat, and disabled the autopilot. Tanis joined her a few seconds later and sank into the other seat.

"Clear?"

Vala checked. "No signs of aerial pursuit, at least not yet." She squinted at the screen ahead of her. "If we can get out of the system without running into any blockades, we should be home free." She smiled at her partner. "Very well done back there, Ms. Reynard."

"You weren't so bad yourself, Mal Doran. What's our next step?"

Vala took out the crystal with Wyrrick's information on it and tapped it against her thigh. "Next, we plan."

CHAPTER TEN

A SECOND team of Marines came through the gate and helped secure the prisoner before she was brought through to Earth. Jack made certain the corridors were kept clear of anyone other than security personnel as Kali was taken to the brig. She was allowed to shower and offered a change of clothing before she was escorted to an isolation room with a table set up in the center. Her hands were shackled to the table in front of her. Once she had been confirmed as a non-threat, she was left alone.

SG-9 briefed Jack about what they had found on the planet, and now they were on a well-deserved standby while he figured out how to deal with their new prisoner. When he finally went down to see her with his own eyes, he was surprised to find Morello in the observation room watching the Goa'uld through the one-way glass. He pushed up the sleeves of his jacket and stood just behind her right shoulder for a moment, watching as she watched the former System Lord.

"Captain."

Her shoulders twitched and tension appeared in her neck, but she kept her eyes on the glass. "General. Sir. I-I didn't know it was you."

"Relax. I learned a long time ago with Colonel Carter that I can't order anyone to stand down no matter what it says on my uniform. And I don't think anyone would mock you for taking a victory lap with this mission. How long have you been assigned here?"

"Two years, sir."

"And you already bagged yourself a Goa'uld. Not one of the good ones, of course. Kind of lower-tier. But still not too shabby."

He could see her fighting the urge to smile. "I'll aim higher next time, sir."

"See that you do. No more slacking off." He uncrossed his

arms to pat her on the shoulder. "I know I said it in the briefing, but it bears repeating. Good work, Captain."

"Thank you, sir."

Jack left her in the observation room and nodded to the airmen outside the door as he entered the holding cell. Kali sat up straighter when she saw him, lifting her chin and narrowing her eyes as she tracked his movements. Jack stood in front of her and crossed his arms. Her lips were pursed in a moue of unimpressed boredom. She looked as if she'd taken a bite of something foul and was trying to find the strength to swallow or find a napkin to spit it into.

"Hi. I'm Jack O'Neill. You may remember me from such events as the Kicking of Ra's Ass and The Death of Apophis numbers one through five."

"Why have you brought me to this place?"

Jack raised his eyebrows. "Accommodations not to your liking? We could try to find somewhere a little gaudier for you... I think Trump's got a few casinos nearby."

Kali sighed. "This war has been fought already, O'Neill. You have nothing to gain by imprisoning me here."

"Oh, that's where you're wrong." He leaned forward and placed his hands on the table. "See, we know all about your little Hail Mary plot. We know you're going after the Jaffa, and we're going to stop you. The only question is whether you get brownie points for helping out."

The Goa'uld smiled. "Aha. Now we have come to the crux of the matter. You consider yourselves fortunate, no doubt, to have discovered the device before it activated. But if you believe you will foil the plot you are sorely mistaken. I have lost everything because of the Tau'ri and the Jaffa, and you will both feel my vengeance."

Jack said, "I think you've forgotten where you're sitting. See, I have some very good friends among the Jaffa. One of 'em is a big guy with a gold tattoo in the middle of his forehead. Nice guy, not a big talker. But if he dies, or if his family dies, because of some pissy Goa'uld with a grudge, you're going to wish those Jaffa of yours had caught up with you. Because what they would have done is nothing compared to what I'll do. Do we have an understanding?"

Kali stared at him.

"Tell us how to disable your devices."

"Begin mourning your friend now, O'Neill."

Jack worked his jaw and pushed away from the table. "How long do we have before it activates?"

"Seconds."

"We're not done here."

Kali smirked and it took everything he had not to smack her. He left the room to find Daniel lingering in the corridor.

"Geneva Convention," Daniel said.

"Doesn't count for zats."

"Pretty sure it does."

"Show me where."

"I don't think the people who wrote it were prepared for the possibility of alien energy guns but if they had they would have been very against the idea of using them on prisoners."

Sam approached and joined them. "Has she given anything up?"

Jack sighed. "No. But I suppose I shouldn't be surprised. What about you? Any luck?"

"The infirmary has gathered a pretty sizable care package. With your permission I'd like to begin preparing to take it to Nicia."

"Yeah, it doesn't look like Kali is going to be much help. We might as well keep chipping away at the other side of the problem. Look, I know she was lying about only having seconds left, but I bought it when she implied time was running out. Is there a chance that even with all of this running around we're still going to come up short?"

"Of course," Daniel said. "There's always a worst-case scenario."

Jack glared at him. "Not the answer I was angling for."

"It's a small miracle we even discovered this plot before it devastated the Jaffa nation," Daniel said, "and every minute spent without disabling it is another minute closer to having it go off."

Jack sighed. "Okay. Forget the scheduled mission departure time. As soon as the medicine is ready to go, dial out and take it where it needs to be."

Sam said, "Are you sure?"

"Yes. I'm the general now. I can do cool things like disagree with myself for the greater good. If Walter gives you any trouble tell him to… Hell, he'll probably have made the decision for me an hour ago." He shrugged. "The clock is ticking, boys and girls, and the fate of an entire newborn nation is hanging in the balance. I think that offsets the expense of an extraneous gate activation, don't you?"

"Absolutely," Daniel said.

Sam said, "We just have to gear up."

"Then go," Jack said. "Gear. Go."

They left, and Jack went into the observation room. Morello had disappeared, and he stood alone in the dark room to look at the former System Lord. She didn't look imposing in the least despite her attempts at posturing. He saw her for what she really was, a frightened woman whose world had been ripped away from her in the blink of an eye. She had exiled herself on a dead planet and scrounged for food and shelter because it was too dangerous for her to do anything else.

After a long internal debate, he picked up the phone and ordered an airman to bring him something. He was very specific about what he wanted, insisting when the airman expressed confusion. He hung up and waited, and soon it was delivered to him.

"Is it all here?" Jack asked, looking under the lid.

"Yes, sir. Everything you asked for."

He picked it up and carried it into the interrogation room. Kali tensed as he entered, giving away her anxiety by dropping her eyes to what he held in his hand. He placed it on the table, lifted the lid, and pushed it toward her. She looked at it and then raised her eyes to him.

"What is the meaning of this?"

"Tuna fish on wheat," Jack said, indicating the sandwich. "Potato chips. Plain, but I didn't know if you would want barbeque or… well, plain is fine. I had them add the Jell-O because Carter seems to like it, but that's dessert. You don't get that until you clean your plate. Oh, and these are a little tricky even if you've had them your whole life." He picked up the pint of milk and squeezed it open. "You can use the foil top of the Jell-O as a spoon. Just give the end a little twist."

Kali continued to stare at him, ignoring the food in front of her.

"We're not you guys. We don't torture for information, and we don't have a sarcophagus to plug you into if we go a little too far. As long as you're here, you're going to be treated humanely."

"Outside of the threats you've leveled at me."

"We're responding to a threat, and you betcha we're not going to just turn the other cheek. But we're going to give you the chance to do the right thing, to concede defeat and give us what we want, right up until the moment that damned bomb of yours goes off. If that happens, we're going to revisit this. But until that time, enjoy your dinner." He picked up a chip and popped it into his mouth, chewing as he walked out of the room.

By the time he got to the observation room, Kali had picked up the milk carton to sniff the contents before she took a tentative sip.

Maybe not a great stride forward, but it at least was a start.

Vala usually enjoyed quick and dirty thefts, the kind of jobs that required only a little planning and netted medium rewards. They put money in their coffers and made sure they had the funds when they went after the big fish. The last big job she'd tried was an attempt to steal a ship from the Tau'ri. They were a big, loud, obnoxious people and she felt they could use a bit of a knock-down to remember their proper place in the galaxy. Besides, what did they need with a big giant ship like that? They were Stargate people, and they could travel between planets by pressing a few buttons and jumping through a shiny wall. Using ships was just lazy, in her opinion, and she could make a tidy profit selling it along to the next person in the line. The Lucian Alliance was always in need of a good ship with lots of cargo space.

Of course that had gone utterly to hell, so she was eager to prove herself with another truly big job. She was tired of pulling jobs to fund the next job. She wanted one big score to fund a little relaxation. A house, if not a home, and some scenery she could take the time to get sick of looking at. And using Kali's treasure to fund that would be just poetic enough to sweeten the deal.

Tanis knew of a planet where they could hunker down and plan their assault on Wyrrick's home, a rat hole known to the locals as Hinterland. The people who called the planet home were exiles and refugees from a more prosperous planet in the same system, thieves and brigands who were no longer welcome on their home soil. For an enterprising pair of thieves like Vala and Tanis, it was the closest thing they had to being amongst family. They only had a handful of days before Wyrrick threw his party, but Vala wanted to make sure they had all their crystals appropriately positioned before they made a play since it seemed unlikely they would get a second chance.

When they arrived, Vala arranged for the temporary rental of a cottage on a large acreage, which cost her at least four times what it would have a few months earlier. The towns of Hinterland were filled to the brim, not a loft or a bolthole to be found. It was bursting at the seams with people trying to get out, to escape, to find some safe harbor after the sudden shift of power in the galaxy.

"Places like this used to be quiet," Tanis said. "You remember?" There was no answer, so she took another drink and answered herself. "I remember." She was standing on the widow's walk looking out toward the bell-shaped harbor. On the other side of the water she could see the lights of the village burning bright enough to cast a flickering shimmer on the waves. Too many people, not enough room. That was the problem with the galaxy, as near as she could figure. She lifted her bottle and used the moonlight to check the level of liquid that remained, then carried it inside.

"I have about a near-tipsy level left if you want."

Vala said, "Nope, no thanks. I do my best work sober."

"Are you telling me I've never seen you sober?"

Vala faked a laugh and looked down at her work again. She had transferred the information from the crystal onto a projector and then traced the lines onto the floor of the parlor. She'd magnified it enough that she could stand inside each room as she examined the weaknesses. Tanis moved along the perimeter of the blueprint with the bottle dangling from her fingers.

"You remember those days?" Tanis asked.

"What days?"

"When places like this were quiet."

Vala said, "Quiet. There's a concept…"

"The past few years it's been getting crazier and crazier. I blame the Tau'ri. Killing Goa'uld left and right, inciting the Jaffa to rebel…"

"The Tok'ra have been doing the same thing for centuries. And would you prefer to have the System Lords still in charge?"

Tanis said, "At least they kept things in line. You can't say things are better now than they were before."

"Of course I can. Yeah, the Jaffa aren't being used as incubators and slave labor, people aren't forced to worship false gods, and those selfsame false gods can't run around taking innocent victims as hosts. So yes, Tanis, despite the fact that your little hideaway is a bit overcrowded, I would say things are very much better now."

She had surprised herself with the intensity of her retort, and she turned away to brush the back of her hand across her cheek. The silence became a third person in the room until Tanis finally risked shattering it.

"I'm sorry."

"We never claimed we had to agree on everything when we started working together. At least we can agree on the important things, like our jobs." She tapped the blueprint with her toe. "Let's focus on making Dys Wyrrick just a little poorer, shall we?"

Tanis didn't take the bait. "This treasure seems to be very sought-after for the spoils of a lower-tier System Lord. Seriously, who cares about Kali's treasure? Now all of a sudden we're racing against the clock and running all over the known galaxy trying to get our hands on it first. I haven't forgotten your behavior on Baleya's planet. You passed up on a sure thing to keep chasing this boondoggle, and you risked our lives to get this information. I said I wanted answers, and I think I've been more than patient."

Vala rolled her shoulders and tilted her head back to look at the ceiling. "Kali and Qetesh had a… history. It never escalated to the point where we would consider each other a nemesis, but whenever the opportunity arose we would strike at one another. It was almost like a game. She would attack one of Qetesh's strongholds, Qetesh would retaliate by hijacking one of Kali's supply ships. When Qetesh was overthrown, Kali had just ransacked one of my temples. She left the place barren. She even took the tapestries from the walls. After years of back and forth, she won by default. So yes. I want this treasure so I can do something good with it, but also because doing this means that Kali doesn't win."

Tanis said, "So it's a vengeance thing, on top of the redemption."

"Basically, yes." She looked at Tanis. "Still in?"

"Sounds like a valid reason to me." Tanis walked around to

the far side of the drawing and put her hands on her hips. "It'll be a tough nut to crack."

"It's a vault," Vala said. "Nothing was ever put into a vault without the intention of taking it out again. There is always a way to remove what you want no matter how strong the defenses. And remember, you cannot spell 'vault' without Vala."

"I think you're missing a letter or two."

Vala grinned, her emotional outburst from earlier already forgotten. "My dear Tanis, when Vala Mal Doran is around, something always goes missing eventually." She clapped her hands together and gazed at the puzzle before her. "Let's get to work."

CHAPTER ELEVEN

A PATCHWORK leather soccer ball bounced toward the active Stargate, and Daniel moved quickly to bump it into a safer trajectory with the side of his boot. The ball narrowly avoided hitting the event horizon and instead went skimming along the dirt as a gaggle of children went scurrying after it, a few of them tossing gratitude over their shoulders as they continued their game. Daniel watched them go, then turned to see Sam smiling at him.

"What?"

"Daniel Jackson, soccer star, for the save."

Daniel said, "I think you mean football star."

Sam rolled her eyes and chuckled as she continued to the FRED. "At least it's a friendlier reception than the last time we were here."

The medical supplies were loaded on the vehicle, and she began unloading the bags. She had seen that Nicia was approaching with a small retinue that had been drawn by the activation of the Stargate, and she began preparing their offering for inspection. Nicia smiled and bowed her head when she reached them, pausing to scan what they had brought.

"Colonel Carter. Welcome once again."

"Thank you."

Nicia scanned the bags on the ground and let her gaze wander over everything left on the FRED. "I must admit, I did not expect quite this large a bounty. We are truly grateful for your assistance."

Daniel said, "We have some rudimentary medical supplies, gauze and antiseptic, but we also included some extra artificial tretonin. It might not be as powerful as the real stuff, but it'll do the job."

Teal'c turned away from watching the children. "It is indeed a remarkable substitute."

"It is something that we will certainly consider. If you will come with me to my home we may discuss my portion of the arrangement. I trust you will be pleased with what I have accomplished in the short time since we last saw each other."

The group had started to move off, but Sam noticed Teal'c was again watching the children. She walked over and stood beside him for a moment and watched the group of boys and girls play the game. It seemed like a universal analog to soccer — or football, if you preferred — in which the children chose arbitrary lines and then tried to get the ball across the other team's line. Finally Teal'c acknowledged her presence with a slight turn of his head and she smiled at him.

"Never thought you'd see the day, did you?"

"Indeed I did not. Those young women bear the tattoo of Camulus. They play on the same team as boys bearing the mark of Olokun. Mere months ago these children were being taught to fear one another, trained to kill each other. And now they conspire to win a frivolous game. I have spent too long in tents and sitting around council tables discussing the far-reaching consequences of our burgeoning nation. I had forgotten about the simple consequences of what we have accomplished. Thank you, Colonel Carter, for drawing me away and opening my eyes."

Sam touched his arm. "If something good can come from such an evil plot, then maybe there's hope. Come on. They're getting ahead of us."

She and Teal'c caught up with Nicia and her people just as they arrived at a small hut. The windows were open to the elements, covered only by thin curtains. Nicia led the way inside and motioned for the curtains to be pushed back in order to let light into the room. A table had been set up in the center of the space, and Nicia rounded to the other side to take a seat. Sam sat across from her with Daniel and Teal'c sitting to her left and right.

Nicia said, "There is a man by the name of Anton Bellee. He is an opportunistic little fool who hires himself out to others as a furnisher of throne rooms."

"The Goa'uld have interior decorators?" Daniel said.

Sam said, "You thought it was a coincidence that they all had similar gaudy taste?"

Daniel shrugged.

Nicia said, "Bellee no longer requires his invitation to Dysmas Wyrrick's party and would be willing to part with it."

"For the right price?" Daniel assumed.

"The price has been paid, Dr. Jackson." She slid a piece of paper across the table. "This is the address of Bellee's planet. Go there and he will give you the invitation and the address of Wyrrick's party. I've also asked discreetly about the items you seek from Kali's palace. I have been assured that Wyrrick is a hoarder of treasures. He will occasionally sell an item once he becomes bored with it, but he would not have done so with Kali's treasure. Not so quickly at least. I have no doubt that the item you seek will indeed be there."

Daniel sighed and looked at Sam. "Well. Two more stops and a party. We're halfway home."

Sam tried to look optimistic. She didn't want to admit she would be more comfortable raiding a ha'tak with her P90 blazing, but at least there she knew where she stood. And at least in those cases she would likely be able to wear combat boots instead of high heels. Attending a party to save an entire race of people and protect the balance of harmony in the universe? She supposed there were worse things, but at the moment she couldn't think of many.

Still, she had hope. If Nicia was confident Wyrrick still had Kali's treasure then the key to deactivating her devices would be found at his home. All they had to do was get there before anything unforeseen happened and before the devices reached zero and began spreading their poison through the galaxy.

Piece of cake.

Frances Morello once spent a high school summer working on cars in her uncle's garage. It was an easy way to get money, and it taught her enough that she would never have to be the helpless woman stranded on the side of the road. She never thought her skills would translate to being flat on her back in an ancient temple with her hands inside the guts of a dooms-day device programmed by a diabolical parasite as revenge for losing a millennia-long war. Then again, it was surprises that made life interesting.

They had traveled back to Kali's planet, much to General O'Neill's chagrin, but Jay Felger wanted to take a look at the Stargate to see if he could figure out how the domino process was rigged. A year earlier, he and Colonel Carter had created a virus that inadvertently spread to the entire gate system. That was a fluke caused by a correlative update, and he suspected that Kali was utilizing the same system to deliver her virus. If he could find a way to disable it, the network would crash. He just needed to find a way to target only the Stargates on Kali-ruled planets rather than the entire galaxy as he had last time.

Morello had convinced O'Neill to let her return to the planet with Felger's team so she could take apart the disabled device. It was built to resemble an altar, and she wanted to see just how it would have delivered its toxins. They had teams scouting for other planets on which Kali had left palaces, but there was no way they could search every palace. One was bound to slip through the cracks, and the result would be catastrophic. She dropped her hands to her side and stared up into the inner workings of the device. The Goa'uld may have been parasites who stole almost everything they had from other races, but there was a certain beauty to their work. The ancient and mys-terious outer shell hid crystalline interiors and beautifully complex mechanical arrays.

She could hear Dr. Felger and his assistant in the main Stargate chamber, arguing about whether disconnecting any particular Stargate from the greater network would be enough to break the connection between the others in Kali's web. She pushed herself out from underneath the altar and examined it once more, knowing she had done everything she could at this particular site. She had disabled one altar, the same as taking a single bullet out of a gun before playing a game of extreme Russian roulette. It killed her not knowing how much time they had left, how long SG-1 had before all their machinations became moot. The lives of every Jaffa in the galaxy hung in the balance.

They were doing everything in their power, but she couldn't help but think there had to be another way they weren't seeing. This was Stargate Command. This was a place where blowing up a sun was a particularly amusing anecdote in the newsletter. It was a place where, at that very moment, an alien powerful enough to convince entire civilizations that she was their god was sitting in a prison cell. Ordinary solutions wouldn't work for extraordinary problems. They could dig around for the looted treasure and hope they were able to figure out how it worked in time. Or they could take a more proactive approach.

She left the altar behind and entered the main Stargate chamber. Felger looked up as she approached the DHD. He'd removed the panel to reveal the control crystals, but she was able to use their interface to dial without reconstructing it.

"Whoa, uh, hey. What'cha doing there, Captain?"

"There's something I need to discuss with General O'Neill."

Felger said, "Well, we're scheduled to dial-in and give a progress report in twenty-five minutes. So if you wait until then we can just slap the DHD back together — "

"This can't wait that long." She finished the sequence and the Stargate came to life. She entered her IDC as she stepped around the dialing plinth and walked without hesitation through the event horizon. It seemed to grip her skin as she entered it, each atom pulled momentarily outward in a slightly different direction as if she was dissolving in a pool of water. Some people claimed to be fully aware of passage through the wormhole; they described a twisting and turning tunnel of blue light shot through with stars. Morello had always seen it as a dreamless sleep on a train. She was aware of movement and a passage of time but she lacked any true consciousness.

From a dark and humid tomb, she placed her foot on the ramp in the familiar confines of the base. Dust from the palace fell from her uniform as she continued forward, unfastening her vest. General O'Neill came into the gate room and raised his eyebrows expectantly.

"Captain Morello. I hope this unexpected personal report means you come bearing good news rather than the alternative."

"I think that depends on your perspective, sir. If we could speak privately?"

He looked intrigued and motioned for her to follow him. They climbed through the control room, and she composed her argument in her head. As they passed the briefing room table, she tried to think of precedents for what she was going to propose, but none came to mind. The general ushered her into his office and shut the door.

"Well, Morello, you have my attention."

"Sir, we're running down the clock here. Any second now we could start receiving reports that the Jaffa are dropping like flies."

"I'm aware of that, Captain."

"We need to take desperate measures to ensure success. Even if SG-1 comes through the gate right now with the item we need, there's no way to be certain we'll know how to operate it. We need Kali's cooperation, sir."

"And how do you propose we get it?"

"Me, sir." She was glad her hands were behind her back so she could grip them tightly together. It helped control the trembling enough that she was motionless as she met the general's gaze. "We allow Kali to take me as host. We convince her that she's pulling one over on us, that it's her chance to escape. But we'll be prepared. We can find a way to ensure I'll remain in control, and I'll access her memories. We use them to stop this plague, and then we find a Tok'ra to extract the Goa'uld from me."

O'Neill stared at her for a long moment, then finally spoke in a slow, measured cadence. "Are you out of your damned *mind*?" The last word was the only one with any emotion, and he all but shouted it. Morello rocked back a step, and lowered her head. "You think you can control a Goa'uld just because becoming a host was your idea? You think you can convince it to share information with us just because you ask it nicely? The Goa'uld do not work that way, Captain. This is without a doubt the most reckless, insane scheme anyone on this base has ever come up with."

He stepped forward, standing directly in front of her, and lowered his voice when he spoke again.

"Seems like you fit right in."

She looked at him, surprised the tirade had ended so abruptly. "Thank you, sir."

"What you're talking about is the nuclear option. It's sending someone into a blast zone to defuse a bomb."

"To be fair, sir, that has happened before. One of Dr. Jackson's deaths."

"Yes, well, that was different. Daniel didn't ask permission." He paused and aimed a finger at her. "Don't take that as tacit approval. I know I would have jumped on that if I were in your shoes, so let's nip that in the bud. If someone on this base became host to a Goa'uld, willingly or otherwise, there is no way we could put any stock in the information they gave us afterward. The Goa'uld lie. Hell, the Tok'ra lie. The only thing that would change would be half the people on this base would see a Goa'uld wearing the face of someone they know. We don't need that emotional element added."

Morello nodded. "I understand, sir. I guess I just got swept up in the idea."

"I understand. I hear that clock ticking as loud as anybody. Where are you on the altar?"

"With all due respect, sir, I'm just poking at the thing now. I'd be much more use here."

"Sure you're not just trying to get away from Felger?"

"No comment, sir."

He smiled. "Judicious. In that case, you're dismissed, Captain." She started to leave. "Captain Morello."

"Sir?"

"There are people in the government who don't trust Teal'c. Don't even like him." He gestured out the window with his pen. "And half the people here have exchanged fire with Jaffa forces. They're keeping quiet right now, but I know a lot of them are wondering why I'm wasting our flagship team's time trying to save them. You just ran in here offering to host a Goa'uld to save them."

Morello nodded slowly. "They're our allies, sir."

"Yes. Still. That attitude isn't as universal as I might like. I'll remember it, Captain."

"Thank you, sir."

He waved her away. "All right. Go do whatever people like you and Daniel do when you're not on duty."

She smiled. "Pretty much the same as we do on-duty, sir, just with fewer guns."

"Have at it."

"Thank you, sir."

She left the office and looked at her watch. There was no way to know how long they had before the devices activated. It was Schrodinger's plague. But until they got word that the deadline was past, she was going to do everything in her power to find an answer. She straightened her jacket and went to the elevator. She didn't have a lab like Dr. Jackson or Colonel Carter, but she had a whiteboard and a brain. She was sure with those tools she could figure something out.

CHAPTER TWELVE

"WOW. This is unexpected."

Sam looked at Daniel as he scanned the mansion. "What? You're surprised? The guy decorates Goa'uld palaces for a living. Some of that grandiosity had to rub off a little."

"No, you're right about that. It's typical Goa'uld excess, ostentatious nonsense. But beyond that it's a… a house. No palace walls, no idols, nothing to make visitors cower in fear at the owner's presence. It's very un-Goa'uld."

Teal'c nodded. "Indeed, it is quite modest."

Sam had to admit they had a point. The house was extravagant by most standards, a sprawling estate built on a rocky cliff overlooking the ocean, but for the home of someone who had turned every Goa'uld throne room she'd seen into a Vegas nightmare, it was quite understated. The green lawn was wide and rolling as a golf course, and portions of the roof looked large enough to land a cargo ship on, but for the most part it was quite demure. It was far enough from the Stargate that she presumed Bellee was also a man who appreciated his privacy.

At the moment Anton Bellee's home was made to appear even less impressive by the flock of security vessels hovering like carrion birds around the property. Sam eyed one of them as she passed, aware that she was being scanned. They had elected not to wear the normal uniform of the SGC for fear of sending the wrong message. Instead they wore clothing borrowed from Teal'c's allies among the Jaffa. Sam wore a sleeveless leather tunic with a wide belt across her midsection, grateful that it wasn't quite as revealing as some outfits she had seen. Daniel was stuck with a shortened black cape that he kept shrugging and tugging at when it would brush the backs of his arms.

Only Teal'c looked comfortable, and Sam was happy seeing him once again immersed in his culture. He'd fought tooth and nail for the right to rejoin his people, to be seen as more than a shol'va, and seeing him in Jaffa robes was a visual reminder of his victory.

The little security drone declared Sam unthreatening and moved on. She noticed that Teal'c and Daniel received a longer examination and wondered if she should be offended that she was cleared so quickly. She fought the inner O'Neill that urged her to make a nuisance of herself just to prove she could cause some damage and focused on the machines themselves.

"What do these things remind me of?" Sam asked.

Daniel watched one of them skim along an air current over the water. "*Batteries not Included*. That eighties movie with the little flying robots."

Sam grinned. "Right. God, I loved that movie."

"Was that before or after you started watching sci-fi just to tear apart the plot holes?"

"There are no plot holes in a movie about cute little robots."

As they approached the front door a man wearing a security uniform stepped out of the house and held up a hand to stop them.

"I apologize for the inconvenience, but Master Bellee is not receiving guests at this time."

Teal'c stepped forward with Sam and Daniel flanking him. "I believe it would be in his best interest to grant us audience."

The security officer started to reply, but he was cut off by a shout from within the house.

"I am supposed to have dark-to-dark security! I am supposed to be personally guarded every moment of sunlight, so where in…" Anton Bellee himself, a short and grumpy-looking man in a silver jacket, appeared in the doorway. "There you are! What are you doing out here when — " Bellee cut himself off when he saw their guests. He stared for a moment, then laughed. "Because of course! Of course the day I'm rebooting my security system and I'm at my most vulnerable, two Tau'ri and a Jaffa are going to show up. Let me guess, you're Samantha Carter and you're Jonas Quinn."

Daniel coughed and furrowed his brow, but didn't bother correcting him.

"And if they're SG-1, you must be the infamous Teal'c. The shol'va."

"I wear that term with pride, Anton Bellee."

"I'm sure you do. Look, whatever you're here for, I can't help you. The Stargate is that way, so kindly shove off…"

Sam said, "Actually we were sent here by Nicia. She said you had an invitation you needed taken off your hands."

Bellee laughed. "The invitation to Wyrrick's party? She was asking for *you*? Oh, that is rich. The three of you want to attend Dysmas Wyrrick's party?" He put his hands up against his lips and chortled quietly. "Oh. The temptation of sending the infamous SG-1 into that den of snakes is almost too good to pass up. But you're lucky I'm not personally vindictive toward you. The invitation is useless to you, okay? Tau'ri aren't getting through the door and a Jaffa certainly isn't going to get very far. Tell Nicia I'm sorry to back out on our arrangement, but I'm not going to give you something you can't even use. I do have a few morals. So if you don't mind, I have to supervise the repairs to my abode."

Sam stepped forward. "Mr. Bellee…"

"That's Master Bellee to you."

"No."

He sighed. "Fine."

"Mr. Bellee, you're in a precarious position here. You've made a living, a very fine living from the looks of it, decorating the palaces of various System Lords. It's because of you that their palaces look as… magnificent as they do."

Daniel made a pained face. Sam glanced at him but didn't comment.

"That's all changed. The System Lords are running scared,

and I think it will be a very long time before you get another commission. They aren't going to be doing a lot of redecorating in the next few months. Or years. Or… well… ever. You just lost your entire customer base and they took their checkbooks with them. You know who will be redecorating in the coming months?" She turned and looked at Teal'c.

Bellee stuck out his chin as he considered her argument. "Huh. You may have a point."

"Teal'c's word carries a lot of weight with the Jaffa," Daniel said. "The Jaffa might be reluctant to work with someone who is so closely associated with Goa'uld excess, but if he vouches for you…"

Teal'c said, "Assisting us in this matter would make great strides in proving you are more than just a hireling for the Goa'uld. It would prove that you can also be a friend to the Jaffa nation."

Bellee pursed his lips, looked at his security officer, then finally threw his hands in the air. "Fine, you know what? Whatever. Everything's topsy-turvy right now anyway so why not help the Tau'ri and the Jaffa? Fine. Come in. But I'm not just going to hand you the invite and let you waltz in looking like that. You may not realize this, but your little troupe is quite distinctive. People will recognize you."

"Apparently not that distinctive," Daniel muttered.

"Quiet, Jonas," Sam said.

Bellee pushed the guard out of his way. "Come inside. I'll find something for you to wear that will help disguise you when you're at the party. If anyone can do it, I can. You're just fortunate this is a masquerade or you'd be out of luck."

Daniel said, "Oh, so getting dressed by a grumpy fashionista counts as lucky?"

"Look at the bright side," Sam said. "We're one step closer to reaching Kali's treasure and ending the threat once and for all."

Daniel sighed. "One step closer… let's hope it's the last hoop we have to jump through."

"Indeed," Teal'c said as they reluctantly followed Bellee into the house.

The next morning Tanis woke to find Vala was still in the front room. She was cross-legged on the floor, elbows on her knees with her fists balled under her chin as she stared at the drawing. Before Tanis had retired for the night they had marked out everywhere that would be a hot spot during the party. The central room of the house was large enough to house a good number of people, and it boasted a large glass wall that would provide a great view for the gathering. A corridor wrapped around the main room with entrances to smaller interior rooms. Vala assumed these secondary locations would be utilized as display rooms. Access would be easy, but getting enough privacy to actually steal anything would be a hassle. She had marked doorways at either end of the hall that could be used for a quick escape to the hangars, and a staircase in the main room could take her to the second floor and provide access to the private landing pad on the roof.

Tanis scratched her head and pushed her hair out of her face, standing with her other hand on her hip as she examined the miniature home spread out in front of her bare feet. "You're still looking at this thing? What else is there to figure out?"

"The biggest problem, the most obvious hurdle. The thing we never once stopped to consider in all of our planning." Vala unfolded her legs and grunted as she stood up. She shook her right foot out to the side to get rid of the pins-and-needles as she walked the line of the eastern wall. "We've determined that these spaces — heavily fortified and sparsely furnished — will be the display rooms during the party. The security will be lessened to accommodate the amount of people moving through the space. It would destroy the ambiance if he had bells and whistles going off every five minutes."

"Exactly. All we have to do is walk in and grab it."

"Yes. How?"

"How… what? How will we make our escape?" Tanis walked to stand next to the exit at the end of the corridor. "We'll go out through this side door to the hangar. We covered that last night."

"Indeed we did. But what I mean, my dear Tanis, is how exactly are we going to move the treasure in the first place? I don't know about you, but I've been working on the assumption he would have it safely locked away in a vault, not sitting out in full display surrounded by people. Either we'll have to carry a huge amount of valuable items past a large group of partygoers or we'll have to make multiple trips as the collection slowly shrinks. Getting it out the door isn't even the biggest problem when you consider that we'll be stealing these items from displays while groups of people are mingling and looking at everything. We're going to be robbing this place in the clear view of over three dozen guests. Care to explain how to accomplish that?"

Tanis stared at the map for a long moment. Her expression changed from sleepiness to full alertness, then to alarm as she realized the extent of the problem. "Damn it."

"Damn it indeed," Vala said, planting her fists against her hips. "I figure we can arrange for some sort of distraction, and there's bound to be entertainment to draw people's attention away from the displays. We simply have to find ways to use those moments to our advantage. By my estimation we can manufacture five trips in and out of the building."

"A lot of risk involved. He's bound to have security, and if any of them notice when stuff starts to go missing, we could get nabbed."

Tanis was speaking in a clipped manner in an effort to control her anger. Vala couldn't blame her for being annoyed. After everything they'd gone through to get this treasure, only to have this final hurdle thrown up at the last second just because neither of them managed to think of it before… Vala had been kicking herself for the same reason all night, but the recriminations hadn't given her insight into how to fix their problem.

Five trips, carrying only what they could conceal on their persons, avoiding security the whole time. It left out the larger, more valuable items that might fetch more in the black market. They might be able to make up for it with enough smaller items, but it always came back to whether they would be able to move very much at all.

"We may have to call this one."

Vala blinked. "What?"

"The chance of being caught in the act is much too high. We're going to rob this house in the broad daylight, with a potential hundred witnesses, and according to Bellee, Wyrrick is the kind of person who holds a grudge. All of that adds up to too much hot water. You say I have a knack for escaping when I'm imprisoned, but the real trick is to not get imprisoned in the first place. I do that by knowing when to call it on account of impossibility."

"It's not impossible."

"Fine, but is it worth the effort? You're the one with something to prove here. This treasure is your way of getting back at Qetesh, I understand that. You want to symbolically fund yourself with the treasures you lost. But is that worth everything we've been going through these past few days? I'm still trying to get over the hangover I picked up on Baleya's planet. It can't be worth the risk of being thrown in some rich man's dungeon if we get caught."

Vala was looking down at the map. "It's not just a symbolic gesture. I don't want Kali's treasure just to own it. Qetesh did horrible things to get her riches, and she used my body to get it." She flipped her hair out of her face. Her cheeks and ears were burning, but she wasn't going to cry in front of Tanis. She took a deep breath and closed her eyes, waiting until her breathing was steady before she continued. "I don't doubt Kali acquired her treasures in the same manner. Gold acquired through bloodshed and torture. I want the treasure so I can do something good with it."

Tanis stared blankly at her through a curtain of fallen hair and Vala waited as if for a firing squad, knowing she would be mocked for her statement, but she didn't care. It was the truth. Finally Tanis broke her silence.

"No one's ever accused me of doing anything good." She looked down at the map. "We'll need a better extraction plan."

Vala stared at her as hope blossomed in her chest. "Yes, it… it makes sense. It doesn't matter how much we get in the ship if we can't escape afterward."

"It won't be easy."

Vala slowly felt her normal self-confidence returning. "Now, Tanis. Let's not get discouraged. This isn't an insurmountable problem."

"I'm open to suggestions. Because right now it's looking pretty insurmountable."

"Ye of little faith. I've had to overcome much bigger problems than this. I'm sure you have as well. We just have to apply ourselves."

Tanis sighed. "Well, we'd better hurry. The party is in four days and if we don't make our move then we won't get another shot. You better hope another female System Lord's loot ends up on the black market if you want to get your good deed." She began to walk around the perimeter of the building. "Insertion and extraction are two big problems, but we can't focus on that right now. If we come up with a plan to move the items that doesn't line up perfectly with our preset requirements we'll be back at square one."

"Okay. So we figure out what we're doing inside and how, and that will inform the rest of the plan. It's what happens inside that matters."

"Right. And what's happening inside is that we need to find a way to move Kali's goods without being seen by any guards or the guests."

Vala pursed her lips and exhaled. "We need to be invisible."

Tanis straightened. "Yeah. That would work perfectly."

"Sorry to get your hopes up. I sold my remaining inventory of Re'tu gland months ago."

"That's okay. I didn't mean we had to be genuinely invisible. We just need people to ignore our presence and look through us even when we're standing right in front of them. Like anyone wearing identical uniforms, moving through the crowd with covered trays or pushing carts covered with large sheets…?"

Vala's eyes widened. "Caterers. Tanis, you genius!" She dropped to one knee and stretched out over the map. "The kitchen shares an access hall here, which connects it to the corridor with the display rooms. We could bypass the main room entirely. And even if someone happened to see us moving back and forth, they wouldn't think twice about it. We could carry out everything we want right under Wyrrick's nose!"

"Maybe not everything," Tanis said. "We'd be limited to whatever we could carry on the carts and trays, so the bigger things will have to stay behind. But this way we could take more than five trips. We could take as many trips as we needed. We just have to get in with the caterers."

Vala tapped a finger on her chin. "Easier said than done, I'm afraid. Wyrrick is sure to take precautions with this sort of thing. He'll have planned ahead and anticipated security breaches. On the day of the party, of all days, he won't relax his guard."

"I didn't say it would be easy. If I wanted easy, I would just put on my Kull warrior armor and walk in guns blazing. Oh, wait. I can't do that…"

Vala rolled her eyes back and slumped her shoulders. "My *God* will you ever let that go?"

"One of the most valuable tools in our arsenal and you just walk off and leave it. Which may have been acceptable if you'd actually succeeded in the job, but no. You lost the ship, too."

"I would like to see you steal an entire ship by yourself."

"Remind me again how many crew members were on the ship when your plan got foiled?"

"If you had been there, maybe things would have turned out differently! Two against one, ever think of that? You wouldn't have even let me keep Jackson on board in the first place. So the entire mess is really your fault for not being there!"

Tanis started to respond, then stopped. "Was… that a compliment?"

Vala straightened her shirt and looked away. "Possibly. You are extremely adept at getting out of tight situations. If you'd been there perhaps the two of us could have overpowered Daniel Jackson, and I'd have not lost the suit, gained the ship, and we wouldn't have to look over our shoulders for Jup and Tenat seeking revenge." She pressed her lips together. "I suppose what I'm saying is that I'm sorry, and I'm willing to admit you have a way with plans. It's one reason I'm always willing to work with you even though I don't trust you. You're good at this, Tanis. Almost as good as I am." She swung her arms in an attempt at casualness. "And that's… all I'm going to say about that."

Tanis blinked. "Okay. I don't trust you, either. For the record."

"Oh, you'd be a fool to." Vala began to circle the blueprint drawn on the floor. Tanis moved in the opposite direction. "There's a solution here, and you've found it. Food service. We get in, we move invisible through the crowd, we get what we came for, and we get out. Most of the hard work is done. The last difficult bit is actually inserting ourselves into the catering crew. How exactly do we go about that if Wyrrick is certain to cover every base?"

Tanis paused next to the kitchen. She tilted her head one way, then the other. Finally she looked up at Vala through her hair again. This time, she smiled.

"Hope you know how to cook, Mal Doran."

Vala grinned.

CHAPTER THIRTEEN

THE MORE she thought about it, the more horrified she became at the idea General O'Neill might have agreed to her suggestion in a moment of desperation. Morello knew that if he'd agreed to it she would currently be frantically searching for a way to back out of the deal. She very much wanted to be the one who came up with a solution, not for the glory but in order to prove herself as a valuable member of the SGC. The mission reports were full of team members doing crazy things in the interest of saving the world. General O'Neill himself had risked court-martial and treason charges on more than one occasion. Daniel Jackson had risked death several times, succumbing more than once. And Samantha Carter... well, the mental acrobatics she'd pulled off in the nth hour would be enough to destroy a normal human's brain.

Morello had set up a workshop in the mess hall, bent over history books and encyclopedias of mythology. She was so wrapped up in her reading that she didn't notice Colonel Getty's arrival until he pushed one of her notebooks aside to make room for his tray. She reached to save it from falling onto the floor and smiled sheepishly as she looked up at him.

"Sorry, sir."

"No need to be sorry. May I?"

She nodded. "Of course. I'm just trying to find some way to convince Kali to help us."

Getty sat down and opened his drink. "SG-1 is on the case, Captain."

"I'm aware of that, sir. I'm also aware that if someone from another planet was looking for the nuclear football, even if they found it that wouldn't mean they could actually launch the missiles. SG-1 is looking for a magic button that can save the day, but even if they find it, it will still be alien technology. There's no guarantee we'll even be able to use it to shut off the devices."

"Samantha Carter is a certifiable genius. She'll figure it out."

"Be that as it may, sir, I'm going to do everything in my power to save them the trouble. We have Kali, we might as well try to use her."

Getty smiled. "Have you always been like this, Morello?"

"Yes, sir," she said, turning back to her book. "Ever since I was a kid. I knew there was a gold standard out there somewhere, some lofty goal that indicated the best and the brightest. I had no idea what it was, but as long as people kept pushing me higher…" She shrugged. "From high school to the Air Force Academy. That's where I first heard about some top-secret elite posting. I knew I had to do whatever I could to get here. So I figured out what I might need to study in order to make the grade, buckled down, went to grad school, and here I am."

"And now?"

"Now I'm angling for the general's chair." She smiled. "In a few years, anyway. But for right now I'm content with just pulling my weight. Justifying my presence to anyone who might question it."

Getty said, "No one is questioning your presence here, Captain."

"I know, sir. And I aim to keep it that way." She tapped her pen against the drawing of Kali. "The people who made this place always go above and beyond what's necessary to do the right thing. Did you know General O'Neill once basically kidnapped an alien girl and took her to an elementary school? Just so she could learn how to be a kid."

"No, I didn't know that."

"Samantha Carter once went into a bomb shelter to comfort a different little girl that everyone else thought was implanted with a bomb that was about to detonate."

Getty nodded. "That I heard about."

Morello said, "And Janet Fraiser once…" Her voice trailed

off, and she looked down at the encyclopedia again.

Getty waited for her to continue. "Captain? What did Dr. Fraiser do?"

"Excuse me, sir."

She stood up and hurried out of the cafeteria. The anecdote she had thought of was more rumor than actual fact, and it hadn't been mentioned in the official report, but even if it wasn't true, her reasoning could still work. She took the elevator down without thinking about what she was doing, walked down the corridor as if she owned it, and didn't realize how presumptuous she was being until she had entered General O'Neill's office without knocking.

She stopped dead just over the threshold, frozen in space as O'Neill and Harriman both looked up at her. She opened her mouth to apologize, tried to force herself back into the hallway where she could hope they would forget what had just happened, but her feet were frozen in place. She reached for the door as if knocking now would help at all, then dropped her hand to her side.

"Uh-oh."

O'Neill raised an eyebrow. "Captain. Was there something you needed?"

"Um. A question. I had… a… question to ask you."

He handed the file he'd been looking over to Walter and dismissed him with a nod. Walter left, pausing before the door closed to give Morello a look of compassionate understanding. Once they were alone, the general gestured at the spot in front of his desk.

"You have the floor, Captain Morello."

"Right. Sorry. Um." She cleared her throat. "There's a rumor about Dr. Fraiser, and I wanted confirmation it was true."

"And this is relevant to our current situation?"

"It could be, sir. Three years ago, Cassandra Fraiser was suffering from an illness. Nirrti was a prisoner of the SGC at the time, but she refused to help. General Hammond offered diplomacy, he negotiated, and according to the reports there was a long discussion between you and General Hammond about whether or not to give in to her demands. In the end the thing that convinced her to help was Janet Fraiser walking into her cell and holding a gun on her."

O'Neill cleared his throat. "Right… but you understand that's not the sort of resolution we condone. Even if I did want to give her a medal for that little display."

Morello nodded. "Of course, sir. I wasn't thinking of a direct duplication, but the mentality of the moment is what matters. We've exhausted asking nicely, sir. We aren't going to offer her anything valuable enough to make her help us. We need to think like Janet Fraiser. She didn't look at Nirrti as a Goa'uld. She saw someone who was withholding treatment from her sick child. She responded to that without any of the other complications. Yes, Kali is a Goa'uld, but she's also a human host. We have to appeal to that side of her."

"I assume you wouldn't have barged in here without a plan in mind."

"Yes, sir. I mean, no. No, sir, I wouldn't have." She winced. "And… sorry, sir."

O'Neill leaned back in his seat. "No, no. You've got my attention. Let's hear what you have."

Jack came down the stairs as Walter glanced back to make sure he was there before speaking. "SG-1's IDC confirmed, sir."

"Bring 'em home, Walter."

The iris slid open and Jack descended into the gate room. "Welcome back, kids. You're home… just in time for the…" He slowed and tilted his head to the side as he registered that his team was dressed rather differently than normal. "Show," he finished lamely.

Sam stopped at the bottom of the ramp and sighed. She wore a black and green jacket with a stiff, high collar that made it seem as if her head had been severed and placed on a pedestal. Two vertical stripes of green makeup ran from her hairline to her jaw to correspond with the color on her jacket, passing over her eyes. Her hair was slicked back away from her face, and Jack had to admit the overall impression was much more masculine than he'd have assumed.

Sam gestured at the blazer and the matching black trousers. "Okay, sir. Get it out of your system."

"Get what out of my system? Oh! Are you out of uniform?"

Daniel had been dressed in a flowing white overcoat with a brown leather placket. "Anton Bellee informed us that a couple of Tau'ri wouldn't make it through the front door at Wyrrick's party, even if we had an invitation. Which we do, by the way. Bellee was willing to part with his invite, so at least as far as that goes, the trip was a success. He assured us that Wyrrick will still have the things we need from Kali's palace. And then he decided to take the extra step and give us something to wear."

"Ah." Jack looked at Sam. "No slinky little black dress? High heels, something simple but chic?"

"Bellee didn't have any women's clothing. We're just lucky he had something in our sizes."

Teal'c said, "He is rather diminutive."

Jack glanced at the sleeveless tunic Teal'c was wearing over a pair of floating linen trousers that draped his feet like bell bottoms. "Yes. Well, it seems to have worked out for everyone. I guess this is to be expected considering how some of the Goa'uld dress."

Sam glanced at the control room and rolled her eyes when she saw everyone watching her. "So. Sir. You said we were just in time for the show."

"Right!" He motioned for them to follow him. Daniel self-consciously rubbed at his cheek as they passed an airman who was trying valiantly not to snicker at their appearance. "Captain Morello on SG-9 has been busy while you guys were out playing dress-up. We've been trying to find a way to get Kali to help us with the device."

Sam said, "How's that been working out for you?"

"Not well. Turns out, the Goa'uld? Not the most charitable folks in the galaxy. But Captain Morello thinks she's come up with a way to convince her."

"Do we have time to change out of this stuff before we observe?" Daniel asked.

"I was just on my way when you dialed in. Morello's waiting for me before she goes in." He put his hand on Daniel's shoulder as they stepped into the elevator. "But I want you to know from the bottom of my heart, even if you did have five minutes, I'd still say we had to go right now."

Daniel sighed. "You're enjoying this way too much."

"Yes," Jack said unabashedly. "It's the first time I think I've been glad I'm not going off-world anymore."

The elevator doors closed on his self-satisfied smirk.

Morello flexed her hands at her sides, opening and closing her fists as she tried to focus her anxiety. General O'Neill approved of her plan. He thought it was a good idea, albeit a little crazy. But he'd added, "Those are always the plans with the best chance of working." She hoped he was right because, at the moment, she was feeling less than enthused. But it was her idea, and she was grateful he was letting her go forward with it. Colonel Getty was waiting with her for moral support, and her heart leapt into her throat when the elevator doors opened to herald the general's arrival.

"Sir, I..." Her words died in her throat when she saw SG-1 behind him. They looked like refugees from *Burning Man*, especially Colonel Carter's oddly flattering face paint. The general smiled at her confusion. It was one thing to try her crazy Hail Mary in front of her direct commanding officer and the man in charge of the entire base, the living legend of the base. But now all of SG-1 would be witnesses to her potentially epic failure? She couldn't even look Daniel Jackson in the eye.

Fortunately O'Neill seemed to think her reaction was due

to their flamboyant outfits. "Don't mind the dress code. Just another day in the wild and wacky SGC, Captain."

"Yes, sir. Ah. I wanted to let you know I was ready. I didn't know Dr. Jackson was back. If you would prefer for me to step aside and allow him to take over…"

He looked at Daniel. "I don't know. He doesn't really seem dressed for it."

Daniel ignored the comment. "Actually, Captain, I think you have a better chance at swaying her than I would. SG-1 might not have much personal history with Kali, but we are kind of infamous among the Goa'uld. Maybe having you at the table, rather than me, is one of the things that's making her talk."

"Right." O'Neill nodded. "Then get in there and get cracking."

Morello looked at Getty, smoothed her hands over the front of her jumpsuit, and went into the interrogation room.

Kali lifted her head slightly and focused on the doorway. She had obviously been asleep sitting up waiting for the next round to begin, but she was trying to hide the fact. Her shoulders were back, her head held high, and she moved her hands to fold them together in front of herself despite the handcuffs. She was determined to look like she was completely and utterly in charge.

Morello pulled out her seat, sat down, and looked the Goa'uld in the eye. "You lose."

A wrinkle appeared between Kali's eyebrows, but she said nothing.

"Whatever happens in this room, whatever goes down with the Jaffa and your doomsday device, it doesn't matter. The only thing that isn't up for debate, the only thing that is an unassailable fact, is that you have lost. There is no possible way you can come out of this a winner. You're on the run from people who once worshipped you as their goddess. They would spit on you if they walked into this room. You think we're holding you here because we're scared of you, but no one on this base is tense. No one cares that you're here. They all pity you."

"How dare you mock me?"

Morello shook her head. "I'm not mocking you, Kali. I'm simply putting things in perspective. When we decided to go looking for you, we found you in a matter of hours. Living in squalor, scrounging for food, and clinging to the last vestiges of the power you once held."

Kali slapped both hands down on the table. "You will know how powerful I truly am once..."

Morello leaned forward. "Once what? Your machines go off? I have a coffee maker at home that will make me a fresh pot even if I don't go home tonight. That doesn't make me a god. You programmed a machine. No one cares. And if we let you go right now and walked you to the Stargate, where would you go? What hole would you scurry down this time, and how long do you think it would be before your Jaffa found you? You lost, Kali."

Kali seethed and curled her fingers until the nails were biting into her palms.

"But Bhavatarini still has a chance to win."

Kali's expression changed just a fraction. "What did you say?"

Morello said, "It's your other name. Redeemer of the Universe. When you lived on Earth, you were seen as a destroyer, yes. But you were also revered as a mother goddess. The great protector. There are myths that speak of you as the kindest and most loving of all the gods in the Hindu faith. Mother of the Universe." Morello smiled. "The centuries of infighting and scheming among the Goa'uld may have hardened you, but I don't think they've completely destroyed the part of you that showed compassion. And I doubt the Mother of the Universe would do something as cowardly and vindictive as poisoning an entire race of people just out of spite."

Kali took a deep breath.

"You can't win. But there's still time to change the game. You can be Bhavatarini again." Morello stood up and tugged at the hem of her jacket. "Threats aren't going to change anything, and offering incentives… we don't have anything you want. We could lock you in a cage and protect you from any vindictive Jaffa who come looking for you, but I don't think that's an ending you'd accept. So all we can do is ask for you to help us and hope you choose to do the right thing." She turned to the one-way glass and nodded. "I realize this room is probably very boring to be locked up in all day, so I thought we'd offer you something to look at."

A projector on the other side of the glass showed the image of a wide green river flanked on either side by bright green fields. Kali leaned forward and her eyes widened.

"We call that area of the world Bangladesh now. It's the area you once ruled over. In fact, it might be the place your human host once called home." She was quiet for a moment to let that sink in. "We have quite a few images that we'll scroll through over the next hour or so. General O'Neill will be in to see you again at some point. No games, no tricks. We're just asking you for help. This is the end, Kali. No more battles, no more vanquished enemies and newly-claimed territory. You're done. Don't let your last act be one of anger and mass murder. That's not who you are. It's never been who you are."

She turned to the door, but Kali spoke before she could leave.

"What is your name?"

"Captain Frances Morello."

"I… thank you, Frances Morello."

Morello nodded. "You're welcome." She left the room and, once the door was closed behind her, slumped against the wall. Her mind had been filled with horror scenarios gleaned from mission reports. Hand devices and superior Goa'uld strength, pain sticks and forcing themselves on new hosts. She had just faced down a Goa'uld without blinking and the adrenaline was leaving her body in waves of violent tremors.

General O'Neill came out of the observation room with Colonel Getty in tow. She steadied her nerves and faced them both.

"Good job in there, Captain," Getty said.

"Thank you, sir." She looked at O'Neill. "Do you think it will work?"

"It's as good as anything else we were trying. Now all we can do is wait and hope she makes the right choice."

CHAPTER FOURTEEN

TANIS didn't trust many people in her life. During her three years of exile, she was forced to rely on Corso and Pender, but she was always aware they could turn on her at any time. It was that distance which allowed her to turn on them when the time came, which led to her escape from custody. She worked alone whenever she could, and she took partners as fresh fish she could leave in the water if sharks started circling too closely. Extra sets of hands often came in useful, and sometimes two heads were definitely better than one, but she didn't let herself get too comfortable relying on someone else.

Vala was different. They argued and they disagreed, and yes, Vala had cost her that damned Kull warrior armor, but the benefits of their partnership far outweighed the losses. She hadn't done a formal accounting but her rough estimate said she had gained more working with Vala than she'd ever made working on her own. Still, she preferred to work solo. She considered herself a solo act with occasional accompaniment. When Vala first started talking about Kali's treasure, Tanis went along for one simple reason: she wanted to take the whole thing for herself. It would be a tidy way to end their association, and she had little doubt Vala would do the same to her given the chance.

But as the days marched on, she started changing her mind. She started thinking about her cut rather than how she would get away with the whole thing. In fact, if pressed, she would have been willing to cut her percentage so Vala could have more. She deserved the majority. She had valid reasons for going after this particular prize and Tanis was just a helping hand. Tanis caught herself and suppressed those feelings with a quick shake of her head; she almost felt compassionate. Those were dangerous waters to tread.

They were still at the rented house, and Tanis was out on the veranda to watch the incoming ships. She had sent a few subspace messages to associates with connections in the food service industry. One of them, she knew, was bound to have information about Wyrrick's party. They had three days to get in and be vetted by Wyrrick's security or their opportunity would be lost. Tanis' hands were clammy and she had a constant buzz of excitement at the possibility of another big score on the horizon. Riches, gold, jewels… she didn't know exactly what Kali had used to decorate her palace, but she knew it would be worth all the trouble they were going to.

She saw Vala returning up the dirt path that led to their temporary headquarters and got up to go inside. Their dinner was still on the table, plates loaded with strips of meat from a local creature garnished with small red fruits. Tanis picked up one of the meat strips, sniffed it, and popped it into her mouth. It was moist but somehow extremely salty, and Tanis made a face as she took a drink from her flask. She was wiping her sleeve across her lips as Vala came in.

"Good news!"

"You brought something to take the taste of dinner out of our mouths?"

Vala swung her bag around to the front and unclipped the top. She withdrew a small pouch and tossed it underhand to Tanis. "Try it with that. I saw some people in the tavern dipping it in the sauce, seemed to be a universal recipe."

"Couldn't hurt," Tanis said. "Do you have any other good news to report?"

"Indeed I do. I know who is providing the food for Wyrrick's party."

Tanis raised an eyebrow. "Do you?"

Vala preened a bit, tossed her hair, and gave Tanis a toothy grin. "Us."

"That's a given. But who are we — "

"No, it'll be us. See, we figure Wyrrick is going to vet anyone who works his party. I intercepted a few subspace messages, discovered he was researching several renowned chefs. I used the Lucian Alliance contacts to make sure he discovered something to disqualify each of them. At the same time, I seeded the network with just enough information to send him looking for the exclusive and reclusive Ai Okano, Lord Yu's former personal food preparer. Most people think that she vanished and became a recluse, but lo and behold, she is getting back into the business of private functions, and she believes Wyrrick's party will be a wonderful place to kick-start her new life."

"So I'll be the waitress. Actually serving food, not just wearing the uniforms and faking it?" Tanis glared at her. "You swore after the last time I wouldn't be thrown into another menial position."

"This is not menial! Bite your tongue! You're providing the food for the biggest party the galaxy has ever seen!"

"You do this every time, Vala. You put me in some subservient position while you're the hero, the one the mark needs to fix everything. I'm sick of it!"

"I do not do that! How dare you?"

Tanis said, "I was the maid at the palace, I was the cargo chief at the depot, I was the file clerk at the registry office... meanwhile you were the doctor, you were the navigator, you were the magistra. I can't believe I was just thinking about how great it was working with you. You are always the elite and I am always the worthless serf. What are you this time, hm?"

Vala kept her gaze steady. "Waitress."

"Waitr —" Tanis blinked.

"Yes, I figured since this job required access to trays, dollies, and carts, that it would behoove us to have someone in position to load and unload said items. I thought it seemed quite lowly, and out of deference for you taking those jobs so frequently, I assigned it to myself."

Tanis winced. "Right."

"No harm done." Vala tossed her hair out of her face and cleared her throat. "The important thing is that we have our jobs figured out. Now we have several days which we will need to use wisely. Can you actually cook?"

"I can fake it well enough for one of these things," Tanis said in a sheepish voice. "The portions will be small enough that no one is going to notice if it tastes like *g'may*."

"*G'may*?" Vala said. "I like *g'may*. It's tangy. Little pungent."

Tanis made a gagging noise at the back of her throat.

"With a little sauce? Perfect."

Tanis rolled her eyes.

"Anyway, I brought some food so you can experiment with some signature dishes." She squinted and looked around the house. "Do you have any idea what a kitchen might look like?"

Sam didn't like going home when there was something big happening at the base. From the moment she took the elevator up to the surface, she felt the urge to run back downstairs just to make sure there was no update or crisis that required her attention. Then when she got home, her first stop was always the phone so she could call someone who had stayed at work and get a sitrep. She had been mocked for this more times than she could count. Daniel and General O'Neill both knew her commute time so well that often she had called only to have them answer and ask, "Eight minutes late, Sam. Did you stop to pick up a coffee?"

She eventually surrendered the self-consciousness that prevented her from keeping quarters at the base. She only used them in extreme cases, and many times knowing she had a bed a few levels away was the only reason she got any sleep at all. When she was still rising through the ranks, she accepted the whispers and rumors that she was burning the midnight oil to prove her worth to 'the boys club'. Now she was a colonel, she had established her credentials with everyone who mattered, and still she stayed at her computer long after everyone else had gone home. Now she accepted she worked so tirelessly because she simply had to know the answers or the questions would never let her get to sleep.

It was times like these when she was glad she had a little corner of the base to call her home. There was nothing for the team to do, nowhere for them to go, until it was time to scout Wyrrick's home planet. They had two days before leaving, and Sam was trying to use her pent-up anxiety to do something useful. The messages from Atlantis still needed to be catalogued, and she was using her free time to collate them for eventual delivery to the proper friends and family members.

She had used the private bathroom to change out of her disguise, scrubbing until her skin was raw and pink instead of the ugly green paint Bellee had insisted on using. The bathroom was another reason she was glad to have the quarters. She appreciated having access to a private shower where she could wash off the dust of alien worlds as soon as possible. She loved exploring, loved knowing she stood where no one from Earth had stood in hundreds or thousands of years, but once she was back home she couldn't help but feel *wrong*.

Afterward she changed into blue BDUs, combed back her wet hair, and settled down to check in on a few of her ongoing projects. She knew Daniel was using their post-war downtime to finally settle in with his catalogue, and Sam was hooked into Area 51 to see what progress research and development had made on some of the tech they'd brought back over the years. She desperately wished she could be there, on the scientific front line, now that she wasn't as necessary on the military side of the fight. The only thing holding her back was the fact SG-1 needed her, but with General O'Neill's promotion and Teal'c spending more time with the Jaffa, it was only a matter of time before it was just her and Daniel on the team with two strangers. And if Daniel was willing to spend more time with his books and the team was being rebuilt anyway...

There was a knock on her door that startled her from

thoughts of defection. She answered and smiled when she saw her visitor. Teal'c had also changed out of the costume Bellee had given him, electing instead for the simple black T-shirt.

"Speak of the devil."

He tilted his head to the side. "Am I unwelcome?"

"No! That's just something we say, uh, when someone… I was just thinking about you, and now you're here. It's based on a superstition that…" She narrowed her eyes as her voice trailed off. "You know, sometimes I think you fake confusion just to make us think about how ridiculous we sound sometimes."

"I would do no such thing, Colonel Carter."

She grinned. "Come in. Any progress with Kali?"

"No. However, I find Captain Morello's strategy to be quite… unconventional. It is not a tactic I would have suggested using on a Goa'uld."

Sam sat at her desk. "Do you think it has any hope of working?"

He gave the question some thought before he responded. "The Goa'uld have been defeated. This was achieved via strategies I would never have considered before I became acquainted with the Tau'ri. I do not know if the gambit will be successful, however I would not be surprised should it bear fruit."

Sam chuckled. "I think that's the nicest version of 'it's just crazy enough to work' I've ever heard."

He smiled and looked at her computer. "Have I interrupted your work?"

"No, nothing that can't wait. What brings you by?"

"The past several days, I have been struggling with the question of my future. When the current crisis ends, I believe I will once again depart the SGC and Earth."

Sam said, "We all understand why you have to leave, Teal'c. No one holds it against you. When you joined us, your goal was to help free the Jaffa. We succeeded, against all odds, and now your place is with them. You've earned your right to help them through this transition period. Of course that doesn't mean we won't miss you like hell."

He smiled again. "And I shall miss everyone here as well. I cannot help but feel ungracious for leaving the moment my goal has been achieved."

"You didn't leave us, Teal'c. You're here now."

"For selfish reasons."

Sam shook her head and stood up, resting one hand on his arm. "No. You're here because we asked you to be here, and you came back. I have no doubt that in the future when we need you, you'll be here for us again. Just like we'll always be here for you. Even if you leave SG-1, you'll still be a member of our team. It's more than just a shoulder patch."

"Thank you, Colonel Carter. You have taken a great burden from my shoulders. I believe I am better prepared to tell General O'Neill of my plans. Although it will be painful to step away from the fight, I must accept that my presence is needed elsewhere."

"Happy to help. You know, on Chulak, when a great warrior retires from the field of battle, it's customary to sing a song of lament."

Teal'c tensed. "We are not on Chulak."

Sam raised an eyebrow at him and assumed what she hoped was a stoic expression.

Her phone rang before he could respond to the mockery, and she chuckled as she walked over to answer it. "Carter." Her amusement faded. "Now? I'll be right there. Teal'c is with me." She hung up and turned back to face Teal'c. "Apparently Bellee is contacting us with important information."

Teal'c lifted his chin and followed her out of the room. "Do you believe there has been a complication with the device?"

Sam knew he was asking if Kali's failsafe had been activated. If it had, Teal'c ran a huge risk just by accompanying her to the control room. "I don't know. We can only hope it's something smaller and less catastrophic."

General O'Neill and Daniel were already in the control

room when Sam and Teal'c arrived. The video screens mounted throughout the room displayed Bellee's bulldog visage. He was holding the recorder at arm's length in front of him, squinting at the screen as if he could use it to see through the event horizon. O'Neill turned to see their arrival and then faced forward again.

"Okay, Belly, they're all here. What's so important?"

"It's Buh-lee, and I'll have you know that it has been very unpleasant speaking with you. I don't know if there's an official complaint I can make, or if there's someone else there I can talk to, but your attitude is extremely — "

O'Neill snapped, "Bellee! The reason you called…"

"Oh. Right. Yes. SG-1? You're all there, right?"

"That's what I just said," Jack muttered.

"I heard that."

O'Neill tilted his head back and rolled his eyes to the heavens. "SG-1! Anton Bellee here."

"They can see you," O'Neill said with a tone usually reserved for children.

Bellee said, "I got in contact with some of my associates who are attending Wyrrick's party. I have some information that you're not going to like. But! But I also thought of a solution to it as well, so don't panic."

Daniel said, "That's promising. What's the problem?"

"Earlier I said that they wouldn't take kindly to Tau'ri crashing the party. Well… it's a little deeper than that. Turns out if a Tau'ri goes to Wyrrick's party, there's a very good chance they won't come back. I couldn't figure out if they meant death or taking prisoners and frankly I didn't feel very much like pushing. But there is good news!"

"Can't wait to hear it," Sam said.

"With a very simple voice modulator, Colonel Carter, you could pass as a Goa'uld. I happen to have two pieces of information that could help you pull it off. One, I know who has been invited, and I happen to know one of them is in no physical position to attend the party." He paused. "She's dead."

"We got that," Daniel said.

"And it's not common knowledge. I can provide you with a modulator if you need one, for a very reasonable price. All you have to do is show up and claim you're her new host."

Sam sighed. "Is this going to affect my costume at all?"

"No, it shouldn't. Goa'uld can get away with pretty much anything when it comes to style. I mean, my goodness, that thing Zipacna wore on his head for so long? I didn't have the heart to tell him it was supposed to be ornamental."

Sam closed her eyes. "Okay. Who am I supposed to be?"

"Callisto."

Daniel was already in motion. "I'll see what I can find out."

O'Neill dismissed him with a nod. He looked at the screen again. "Well, Bellee, I suppose we owe you our thanks for bringing this to our attention."

Bellee said, "Well, I didn't do it for the gratitude, but a little — "

"Great." O'Neill slashed two fingers across his throat, and Walter disconnected the gate in the middle of Bellee's declaration of humbleness. He turned to Sam. "Are you up for this?"

She nodded. "All it should take is a voice modulator. If they have any sort of security to go through, the markers left from Jolinar should get me past. Hopefully Teal'c and Daniel can provide enough backstory for me to bluff if I need to."

"Right. And speaking of Daniel and Teal'c, how exactly can we explain their presence? A mask might help you and Daniel, but Teal'c is basically a celebrity. The kind of people I assume will be attending this soiree will recognize him no matter what disguise we try to give him."

Sam looked at Teal'c. "We can claim that he was captured and brainwashed."

Teal'c said, "Recently, as support for the Free Jaffa has risen, several Goa'uld have begun experimenting with mental manipulation. I believe it would be plausible for one to have succeeded."

Sam nodded uneasily. "We can just say Callisto found a way to change even the most stubbornly convinced mind. If it were true, she would definitely want to show him off like a trophy. If that's acceptable to you, of course, Teal'c. I don't want to force you to go along with a plan that would make you uncomfortable."

Teal'c inclined his head in agreement. "I can bear it for the greater good," he said. "As for Daniel Jackson, despite Bellee's insistence that no Tau'ri may attend, I believe exceptions will be made for lo'taurs."

"What's a Goa'uld without a human slave, eh?" O'Neill said. "Looks like this mission is shaping up to be a real wingding for you, Carter."

She smiled mirthlessly. "Oh, definitely sir. What little girl doesn't dream of being a Goa'uld for a day?"

CHAPTER FIFTEEN

DYSMAS Wyrrick slept thirteen hours a day when he truly wanted to spoil himself. Anything he couldn't get done in the remaining fourteen hours wasn't worth his time. After waking he accessed his files from the bedside management screen before he finally threw back the blankets and rose as if meeting a challenger for fisticuffs. He extended his arms out in front of him, twisted at the waist, and let out a satisfied sigh at the stretch of tight muscles. For the past few years, his time had been filled with meetings. He was constantly trying to set up meetings with one Goa'uld that didn't overlap with one of their enemies, avoiding conflicts on his front step, conducting long and tedious negotiations with First Primes and majordomos. Now his days were mostly empty, dull, boring. That was the public purpose of throwing a party and inviting the bulk of his client list. He could show off his treasures, maybe sell a few things to make some money, and maybe he would find something to occupy his time now that the System Lords were out of the picture. Of course his true purpose was something far grander than a simple exhibition. He had wealth and respect, but he lacked any kind of true power. Hopefully that would all change after the party.

He dressed in clothes that would have constituted the finest outfit in almost anyone else's wardrobe and left his master chambers. Perhaps he would take a walk to clear his mind. His party was in two days and he felt as if there were still a hundred thousand decisions to be made. He had only just recently settled on a caterer after an extremely detailed search through a myriad of potential chefs. The food was an utterly important piece of his party's success; no one would care about admiring his riches if the food made them retch. His final choice was due to arrive that afternoon, and he couldn't wait to taste their sample meals to ensure he had made the right decision.

Wyrrick was a monument of a man, nearly six and a half feet tall with broad shoulders and a barrel chest. The muscles of his gut had gone to flab, leaving him self-conscious about his midsection, but he was rich enough to afford tailors who could hide his paunch. His hair was thick, peppered with grey so that it became the color of ash, and his chin jutted out in front of him like the prow of a great ship. In the past, no more than five Goa'uld had offered to take him as host. When directness failed they tried subterfuge and coercion, had offered him riches beyond his wildest dreams, but he'd shaken them all off time and again. He could have stayed young and pretty forever with one of them riding his spine, but he was starting to enjoy the dignity that came with age.

He followed the curved corridor from his bedroom to the tranquility grotto and slowed to enjoy the view out the windows. This side of the house faced the ocean, and he could see that the sea was calm as glass this morning, visible as a thin blue ribbon along the horizon just beyond the edge of the cliffs. He owned the entire region, purchased for a flat fee and then kept up through taxes and fees from the inhabitants. He had already earned back what he'd paid for the land but the money kept coming in. It was as if he had built his home inside a well that never ran dry.

In two days, his home would be filled with dignitaries and representatives of several key players in the new galactic order. The Lucian Alliance represented the thieves and brigands; old rulers who had paid homage to their Goa'uld overlords for generations would find themselves courting a new overlord; he'd even extended the invitation to a few select Jaffa just to cover his bases in case their new government found its footing before they were overwhelmed by new enemies. His advisors urged him to invite some displaced System Lords, and he overcame his initial misgivings to send out invites to a few choice names. The party was intended to show those left behind that things had changed, but just because the Goa'uld had been defeated was no reason to shun them as individuals. Those who were in a position to attend a party could prove to be good assets in the future.

When he reached the grotto the central lighting fixture had already been activated by his hardworking household staff. He stepped inside and took his standard position next to the structure. Waves of undulating white, purple, blue, and silver light cascaded upward toward the ceiling in a liquid rhythm. Wyrrick felt himself slipping away into blissful distraction as he tracked its movements. His eyes glazed over and a dull smile spread across his features as he watched the light bend and fold and twist around itself.

"Master Wyrrick."

It was absolutely gorgeous... weaker-willed individuals could lose entire hours staring into the shine, but Wyrrick was mostly immune to its effects. There were other devices which induced an addiction in those who partook of its enjoyment, but he'd had his one specially designed to prevent that. The light still found a way to utterly engross him, to wrap around his brain like a blanket and take away his concerns and worries. It was an easy way to clear his mind in case he needed to tackle a particularly...

"Master!"

He blinked and turned to find his aide, Athen, standing beside him. He was suddenly assaulted by the strength of his hunger, and through the open door behind Athen he could see that the sun had made quite a bit of progress across the sky since his arrival in the grotto. He shook his head to clear the lingering cobwebs and turned to face his assistant fully.

"Yes?"

"Apologies, Master Wyrrick. You wished to be informed when the workers for the party began arriving." He removed a small pad from the breast pocket of his uniform jacket. "The landscapers are outside and I have already started them preparing the garden, we have the interior decorators coming to set up display cases for your treasures, and the chef is here to meet you before she begins work."

"And the grand finale?"

"Everything is prepared. The items you requested are safely locked away upstairs."

Wyrrick clapped his hands together. "Fantastic! And you said the chef is here as well? Where did you leave her?"

Athen led Wyrrick through the house, purposefully choosing a route that took them through his collection rooms. Soon decorators would transfer all of this finery to their proper positions in rooms where his guests could enjoy them without worrying about the security systems sounding. But for now they were nestled within vaults in the private section of his home. He passed some of his most prized items — a golden altar that had stood in one of Ra's temples, a bladed weapon that had once been displayed above Khonsu's throne, a stately throne crowned by a representation of Ba'al's symbol backlit with a glowing blue globe — and smiled as he remembered acquiring each one. Athen was accustomed to his master's ruminations and slowed his pace to keep from getting too far ahead.

Eventually they passed through the vaults and arrived at their destination. The kitchen occupied its own wing, covering more ground than most private residences. The machinery gleamed, appliances looking as if they had been formed from pure light. Wyrrick assumed he paid people to come in and clean everything but he had never seen them, nor did he want to. Athen had been hired to take care of those small things for him.

At the moment the only other people in the cavernous kitchen were two women standing near the burner top. One wore a lovely outfit befitting her former position with the Jade Emperor; a red blouse with yellow piping, billowing black slacks, and the look was completed with the dark hair which hung loose on her shoulders. When she turned, Wyrrick was surprised to see how beautiful she was. The woman with her was equally beautiful, wearing a matching outfit and leaning against the counter with a disinterested air. They looked similar enough to be sisters, but he had no doubt which of them was the woman in charge.

Wyrrick smiled. "Ai Okano, I presume, late of Lord Yu's scullery. It is an honor to have you here in my home. I am Dysmas Wyrrick, but you may of course call me Dys."

Okano smiled. "It's an honor to be chosen for such a prestigious event. Considering our competition we didn't hold out much hope that we would be fortunate enough to win."

"Between the people in this room, your competition all had an unusual amount of disqualifying information in their records. Some of them tried to hide it, but there is no hole too deep to hide from my hounds. You should be grateful you cleared the examination."

Okano shrugged. "I'm not surprised. Lord Yu brooked no controversy. We were forced to remain above reproach lest we be relieved of duty."

"Excellent. I'm glad to hear it." He looked at the assistant. "And I assume she will be helping you on the evening of the party?"

"Yes, this is my associate and right-hand woman, Oshin Kaori."

"A pleasure to meet you, madam."

Kaori grinned, showing her teeth. When she spoke it was with an accent he couldn't quite pinpoint. "Oh, yes, it's an honor, sir."

"Now, I don't want to get onto a touchy subject, and I know that the Tau'ri wasn't one of the great many worlds under Yu's dominion. However, I must confirm…"

"We're both Hebridian," Okano said. "We left home early to find more exotic culinary worlds, and along the way we ended up in Yu's domain."

"Good, good, good. I just want to make certain the party is

Tau'ri free. I mean, I'm as open as the next man when it comes to that sort of thing, but some of my guests… I mean, those SG teams cut straight to the bone of the galaxy in the past few years, you know? For a lot of people who will be at the party, those wounds are still fresh."

"I completely understand," Okano said. "We lost our god. If any Tau'ri even think about crashing this party, we'll have a special treat prepared just for them."

Wyrrick laughed and pointed at her. "You. I like the way you think. You're definitely officially hired to provide catering to my party. Congratulations. This kitchen is now your domain. Everything you find here is yours for the taking, just let me know if you need any supplies refreshed or if there's something special you need for the menu. The galaxy's pantry is just a Stargate away. I'll check in later."

"We'll have a few items ready for you to taste by this afternoon."

"Excellent, excellent." He clapped his hands together. "I have a good feeling about this."

Kaori said, "Oh, so do we, Mr. Wyrrick."

He laughed and winked at her, then motioned for Athen to follow him out of the kitchen. He paused in front of the large glass windows and looked over his shoulder to make sure the women were out of earshot.

"Lovely choices, my friend. Be sure they don't venture upstairs for any reason. I would hate for anyone to spoil the grand finale of my big night."

"Of course."

Wyrrick leaned closer to the glass and pointed at something in the sky. "What do you think that is? Bird?"

Athen followed the line of his employer's finger to a small black shape just as it disappeared into a cloud bank. "Yes, sir. A bird."

"Huh. I've never really liked birds. Except for the ones which find their way onto my plate." He tugged at the lapels of his shirt and rolled his shoulders. "All this talk about food has made me hungry. Why don't you go into town and see what the bakery has rolled out today?"

"As you wish, sir."

Athen bowed sharply and left, but Wyrrick waited a moment to watch when the flying object emerged from the clouds. The wings were rigid, and it seemed to be flying on an artificially straight trajectory that most animals wouldn't have bothered with.

"Most peculiar bird I've ever seen."

He shook his head and patted his stomach as he walked away. He was no ornithologist, but he thought birds had to flap their wings every once in a while even if they were riding a current. Perhaps it was a guest arriving early, or maybe it was in fact a bird in flight. Either way he would be certain to alert his security officers to the potential issue. But first, he would return to the Grotto to finish what Athen had so rudely interrupted.

"UAV feed is live," Sam said, looking away from the Stargate to watch the aerial footage of Wyrrick's planet. The planet's Stargate stood in the foothills outside a small village, but according to the intelligence they received from Bellee, Wyrrick lived on an estate near the coast well away from the common people. They had anticipated security measures or surveillance at the gate, but there didn't seem to be anything of that nature impeding their arrival.

Teal'c noticed the lack of precautions as well. "Perhaps he is more concerned with security on his property and leaves policing the Stargate to the villagers."

"Let's hope," Sam said. "I doubt we'll be as lucky on the day of his party."

She angled the drone into the low atmosphere where it would be less obvious from the ground and flew northwest. After a buffer space of fields and winding dirt roads the camera found a sprawling house near the rocky edge of the coast. It looked more like a museum than someone's home, and a half dozen statues stood in a semi-circle at the front of the building, their carved faces looking out toward any visitors as they arrived. An al'kesh was parked behind the building on an inclined display, like a truck on sale at a used car dealership.

Standing behind her, Jack, Daniel, and Teal'c all examined the building. "Looks like the Goa'uld aren't the only ones who like their palaces to be a little gaudy," Jack said. "How many square feet you think that thing's got?"

"I'm more concerned with the defenses," Sam said. "If Wyrrick discovers who we really are, we don't want to end up trapped in there."

"I still don't understand why we don't just sweep in, blow out the doors, and take what we need." The team all looked at him and he grimaced. "Wishful thinking. I'm the boss now, so of course I understand why we have to go the diplomatic, quiet route. But still... if I wasn't here, I would definitely suggest ignoring the general's orders and just taking what we need."

Sam said, "We'll take that under advisement, sir."

"Just don't let me find out if you have to take extreme measures. Deny, deny, deny."

Sam nodded. "Yes, sir."

The phone near the stairs began ringing, and Jack glanced over as a technician answered it. He listened for a moment, then handed the receiver to Jack.

"O'Neill."

"Sir, Kali has requested a conversation. She said she'll only speak with Captain Morello."

Jack raised an eyebrow. "I'll track her down." He hung up and looked at the team. "Looks like Captain Morello may have one-upped you in the negotiating world, Dr. Jackson. Kali is willing to talk."

Daniel blinked behind his glasses. "Wow. That—that's great."

"Yeah. Any idea where the captain is right now?"

"She's been researching Kali," Daniel said. "She wanted to

use some of my books so she's probably in my office."

"I'll go grab her. Daniel, want to sit in?"

"Sure. It's not every day we see a Goa'uld offering to help us out."

Jack said, "Carter, keep up the recon. Let me know if you find anything."

"Yes, sir."

Jack led Daniel to the elevators and rode up to Level 19. As expected, Morello was stationed behind Daniel's desk with one book open in front of her and her body twisted so she could refer to something on the computer screen.

"Well, this looks familiar…"

Morello turned when she saw who had arrived. "General! Doctor! Um." As she stood up she accidentally displaced one of her books and shot one hand out to grab it. Putting it on the table she checked to make sure it would stay, then straightened and smiled. "Sorry. Kind of messy."

"You work with Daniel Jackson, you get used to messy," Jack said. "Just got word from one of the guards watching Kali. She's ready to talk."

Morello blinked. "That's fantastic! What did she say?"

"She hasn't yet," Daniel said. "She's waiting to talk to you."

"Me?"

"It was your idea," Jack said.

Morello said, "Oh. Okay. Um. Yes." She cleared her throat, looked back at her work. "I've been trying to find an angle, something that will further sway her if she needs more convincing. I've found a few things, so I'm — I'm confident."

"Good," Jack said. "Then so am I. Shall we?"

Jack noticed that Morello's nerves only got worse as they walked to the holding cells. "No reason to be nervous," he said. "There's one person in that room with any power, and she's a captain in the United States Air Force. The other one is a has-been trying to hold onto the last little bit of her power. She's going to play games, she's going to try and intimidate you. Don't let her."

"Yes, sir. I'll try, sir."

Jack nodded to the guard to open the door, then he walked into the observation room. Through the glass he saw Kali watching as Morello came in and took a seat across from her. The captain's voice was calm when she spoke, but Jack could tell she was still quaking on the inside.

"I hear you wanted to speak with me."

"You are foolish if you believe you can sway me with sentimentality," Kali said. Again, her voice was strong and full of confidence, but Jack knew it was just a front. Morello had gotten to her. "Are your people still flailing about in an attempt to stop my vengeance?"

"We're trying to stop your petty revenge, yes."

Kali took a deep breath and slowly blinked. "I will not help you in this matter. But I will tell you this; I left my palace three hundred days ago. If I do nothing, the failsafe will be enacted and the plague will be released in four days' time."

Jack looked at Daniel. "Party's in two days. Gives us plenty of time to get what we need and plug it in. If she's telling the truth."

Daniel nodded. "And that's a big if."

"Still, Sam has worked miracles in thirty seconds. If we give her forty-eight hours to figure out how the thing works, I have no doubt she'll pull it off. It's nice to have a little wiggle room." He noticed Daniel's pensive expression. "Right?"

"Right," Daniel said. "If we can find the master switch, and if we can figure out where the signal is supposed to originate so we can cut it off at the source. There's a chance success will mean cutting a genocide down into a mass murder."

Jack hissed through his teeth and glared through the glass. "Right."

"I suppose there is one good thing about knowing when the plague will be released. If the deadline is approaching and we're still coming up empty, we can get Teal'c to safety and warn as many planets as we can that they should bury their Stargate. The Jaffa can protect themselves so that even if the failsafe is enacted the actual lives lost will be minimal."

Jack said, "It would only take one."

"Exactly."

"Damn. Every time I start to get a little hope…"

Daniel looked at him. "Are you serious? This is huge, Jack. Morello got Kali to give us a timeline. She got a Goa'uld to tell us how much time was left on her master plan. That's big." He looked through the glass again. "I think Kali is just trying her best to save face by giving us as little as possible, but Morello got through to her. With time, I think she could break through."

"Four days," Jack said.

"Hopefully it'll be enough."

CHAPTER SIXTEEN

OVER THE past twenty-eight hours, Wyrrick's kitchen had become a battlefield. Vala and Tanis alternated tasks, moving between burners and iceboxes, mincing and dicing everything they could get a blade near. Vala swept up a handful of spices and moved to dump them into a pot, but Tanis stopped her and spoke to her in a low but firm voice. "Unless you've changed the plan to involve killing everyone at the party so we can take the time clearing this place out, I would suggest not combining *tacyhek* root with *baccetel*. That would be less appetizer and more poison."

"Sorry we all can't be the culinary geniuses like yourself."

Tanis sighed and Vala felt a twinge of guilt. They'd been at each other's throats more than usual since they started working on the feast. The downside of Vala's plan to get them into the house meant they were actually responsible for the food prep. Tanis had enough rudimentary skills to pull it off, but Vala was just following directions as best she could and trying not to set anything on fire. She knew the next day they would have to be on good terms, so to defuse the tension she wiped her hands on the apron and looked over her shoulder to make sure they were still alone.

"I'm going to take a quick peek around, see if I can get the lay of the land."

"Fine."

Vala left the kitchen before Tanis could snap at her again. Wyrrick had given them a small guest room near the kitchen, an attached cottage that was almost twice the size of their tel'tac. The downside to comfort was that the door had been locked from the outside overnight. "A precaution," Wyrrick's man had assured them. "We have many priceless artifacts here. It's not that we don't trust you, but…"

Certainly not, Vala had thought, but she noticed he hadn't finished the sentence. Fortunately they had already scanned the building from their tel'tac, and Tanis still had the blueprints they'd gotten from Bellee. She plugged the two scans together and got an up-to-date view of what the house looked like. The treasures were represented by large but obscure blobs. From the scan she couldn't tell which specific collection had once belonged to Kali, but she was confident that she would know it when she saw it.

The private residences, kitchen, and laundry, were all clustered in a separate hive of rooms connected to the main house by a grand central corridor. Vala checked to make sure Wyrrick or Athen weren't lurking before she set out to explore. She had a menu question tucked away just in case she happened across either of them in her snooping.

A pair of double doors led from the private areas of the house to the public rooms, the places where the guests would soon be gathering. The main ballroom was enclosed by a curving hall from which all the collection rooms could be accessed. Currently the doors were all standing open so the decorators could prepare Wyrrick's toys, and Vala paused to examine some of the fancier items. She saw items she recognized from Ba'al's palaces, and she saw a multitude of antiques with the mark of Osiris and his queen. Every room she passed was a veritable fortune waiting to be made on the black market. Nothing she saw bore the mark of Kali, however, and she forced herself to keep moving.

In the ballroom she could see the central island where musicians and food stations would be set up. There was room for five hundred guests, perhaps more, and she could just imagine the swarm of attendees mingling with the wait staff she and Tanis were going to hire from the local populace. They just had to be sure to hire people who wouldn't think it unusual when the head waitress commandeered their carts and covered trays. The sheer number of people should keep her activities under the radar.

The stairs were blocked by a tri-fold gate that prevented any-one from going up to the second level. Vala slowed to look up at the landing and idly wondered what could possibly be worth segregating when all the treasures were on the ground floor.

She was about to admit defeat and make another round when she reached the final room on the circuit. She stopped in the doorway and stared, jaw dropping as she gazed at the riches of Kali. She had a moment of nostalgic sadness; she despised Qetesh, but after being freed she had spent several glorious months impersonating her former tormentor and living the life of luxury in temples on a half dozen scattered worlds. There were planets she could have visited that very evening where the people would bow down to her as their god. Word of deicide didn't exactly travel quickly, contrary to what some might believe, and the backwater worlds were slow to believe their god was dead when she was little more than a vague idea in the first place.

But being revered as a god and actually walking back into a golden palace replete with wealth were two very different things. Even her most modest sanctuaries would have been picked clean by now, her glorious and magnificent toys had all been taken away from her and she'd gotten nothing in return. But Kali's loss could be her gain. Even the light fix-tures, golden cylinders with hieroglyphics shapes carved to let the light through, were magnificent. They could sell those without blinking on any of a dozen worlds. Tapestries would be a bit more difficult to unload without provenance, but in the current climate, who was going to worry about something like that? These weren't just any goods. They were spoils of war. People would want mementos and damn the cost.

Vala didn't realize how deep into the room she was until Wyrrick spoke and broke the spell.

"I assure you, no one will be eating in here."

Vala spun to see him standing in the doorway, blocking her exit with his bulk. His arms were crossed and, despite his neutral expression, she could tell he was leaning closer to amusement than anger. Her life had depended on navigating such thin lines before, and she was confident with her ability to read them. She crossed her arms behind her back, smiled, and affected a nervous sway when she moved toward him.

"Master Wyrrick! I thought you would be so busy with… I mean, this place has been such a madhouse, and all these treasures…" She hunched her shoulders and looked at him through her eyelashes, aiming for defenseless ingénue. If it worked, she would see it around his eyes and in a softening of his lips. "I knew I wouldn't get a chance to appreciate them during the party, so I thought… what's the harm in taking a quick peek now?"

The lines on either side of his mouth softened. Vala resisted the urge to smile at her victory.

"I could have you arrested on suspicion, you realize."

Vala widened her eyes. "No! Please, you wouldn't! Even if they merely held me until the party was over, Madame Ai would certainly have my job for leaving her in the lurch. Please, I promise, I won't overstep my boundaries again!"

Wyrrick finally allowed himself a full smile. "Relax. I don't blame you for being curious. In fact, it would have been suspicious if you weren't tempted to have a look around. Someone who resisted such an urge would make me think they were overcompensating. Make me wonder why they were trying so hard to act unimpressed. So you can relax. You've set my mind at ease."

"Phew!" Vala said, masking her authentic relief with an overacted swipe at her brow. "Madame Ai only let me steal away from the kitchen if I promised to tell her what I saw." She gestured at the room they were in. "Where did all this come from, if I may ask?"

"Ah, this room." Wyrrick stepped inside, thus giving her an escape route. The knot of tension in her chest relaxed and Vala allowed herself to follow Wyrrick further into the room.

There was a dialing pedestal nearby and she leaned against it, feigning nonchalance as Wyrrick gestured at the treasures. "These are the pickings from the realm of the once-great Kali."

"Kali! I think I know of her. She was an enemy of Lord Yu." And of Qetesh, but she didn't include that little tidbit of history. "Did she survive the downfall of the Goa'uld?"

Wyrrick shrugged. "She was an ally of Anubis. When he fell, the System Lords who sided with him fell. Not that many System Lords are welcome anywhere these days. Their treasures, however, are always welcome…"

Vala laughed. "Too true! Too true. Um…" She cleared her throat and looked down at the object she was resting against. It was a multifaceted pedestal with a control panel on one side and a cluster of Stargate glyphs in the center. "This, for instance. This is the most gorgeous dialer I've ever seen!"

"That's not actually a dialer," Wyrrick said. "I'm not sure what it does. I've heard rumors, of course." His voice dropped to a conspiratorial whisper. "Would you like to hear one?"

Vala raised her eyebrows. "Of course! I adore rumors."

"I hear it controls a doomsday device, one which any day now will wipe out every Jaffa in the galaxy. Without this to stop it, the plague will be unleashed throughout the Stargate system."

"Really!" Vala gazed wide-eyed at the pedestal. "And to think, the one thing that could save an entire race is sitting right in this room. That's a lot of power to wield, Mr. Wyrrick."

"It's only power if I intend to do something with it."

"You're not?"

Wyrrick said, "For hundreds of years, the Jaffa laid waste to this galaxy. They stormed through the Stargate in their fright masks, staff weapons ablaze, and dragged children away from parents, left people crippled and villages decimated in their wake. The Jaffa are as much a pestilence as the Goa'uld, and I view this plague as a great flood coming forth across every planet in the Stargate system… the Goa'uld may be gone, but we won't be cleansed until their foot soldiers have followed them into the grave."

"A bit odd to invite them to your party in that case, isn't it?"

Wyrrick smiled. "The art of scheming did not die with the Goa'uld, my dear. All will become clear soon enough."

Something in his smile made Vala sick to her stomach. She swallowed the lump in her throat and resisted the urge to cringe away from Wyrrick when he touched her elbow.

"Shall we continue? There are a lot of treasures to explore."

"Yes, of course."

Wyrrick walked past her to the door, but Vala lingered by the pedestal a moment longer. Again with a rumor about a plague that threatened the Jaffa. She still didn't quite believe the plague was real, but if it was… she was standing next to the means with which to stop it. The Jaffa had done unspeakable evil through the galaxy, without question. But she also knew they rarely had a choice in the matter. Obey your god or die. Obey your god or your family will be exiled and left to starve. The Jaffa were victims of the Goa'uld as much as any other race. More so, perhaps.

She reached out and brushed her fingers over the control panel and thought of how many people would move the heavens and its stars just to know where it was: altruists, do-gooders, crusaders for right. Vala was quite sure she didn't know anyone like that and, if she did, they would go out of their way to squash her like a bug. She and Tanis had sacrificed too much already to risk everything on a good deed. Her altruism would begin just as soon as the treasure was in her hands.

"Coming?" Wyrrick asked from the doorway.

"Yep! Just taking one last look."

She walked out and followed Wyrrick to the next room. She still had her heart set on leaving with as much of Kali's wealth as possible, but there was a lot more in the house just waiting to be pilfered. Tanis had to get her cut somehow, and who was she to refuse if the master of the house wanted to give her a guided tour of potential targets?

She glanced back once more at the pedestal and then put it out of her mind. She had been telling the truth when she told Tanis what she wanted to do with Kali's treasure, but maybe it had simply been her better angels trying to sway her. She wasn't the kind of person who sacrificed to help a stranger. As disappointed as she was to discover her reluctance to do the right thing, she didn't have time to dwell on that shortcoming.

She had a heist to plan, and she wasn't going to distract herself with thoughts of heroic nonsense.

Morello didn't go home. She couldn't justify it when so much was hanging in the balance. She was in Daniel's office, seated at the main table with her head propped up on both fists. She closed her eyes just to rest them enough to focus on the words in front of her and was startled awake by a hand resting gently on her arm. She chided herself for falling asleep even as she blushed at the realization that Daniel had just found her sleeping at his desk.

"Oh. Damn. I'm sorry. I'll get out of your way, sir."

"You're fine." He put down a cup of coffee in front of her. "And I think there are enough sirs running around the base. How about you just call me Daniel?"

She nodded as she sipped the coffee, savoring the taste and the smell of it before she spoke again. "I'm sorry to stomp all over your territory here."

"No, that's not, no. You're doing a fine job. If I'm going to be off-world with SG-1, I like knowing someone is back here doing the heavy lifting with the resources." He picked up one of the books and read the spine. "Some of the team leaders don't realize that sitting down with a book all night is as important as blowing up a Goa'uld mother ship."

Morello smiled. "I got lucky on that score. Colonel Getty knows that most of the time the answer is in a book. I'm starting to think this isn't one of those times, though."

"You've been doing a good job so far."

"I've been flailing," she said. She looked at the scattered books with despair. "General O'Neill is treating me like I've got the magic touch, but the truth is I've gotten lucky at every turn. If you hadn't been on the planet, I never would have found that secret chamber. I wouldn't even have known to look for it. And now I'm just flying by the seat of my pants trying to stay one step ahead of Kali. I'm worried that I'm coming up fast on the end of my luck."

Daniel chuckled. "You want to know my secret?"

"Yes. Please."

"Riding by the seat of my pants when luck is running out. Nothing can prepare you for this job, for the scope of it. We're dealing with aliens so powerful they've convinced entire planets that they're gods. There's not a college course for that. We do our best and we look for openings. The trick is to be ready when that opening presents itself. Make sure you're well-armed."

"Thank you. That actually helps." She looked at her books and pushed her chair back. "I'll get out of your way."

"No, please. Stay. I just came by to pick up a fresh notebook. We're trying to learn as much about this Wyrrick character so we don't go in blind. Make yourself at home. In fact..." He looked around the office and thumped his knuckle on the table before he walked to the desk in the corner. "The most important item in the entire office." He pulled a plump pillow from the drawer and brought it over to her. "It's gotten me through more than one long night."

"Thank you, sir. Daniel."

"Stick with it, Captain. Luck, planning, and cleverness. You've got everything you need."

He left with the notebook tucked under his arm, and Morello looked at the pillow he'd given her. The thought of a nap was still appealing but the urge to curl up and pass out for a few hours had passed. If there was an answer to be found, some piece of information she could use to their advantage, it was best to find it as soon as possible. She put the pillow aside, moved her coffee mug closer, and bent over the book again with renewed energy.

Jack was awake so early that he couldn't swear to the fact he'd actually been asleep. But he knew that he must have left his office at some point because there were new updates waiting to be read on his desk. Over the past twenty-four hours, Morello had continued to look through past mission reports and historical documents regarding Kali's reigns on various planets. She reported that there were plenty of references to her being a benevolent god, showing mercy and shepherding her people. She followed the path of least resistance because it led to less war and fewer deaths. Her treaty with Bastet wasn't like other System Lord alliances. Ba'al might have allied with Anubis as a power grab, and Apophis may have offered Heru'ur peace as a way to lower his guard, but Kali and Bastet were true comrades. Morello was convinced that somewhere in the literature there was a way to appeal to that side of their prisoner. The walls were showing signs of weakness, now they just had to find a way to knock them down completely.

Sam made contact with the Tok'ra while Daniel, who would have been buried just as deep in the books as Morello if he had the time, had reached out to their other allies to see what he could discover about Wyrrick. At first glance the guy sounded like an alien version of Donald Trump. He was a collector of fine things, well-known simply for his wealth and decadence. He was definitely not a Goa'uld, and relatively harmless. Unless, of course, one happened to be a Tau'ri. He had never chosen a side in the larger galactic conflict, so he didn't really care either way about the lesser Goa'uld or the Replicators, but the System Lords had been unofficial patrons of his collecting so he tended to be more sympathetic to them. Plus he was one of many who blamed, or credited, the Tau'ri for everything that had happened. Everyone was scrambling to fill the power void and Wyrrick's nice, tidy world had been completely shaken up in the aftermath. When it came down to brass tacks, no one from Earth would be treated kindly.

Jack closed the files and fought a yawn as he checked his watch. He'd done none of the actual work, but he still felt tired just looking at the results. For the eightieth time that morning he wondered how he had been conned into giving up a plum position as leader of SG-1 to play intergalactic doorman and hall monitor. Weir would have been great in his role, and he had no doubt she'd have no problem solving the problems he struggled with. And while he was wishing, maybe Hammond would be willing to come back in an advisory position. A man could dream.

His sour mood was partially lifted by the sight of SG-1 arriving in the control room. They still had a few hours before they were due at Wyrrick's party, but they needed to arrive from a secondary Stargate so there was no record of travel from Earth. Walter glanced over as the team arrived, then promptly looked back at his monitor so they wouldn't see his expression. The team had caused quite a few sideways glances on their way from the locker room to Level 28.

To maintain their cover, they couldn't leave in their SGC uniforms, so they were dressed in their outfits from Anton Bellee's closet. Sam's face was once again painted, and Daniel awkwardly adjusted his tunic. They all wore pouches slung casually over their shoulders, and Jack was confident that the bags held zats, pistols, radios, and their GDOs so they would be able to get back home. Sam's veil was tucked into her belt, and Jack assumed she was waiting until she actually arrived on Wyrrick's planet to put it on.

"Well, kids. After seven years of raiding Goa'uld motherships, wading into war zones, and dialing the gate while dodging enemy fire, you face the toughest mission of all. Prom. It's like you waited until I was gone to get the easy gig."

Sam looked down at her outfit, then gestured at Daniel and Teal'c. "Are you saying you wish you were going with us, sir?"

"Hm. When you put it that way… have them home at a reasonable hour, Colonel. These boys have a curfew, you know."

"I'll do my best, sir."

Jack smiled. "Try to have fun, Carter. Everything else aside, it is still going to be a party."

Sam lifted her eyebrows to indicate she was skeptical, but she said nothing as Walter began to dial. Daniel took out his notepad and flipped through. "We're going to cover our tracks by going to three different planets. Uh, P5X-871 is first. It's a relatively busy emporium planet. Dozens of gate addresses every day. From there we'll go to M71-832. Uninhabited. Then back to Lucia, the planet where we met with Siero. Even if someone wanted to take apart the DHD and dig through the recent dialed addresses, they'd have a hard time convincing the locals to go along with it. From there, to Wyrrick's planet we go."

Jack nodded and watched as the event horizon formed. Nope. Never got old. He faced his team again. "Okay. You'll be deep on this one, so we're not going to expect updates from you. If we don't hear anything in twenty-four hours, we'll dial Wyrrick's planet. Hopefully you'll be able to get a message through."

"We'll do everything in our power, sir."

"I'd expect nothing less, Carter. Meanwhile we'll keep working on Kali. Daniel seems to believe Captain Morello is making progress, so we're going to keep at her. Maybe she'll have an epiphany while you're gone."

"That would be nice," Sam said. "In the meantime, unless we want to be fashionably late, we should get going. We have a lot of gates to pass through in the next few hours."

"Good luck."

The team walked out into the gate room, and Jack felt the familiar pang of being left behind as they started up the ramp. Any trace of amusement left his face as they passed through the shimmering blue surface and vanished. The truth of the matter was, he had just sent his team into an incredibly dangerous situation. They had forty-eight hours to get the pedestal, bring it back, figure out how it worked, and counter Kali's plot in order to save the Jaffa. They had sent out a warning to any Jaffa who would listen, telling them to bury their gates just in case. To no one's surprise, some of the Jaffa refused to take heed, viewing it as an act of cowardice. If Jack heard one more 'We die free,' it would be too soon.

Walter glanced up at him. "I'm sure they'll be fine, sir."

"Yeah? Is that what you used to tell Hammond when SG-1 went off-world?"

"Yes, sir. And I was never wrong."

Jack grunted. "Yeah, well. It only takes one. Keep me informed, will you?" He turned and headed up to his office, hoping he could somehow occupy his mind for the time his team was out of contact.

CHAPTER SEVENTEEN

THE VEIL hooked over Sam's ears, draped the bridge of her nose, and hung down over her chin to obscure her mouth. Teal'c helped her make sure it hung properly before they went through the Stargate to Wyrrick's planet. Her voice modulator was concealed in the collar of her costume, and she could feel it resting against the skin just above her sternum. "Callisto," Sam said, wincing at the hollow and reverberant sound of her voice. "I am Callisto. Are you sure she's not a manifestation of Kali? A cultish off-shoot or something?"

"I'm positive," Daniel said. "Completely different continents, wholly different mythology. You'll be fine."

Sam knew she could trust him when it came to myths and legends, but the names were too similar for her to relax very much. They were about to walk into a party thrown by an anti-Tau'ri eccentric, and the guest list probably read like a who's-who of SGC adversaries. Teal'c dialed and they stepped through. Teal'c went first, followed by Daniel, and then lastly Sam. They went from the gloom of Lucia to a sunny plain, and Sam resisted the urge to bring up her hand to block the sun.

The area around the Stargate had transformed in the day since they sent the UAV through. A wooden corral had been built around it with men posted every few feet. Sam couldn't see any weapons, but she knew they were present. One of the guards was posted next to the DHD, and he approached them as soon as the Stargate disengaged. Sam held out her hand without looking, and Daniel obediently placed the invitation in it.

"I am Callisto. I have been asked to attend Master Wyrrick's party."

"I see." The guard examined the invitation. "And your retinue?"

Sam nodded at Teal'c. "A former First Prime who has been unwavering in his faith to me since declaring his loyalty. This is Teal'c."

"Teal'c," the guard said. "The infamous leader of the Jaffa rebellion?"

Sam smiled. "I have taught him the error of his ways. Tell him."

Teal'c said, "The Goa'uld are false gods. There is but one god in the whole of creation, and she is my mistress, Callisto."

Sam smiled, even though it turned her stomach to hear Teal'c say those words. She tossed her hand dismissively to Daniel. "And my servant, Wiggum."

"He is Tau'ri?"

"He is a lo'taur," Sam corrected. "He was raised in my temple."

The guard looked skeptical but finally handed the invitation back. "There is a transportation cart waiting to take you to Wyrrick's home. I trust you will enjoy the party."

"I am certain we will," Sam said.

They walked through the gauntlet of security and Daniel reached up to scratch under the edge of his mask, cupping his hand so the guards couldn't see him speak. "I'm still not sure about the name…"

"Don't look at me. General O'Neill chose it." She looked at Teal'c. "I'm truly sorry for…"

"There is no need for your apologies, Colonel Carter. I am unshaken by spouting such a ludicrous untruth. However, I appreciate your sympathy."

Daniel paused at the row of carts and took a moment to process what he was seeing. Each cart consisted of a padded seat with a high back that curved above the riders' heads, and each side extended out into long, slender rods. Each rod was fitted with rubber grips on the far ends. A quick scan of the area revealed no pack animals waiting to be lashed to the vehicle. Finally he reached an unavoidable conclusion.

"Um. These are rickshaws."

"Indeed they seem to be," Teal'c said. "And seeing as you are Callisto's primary servant…"

Daniel looked at him. "I don't suppose her loyal First Prime could be enlisted to lend a hand."

Teal'c smiled. "It would be unseemly."

"Of course it would." Daniel sighed, spit into his hands, and rubbed the palms together. "Okay. Here's hoping it's not very far to the party."

Teal'c offered his hand to Sam, and she took it for leverage as she climbed into the cart. Teal'c climbed in behind her, settling next to her on the padded seat. She winced in sympathy as Daniel took up position and scanned the horizon for any sign of Wyrrick's homestead on the horizon. It was nothing but rolling hills and long, unbroken plains.

"It's not very far, right?"

Sam considered not answering, but finally she said, "According to the UAV telemetry —"

Daniel interrupted her. "Not very far. Here's hoping it's… not very far. And mostly on a downhill slope." He bent at the knees to wrap his fingers around the grips, lifted, and exhaled as he tested the weight. "At least Jack isn't here to see this." He looked over his shoulder to make sure Sam and Teal'c were settled, then started forward.

The morning of the party, Vala and Tanis met up before their scheduled duty shift began so they could once more go over the timeline of their plan. Wyrrick would let his guests mingle for the first few hours, giving them time to appreciate his collection. Once everyone was suitably impressed they would be guided back toward the ballroom for a speech from their host, at which point an avalanche of victuals would sweep through the house on a flood of wine and stronger spirits.

"And that's when we'll get to work." Vala tapped her finger on the map. "This is where Kali's treasure is being displayed. While everyone is busy getting drunk and filling themselves with Wyrrick's food, we'll be carting everything out through this side door. Fortunately Wyrrick's tour yesterday included a side note about the security measures in this wing of the building."

"I believe I heard you slipping out of our private quarters last night," Tanis said. "Could you possibly have done something to disable those security measures?"

Vala pulled an innocent expression. "I'm sure I don't know what you mean. I slept like a priest all last night. What were *you* doing awake at such a late hour?"

Tanis twisted her lips and focused on the map again. "We should erase this information when we're done refreshing our memory. We don't want anything incriminating lying around while we're working, just in case Wyrrick gets suspicious."

Vala started to nod as there was a knock on the door. She straightened and looked across the room. "Yes? Who is it, please?"

"It is Athen. I bring a message to Miss Oshin from Master Wyrrick."

"One moment!" Vala looked to see Tanis had already started deleting the files. She nodded her approval as she stood up. "I'm just getting ready for work. Big day today, I'm sure I don't have to tell you." When Tanis signaled her that the blueprints were gone, Vala smoothed down the front of her uniform blouse and went to answer the door. Athen was a slender-framed man with close-cropped blonde hair, and the fact that his forehead was slightly wider than his chin gave him a top-heavy appearance that Vala found amusing.

"Yes? Sorry, Wyrrick said we were to report for duty at five chimes. Did we miss it?"

"No, but there has been a change in plans."

Tanis joined them in the front hall. "I hope it won't affect my menu."

Athen shook his head. "No, but it may have an unfortunately detrimental effect on your actual work for the event."

He focused on Vala. "Master Wyrrick has requested your presence at the party as his personal guest."

Vala's eyes widened, faking surprise to mask her sense of rising dread. "His... guest?"

"Indeed. The master was quite taken with you yesterday. He asked if Madame Ai would be so kind as to let her out of her duties for the duration of the event. He can replace Miss Oshin with a local artisan chef who would be more than capable of filling your absent assistant's shoes."

Vala and Tanis stared at each other, unsure of what to do. Turning down the offer certainly wouldn't sit well with Wyrrick, but accepting it meant they would both have babysitters watching over them. Vala couldn't clear out Kali's treasures if she was hanging from Wyrrick's arm, and Tanis would be stuck in the kitchen with a member of the household staff.

Athen cleared his throat. "Would you like a moment to discuss this? I realize you're being put at an imposition, Madame Ai..."

"Yes. Quite an imposition." She cleared her throat and furrowed her brow. "But if it's what Master Wyrrick wishes, we cannot refuse him. It is his party, after all." She rubbed her thumb in circles against the tips of her first two fingers, one of the nervous habits that, in Vala's experience, meant that her mind was working at a solution. "Tell Master Wyrrick I would be glad to let Miss Oshin out of her duties for the party. Of course, if an emergency arises and I require her expertise..."

"Of course," Athen said. "He extends his apologies and his gratitude. If Miss Oshin would come with me, I believe we can find her something more appropriate to wear."

Vala nodded, smiled, and glanced back at Tanis as she was led out of the room. She followed Athen down the main hall, looking out the windows she passed as if the answer to the predicament was to be found outside. All she saw, however, was a rickshaw being pulled down the road to the palace, the carriage occupied by a masked man and woman while their companion strained to pull the vehicle the remainder of the distance to Wyrrick's front door.

"There's no need to look so glum," Athen said as he escorted her into a private dressing room. "It is a party, after all, and you have just been freed from servitude. The only thing you have to do now is try to have a good time."

Vala forced a chuckle and made an expression she feared was more grimace than grin. "Yes. I shall certainly endeavor to enjoy myself."

Athen smiled and pulled the doors shut behind him, leaving Vala amid the finery. She looked around at the hanging dresses, but all she could see were the shattered remains of their plan. She sighed heavily, let her shoulders slump, and pushed her hair out of her face.

"Well. Bugger."

Daniel dropped the rods and tried to catch his breath, looking down at his hands before shaking out his arms. He turned as Sam and Teal'c dismounted from the carriage. "We're, uh, taking a different way back to the Stargate, right?"

Teal'c said, "If all goes to plan, we shall require a much faster escape than is possible with this method of conveyance." He noticed the al'kesh displayed behind the house. "Perhaps that vessel can be put to use."

"Good. Fantastic. I like vessels. Vessels are… vessels are good." Daniel frowned and rubbed his shoulder. "Wait, are you saying I was slow? That thing wasn't exactly light, you know. And with you and Sam weighing it down —"

"Excuse me?" Sam said in her Goa'uld timbre. "What exactly do you mean I was 'weighing it down'?"

"Mostly him. Muscle mass and…" He gave up and waved them off, sighing with exhaustion as he wiped his brow. "Forget it. As long as we're not doing it again, I'll be fine."

Sam patted Daniel on the back with a smile. She walked between him and Teal'c to the front entrance. She knew it was Wyrrick's house, but it certainly felt more like visiting a museum or some sort of concert hall. It had looked big on the UAV but in person the place was immense. She quashed the rising fear that they wouldn't even be able to find the pedestal amid all of Wyrrick's collections. If push came to shove, they could take extreme measures to make sure they didn't leave empty handed. One man's hurt feelings didn't matter when compared to the lives of every Jaffa in the universe.

The doors opened and Wyrrick stepped out to greet them. He smiled, showing a perfect row of shining white teeth. He looked like a college football star gone to seed, a has-been who refused to acknowledge his muscles had given way to fat years ago. He clapped his hands together and bowed slightly from the waist.

"Callisto!"

"Master Wyrrick. Thank you for inviting me to your event."

"The honor is mine. It is wonderful to at last make your acquaintance. And Teal'c. It is an honor to welcome such an esteemed name into my home. I'm glad to see you've come to your senses. Surely such a seismic shift could not have come easily." He eyed Sam suspiciously. "Callisto must be quite the persuasive queen."

Sam arched an eyebrow. "Perhaps if today goes well, I can arrange for you to examine the device which made my victory possible."

Wyrrick smiled knowingly. "Aha. I should have known. I had heard that Ba'al was exploring mind control technology, but I never dreamed he would share it so early in its development."

Sam lifted her chin and affected what she hoped was a haughty look. "I know nothing of Ba'al's research. My work is my own."

Wyrrick placed a hand on his chest and bowed his head forward in apology. "I did not mean to offend. To sway so obstinate a mind... I shall raise a toast to you this evening, Mistress Callisto."

Sam bowed her head. Teal'c only offered a smile and bowed his head in acknowledgement.

Wyrrick looked at Daniel. "And the lo'taur. Wiggum, you said his name was?"

"Indeed," Sam said.

"So long as he remembers his place." He held his glare on Daniel a moment longer, then looked at Sam again. "Enough of that. This is a celebration, after all. Please, come inside."

Sam nodded slightly and, with a sideways glance at Teal'c and Daniel, she crossed her arms behind her back and stepped into Wyrrick's home.

CHAPTER EIGHTEEN

DANIEL and Teal'c had refrained from donning their masks until they were actually in the party. Daniel wore a small harlequin mask that reminded him of the Lone Ranger, while Teal'c had a more elaborate feathered piece that served to conceal his golden marking. They passed through a receiving area decorated with potted plants and extraordinarily elaborate artworks. The double doors to the main ballroom were open and the team paused to examine the crowd of disguised attendees.

Daniel adjusted the strap of his mask, then tucked his thumbs into his belt to prevent further fiddling. "We're not supposed to mingle, are we?"

"Don't look at me," Sam said, still wincing every time she heard her own voice. "I've never exactly been the life of many parties. I'm usually in the corner somewhere reading spines on the host's bookshelf." She looked at Teal'c, who was carefully scanning the crowd. "See anyone you recognize? Sorry. That's kind of a silly question to ask at a masquerade party."

"Obscuring one's face does little to conceal identity if you are trained to look deeper. There are several people here familiar to me. And despite my disguise I have noticed several of them recognizing me. In order to maintain our ruse, I may have to continually avow that I have broken with the people of Earth and with the Jaffa." He grimaced. "I do not expect this to be an easy task."

Sam said, "The people who matter will never believe those words coming from you. You're doing it for the greater good of your people. Just remember that when the going gets tough."

He bowed his head in thanks.

"Okay. Let's spread out and see if we can find Kali's treasure. It's probably not going to be easy to get the pedestal out of here without drawing attention to ourselves, so I'd like to know where it is as early as possible. And let's try not to draw attention to ourselves."

"Inconspicuous. Right." Daniel nodded and moved off to the right, while Teal'c strode confidently into the crowd to begin his subterfuge. Sam adjusted the veil so that it sat higher on the bridge of her nose, then squared her shoulders and set off to explore.

Vala chose a dress that would still allow her to run if necessary, a dark green thing that hung off one shoulder and left the other bare. It came with black gloves which would be helpful. Some planets were starting to keep track of fingermarks, and she didn't want hers on anyone's file. She had made certain that she touched as many surfaces as possible during her impromptu tour, but there was still a chance that they would end up somewhere incriminating. She felt it was better to take the precaution than worry about than leaving her mark on a security pad somewhere. Wyrrick had provided a mask that covered her entire face except for a small half-moon at the bottom to leave her chin free. She adjusted it until the eyeholes lined up properly and brushed her hair forward over the edges to hang down on either side of her face.

She stepped out of the changing room and saw that Wyrrick had just arrived. He was wearing a white double-breasted jacket over red pants, his hands also covered by gloves. He held his mask in his hands, but Vala could see that when he put it on it would cover everything but his lips and eyes. Vala forced a smile and held her hands out to the side so he could see the dress she'd chosen.

"I hope you approve of the outfit."

"It looks magnificent on you, Miss Oshin."

"Oh, please, call me Kaori. After all, I'm supposed to be your date, aren't I?"

He smiled. "Of course. And you must call me Dys."

She inclined her head in acknowledgement as he donned his

disguise. The few moments he couldn't see her, Vala twisted her features into an expression of frustration, crossing her eyes and sticking her tongue out before composing herself. The front of Wyrrick's mask was painted gold, with flecks of white and silver along the edges to draw the eyes up. It gave the impression he was even taller than he was, and Vala hated how it made her feel inferior to him. She compensated by standing a little straighter as she offered him her arm.

"I trust Madame Ai wasn't terribly put out by my request. I provided her with the most respected chef in the village to take your place."

"Oh, I'm certain she'll make do," Vala said. "In the meantime, I'm very excited about the party! It's been far too long since I attended a party I could actually enjoy."

He tightened his arm around hers. "Just stick by my side, Kaori, and I'll make sure you get the most out of today."

Vala chuckled without humor as she was led out of the changing room. Somehow she doubted his assessment; the only way she would get anything out of the party would be if she could get out from under his gaze. Based on how fervently he was holding her arm she had a feeling that would be easier said than done.

Tanis knew Vala would chide her if she killed the woman Wyrrick had sent to help her in the kitchen. It was a simple enough solution; just a quick blow to the head, hide the body somewhere dark, and tell anyone who asked about her that she was out gathering more ingredients. But her time with Vala had taught her that killing wasn't always the best solution to her problems, so she forced herself to consider alternatives. The woman was named Timony, a native of the nearby village and a chef so well-regarded that the wait staff seemed cowed by her mere presence. She was a tall woman, over six feet, and she wore an all-purple outfit with her name embroidered on the chest. Her hair was tri-colored, black mixed with white and blue, and she wore it in a strange complicated braid that hung over her right shoulder.

Tanis introduced herself as Ai Okano and welcomed Timony to her kitchen. Timony's response was a derisive snort and an arched eyebrow as she scanned the food she and Vala had already prepared. She dipped a spoon into a bowl of broth, brought it to her lips, and slurped. The lines of her face deepened in distaste, and she sputtered her lips quietly as she returned the spoon to the counter.

"You prepared meals for Lord Yu? It is difficult to believe he survived so long in a single host without succumbing to food poisoning. This kitchen is a travesty. It is the mess hall of an amateur playing at gourmet." She put her hands on her stomach as if she was going to be physically ill. "I can only imagine what the rest of this trash tastes like."

The knives called to Tanis. She ignored their siren song and kept her voice steady. "Lord Yu was a great admirer of my food."

"Then the man had no taste."

Tanis kept one hand behind her back, digging her nails into her palms. It would be so easy to take the condescending wench into the supply room and quiet her once and for all. Instead she took a deep breath, smiled, and let the tension fade from her muscles. The solution came to her in a flash, and it was simple enough that she was angry at herself for envisioning homicide first. Her hand relaxed. Her breathing slowed, and when she spoke her voice was calm.

"I was moments away from preparing the main dish. It's quite complicated, so I'll have to ask you to stay out of my way."

Timony's eyes flashed. "Stay out of your way…?"

"This is my kitchen, and I will not have you ruining my *rey-alee* with *inaro* sauce."

Timony laughed. "You must be having delusions! You think you can pull off a complicated meal like that for a crowd this large?"

"I could do it with my eyes closed."

"You would fail. And I will not have my name associated with failure on that scale."

Tanis shrugged. "Very well. I will inform Wyrrick that you won't be assisting today…"

"You will do no such thing." Timony examined the counter and sighed. "You will be assisting me. If this is to be done, it will be done correctly. But not with the garbage I have here." She picked up one of the tools, sneered at it, and dropped it. "I left my tools in town because I foolishly believed Wyrrick hired professionals. Clearly I was mistaken. You will retrieve them while I attempt to recover from the incipient disaster you have created here."

Tanis said, "You can't simply take over my kitchen!"

"This is my kitchen now. And I have given you an assignment. You should be thanking me. The credit for this meal will go to you, and you'll do none of the work. Now run along and hurry back."

"I will not stand for this," Tanis said, her voice trembling with unshed tears. She spun on her heel, stormed from the kitchen, and broke into a smile as soon as she was in the hallway. The odds were good that Timony wouldn't care much if Tanis never returned with the supplies; the assignment to retrieve them was obviously just a ploy to get rid of the irritant. Tanis unbuttoned her shirt and shrugged out of it, hoping her underclothes looked fancy enough to pass for formal wear.

Freed from her duties in the kitchen, her next job was to find a mask so she could blend in with the rest of the partygoers. She dumped her chef smock in the first trash receptacle she passed and went to join the party.

Sam watched as Wyrrick led a brunette woman in a green dress out into the crowd. Once she was sure he hadn't seen her, she slipped out through the same door the host had just used. Multiple rooms branched off the corridor, and she tried to act inconspicuous as she walked past each open door and peered inside. A few people were touring the collections, but Sam only needed a couple of seconds to identify which Goa'uld each treasure belonged to. If it didn't have Kali's mark, she moved on.

Finally she found the room she was looking for. She looked over her shoulder to make sure no one was paying undue attention to her as she stepped inside. It was all the typical Goa'uld excess, golden everything and self-indulgent carvings, and it wasn't long before she found the pedestal Nicia had described to them. It shared the design of a dial-home-device, only being tall and slender rather than short and stocky. She put her hand on top of the device and pushed it just enough to get an idea of its weight, and the pedestal shifted easily on its oblong base. The other guests were moving too slowly to have reached Kali's room, so Sam stepped behind the pedestal and crouched down. If she could figure out how the pedestal worked, there was a chance she could duplicate it without actually stealing the physical object.

The back came off without much difficulty and she set it aside. The guts of the device were like most Goa'uld tech she'd come across in the past few years, and she was confident she could at least get an inkling of how it came together. The main console would operate much as a DHD, only it spoke to the receiving dialer to input the next address. It operated like dominoes; the pedestal would disable the first device, which would in turn disable the next device, and the next, and the next, on down the line.

"So maybe we just have to figure out what this does to cause that first domino to fall," Sam whispered. She bent down, angling her head forward so she could see into the shell of the machine. She had just reached up into the control systems when she heard the doors to the treasure room click shut.

She had two options; she could confront whoever had just joined her, or she could expose herself and try explaining why she had taken apart the pedestal. Then again, there was the third option of simply ducking out of sight. Hiding seemed like it would be the better part of valor so she tucked her legs against her chest, pulled one of the cast-aside drop cloths over her head and shoulders, and hoped no one looked too closely at the space behind the pedestal.

Tanis closed the doors to the Kali room and began a mental countdown. She had watched the guests and came up with a conservative estimate for how quickly they were moving from one room to the next. If she was right, she had three minutes before anyone got this far. She had worked on tighter timetables. She turned and examined the wealth spread out in front of her. Soon Timony would start sending out servers with covered trays of hors d'oeuvres, and she wanted to be prepared to fill the empties with as much as she could and as quickly as she could.

She started with a large golden globe near the door. It was set in a wooden framework and she had to strain to get the whole thing moved even a foot. Once it was out of the way, she replaced it with smaller, more easily moved items such as jewelry, coins... she tried not to count the coins as she moved them, but she still got a rough idea of how much there was. Her estimate was enough to make her hands sweat, so she rubbed them against her trousers as she looked for more items that would be easy to move. Braziers, golden bowls, a knife with a hilt engraved with golden fleur-de-lis... she moved the bowls closer to the door, and glanced at an unusually ornate pedestal that was standing near one wall.

It definitely wasn't one of the 'easy to move' items, but it was certainly eye-catching. If it was closer to the door people would be less likely to notice the rest of the room. It would offer her a little misdirection if it was placed in a more central spot. She checked her mental chronometer and moved toward the pedestal to see if it was light enough to be moved.

CHAPTER NINETEEN

THE AIRMAN standing guard unlocked the door to the holding cells and followed Morello inside. Kali was standing on the other side of the bars, looking oddly vulnerable in her standard-issue jumpsuit. It would have been easy to forget that this woman, who was actually a few inches shorter than Morello due to her plain white sneakers, was a Goa'uld. Morello forced that fact to the front of her mind as she stood before the cell, feigning disinterest while mentally counting down the hours they had left before the device was activated.

"I was told you asked to see me."

"I did." Kali said. "Tell me the name of someone you've lost."

Morello frowned. "Someone I've lost?"

"How long have you fought for the Tau'ri?"

"If you're asking how long I've been a member of the SGC, two years."

"And in that time, have you lost any friends or loved ones on the other side of the Chappa'ai?"

Morello nodded slowly. "Yes. Of course. We all have."

"Name one."

Morello tried to determine if the Goa'uld was feeling out a vulnerable spot, something she could use for future manipulation. Answering was a judgment call, one she would have to make for herself.

"I wouldn't call her a friend, but Dr. Janet Fraiser meant a great deal to me."

"Why?"

Morello knew she was risking a lot by opening up, but she also knew rewards required risk. "Two years ago, I didn't believe in aliens. I worked my whole life to get to this point and when I got here, I found out that everything I believed was wrong. One day I was a good Catholic girl, the next I was fighting false gods." She chuckled, momentarily lost in the memory. "It was terrifying. I was paralyzed with fear before my first mission. We have these medical examinations before we go through the gate, and Dr. Fraiser was clearing me for duty. I guess she sensed how nervous I was because she sat on the bed next to me, took my hand, and told me it was okay to be freaked out. She said everyone's minds got blown open by the Stargate, and the important thing was to just keep focused on the job at hand.

"She didn't cheerlead. She didn't tell me she knew I was going to be great, because she didn't know me yet. She didn't assure me it would all be okay because she couldn't have known that. What she said was that I'd made it this far, so I belonged here. As long as I remembered to breathe, I would be fine. She gave me the confidence I needed to focus on the mission. Since then, every time I stand there and watch the Stargate dial, I hear her voice in my head saying 'Just breathe.'"

Kali said, "What became of her?"

"She… died. About a year later. She was tending to a patient in the field, and a Jaffa killed her."

"And yet you go to these lengths to defend the people who killed your friend? The Jaffa responsible for Janet Fraiser's death may yet live. Your efforts here may be saving the life of her executioner. How can you possibly abide that?"

Morello said, "Because it's the right thing to do. The Jaffa have always been victims of the Goa'uld. They were foot soldiers who were conditioned to fight against the enemies of their enslavers. They did it because they had no other options. Even if they weren't, I couldn't stand idly by while an entire race of people were wiped out of existence no matter who they were or what they'd done. I know that if Janet Fraiser came back today, she would be right here with me trying to convince you to help us. Because we don't ask why we should save people. We ask how. That's what makes us different from the Goa'uld."

Kali held eye contact with Morello as if daring her to look away. Finally she lifted her chin, exhaled through her nose and said, "I will help you in exchange for my release."

Morello tried not to betray her excitement. "I'm not sure General O'Neill will go along with that arrangement."

"Those are my terms."

"I'll let him know."

She turned and walked out, standing in the corridor as the airman locked the door behind her. She turned to him. "What the heck just happened in there?"

"I'd say you just won a staring contest with a Goa'uld, ma'am."

"Right." After a moment she allowed herself a grin. "Yeah, I think you're right. Okay. I guess I should go report to General O'Neill."

She suppressed her giddiness as she walked to the elevator. There was still a chance the general could refuse Kali's terms. Releasing a Goa'uld into the wild wasn't as dangerous as it would have been a year ago, but there were still plenty of reasons to hold onto her. And even if he did agree to let her go, it would all be for naught if SG-1 didn't manage to find and retrieve the pedestal from Kali's palace. Once she was in the elevator she put her hands behind her back so anyone else who got on wouldn't notice she was crossing her fingers.

Tanis had just touched the sides of the pedestal to see how difficult it would be to lift when she was interrupted by a noise near the door. She took her hands off the treasure and looked for a hiding place, but nothing presented itself. The door opened and she reached for the knife she'd taken from the kitchen and tucked into the waistband of her trousers. The hilt pressed reassuringly against the small of her back, and she wrapped her fingers around the warm leather as one of the guests came inside and closed the door behind him. He wore a harlequin mask that barely disguised his features, and she saw his blue eyes widen through the holes when he saw her.

"Oh." He looked left and right, then focused on her again. "I was looking for someone else. Ah. Sorry."

Tanis smiled and sauntered closer, within striking range if the man was less bumbling than he appeared. "Sneaking away for a little tryst with another guest?"

He was silent for a long moment, then said, "Yes. Exactly. I, uh, thought she was going to meet me here, but apparently our signals got crossed…"

Tanis moved to the left to sidestep the man so he was no longer between her and the exit. "Or maybe you were just a little eager and she hasn't arrived yet." She suggestively raised one eyebrow. "I won't tell anyone you're in here if you want to wait for her to show up."

"Thank you. That's, uh, that's very kind of you."

Tanis offered him a wink as she slipped out of the room, her smile fading as soon as she was out of sight. The lovebirds would be frightened away when the other guests began filtering in. Still, her trip hadn't been wasted. There was plenty of wealth near the door where it could be easily grabbed, and she'd gotten a sense of the room's dimensions. She was confident that when the time came she would be able to get in and load up a tray or a cart without wasting too much time.

She stopped in the doorway of the party and tried to spot Vala in the crowd. Her view was momentarily blocked by a redheaded woman disguised as a symbiote, but she saw enough to convince her that Vala wasn't present in the room. Hopefully wherever she was, her actions were furthering their cause. Tanis wasn't terribly worried about her partner. If anyone could evade the affections of Dysmas Wyrrick, it was Vala.

As soon as the woman was gone, Daniel turned to scan the room. "Sam? Are you here?"

"Right here." She rose from behind the pedestal. "I was trying to get a look at how it was put together in case we have to MacGyver something back at the base." She looked around the room and narrowed her eyes. "Did the woman in here look like she worked for Wyrrick?"

"I don't think so. Why?"

"She was moving everything around. I had to go by what I could hear, but it sounded like she was rearranging everything at random."

Daniel looked around to see if he could spot a pattern. "Huh. Everything near the front of the room is small, easy to move."

"Easier to steal." He looked at her and she shrugged. "I worked a couple of retail jobs in high school. The manager told me that anything small that was stocked near the door was just asking to be stolen. Whoever that was, she's stacking the deck." She narrowed her eyes and tilted her head to the side. "Did you recognize her?"

"No. Should I have?"

"I don't know. Something about her voice seemed familiar. I can't place it, but I could have sworn I've heard it before."

Daniel searched his memory. "She was wearing a mask, but she didn't strike me as at all familiar."

"Probably just hearing things," Sam said.

"Well, whoever she is, we may have competition. If someone is targeting Kali's treasure, they could take the pedestal before we have a chance."

Sam pursed her lips. "That might not be a bad thing. There's an exit to the exterior of the building nearby, isn't there? I think I saw it when I came in." Daniel nodded. "Okay, so. It stands to reason they have some sort of getaway car waiting. Or it's probably a ship."

"Yes, and…?"

"And," Sam shrugged, "a ship is easier to rob than a party filled with security officers. We just have to make sure we can either get on board before it takes off or find a way to track it once it's gone." She looked at the pedestal. "And we have to make sure they take this. Give me a hand."

In less than a minute they had lifted off the heavy pedestal top from its base. She gestured for one of the tarps that lay folded in the corner and wrapped it around the two pieces. Outside the door she spotted an unattended catering cart, brought it in and helped Daniel lift the pedestal onto it. Sam assumed the thieves would look under the tarp, see gold, and take it just because it was conveniently mobile.

"You realize we could just be setting ourselves up for another wild goose chase across the galaxy?"

"We'll just have to make sure they don't get very far with it. You know what one of them looks like. We'll have Teal'c keep watch for her to make a move on the treasure."

"Okay. While he's doing that, I actually came to find you because we may have a bigger problem."

Sam raised her eyebrows. "That would be impressive."

He tilted his head quizzically. "Yes, but we're us."

"Right. Bigger problems are our stock in trade. Lead the way."

"Teal'c."

He cringed at the voice, fortunately facing away from the Goa'uld that had spoken. He recognized the voice so he was prepared when he turned around to see Morrigan gliding through the crowd toward him. In lieu of a mask, she had disguised herself by painting her face jade green and applying a row of feathers down the sides of her neck to give the appearance of fins. He recognized it as japing the vague appearance of a mature Goa'uld symbiote, and the sight turned his stomach almost as much as Morrigan did. She smiled, showing her teeth as she circled him.

"I would never have imagined encountering you here. You, of all people... the Jaffa who led so many of his people into slaughter at the hands of their brothers. And now that they have the freedom they fought so foolishly for, you abandon them?"

"My Queen Callisto has taught me the error of my ways."

"Yes, the mental conditioning," Morrigan said softly. "I've tested those waters myself, but the process is hardly foolproof.

In my experience, a strong mind can resist what it believes to be a distasteful lie no matter how it is delivered. But I seem to recall another instance where your loyalty was shattered with very little effort. You turned your back on your Tau'ri friends and scurried back to once again serve Apophis. For all of your legend, the truth is that you are a weak-willed disgrace, Teal'c of Chulak."

He fought his initial instinct, the rage that insisted he respond with the truth. "I have found the truth after years of searching."

"And that truth is Callisto?" She scoffed and looked around the room as if to see whether the object of her derision was nearby. "She is a half-rate goddess, a joke among the System Lords. Has she regaled you with the story of how long she spent with a bear as her host? She was kept as a pet by Artemis, another minor Goa'uld, until she proved so pitiful that her captor let her go. That is the singular true god you chose to follow after years of fighting for your freedom?"

"Indeed. She lacks a quality I've found often overwhelms the personalities of false gods."

Morrigan raised a ginger eyebrow. "And what is that?"

"Hubris. Vainglorious arrogance."

Morrigan's smug smile crumbled, and her eyes turned hard. "Your brother Jaffa would do well to surrender themselves, Teal'c. One day this will all be but a footnote in the glorious history of the Goa'uld, and people will tremble when they think of the idiocy your people demonstrated by—"

Teal'c held up his hand to stop her. "One thing has not changed. I shall never again have to bear the pompous diatribes of a false god." He inclined his head and stepped around her. O'Neill would surely have prompted him to nudge her shoulder as he passed, but Teal'c did not feel she was worthy even of that minor indignity. He left her fuming and refrained from looking back. He did not care if she was angry, for now it no longer mattered. She was a false god without an army to do her bidding, a toothless dictator whose delusions of grandeur now fell on deaf ears.

He caught sight of Samantha Carter and Daniel Jackson and cut through the crowd to intercept them. Daniel saw him and changed course so that they met halfway.

Sam reached under her collar to deactivate her voice modulator as she approached. Teal'c did not know if she did it because she saw he had just been speaking to a Goa'uld or if she was just weary of hearing herself sound like one. Whatever her reasoning, it was a relief to hear her true voice when she spoke. "We've found the pedestal."

"That is indeed good news."

"Yeah, so we've established it's here." Daniel looked around. "The problem is that we think someone else is trying to steal it. There's a woman, she's wearing a sleeveless white blouse with lace trim and a horned mask. She has black hair, about Sam's height, could have some sort of weapon tucked into the back of her belt." He caught Sam's look and shrugged. "I saw her reaching for something, but her arm relaxed when she determined I wasn't a threat. Anyway, the pedestal is on a cart in the last treasure room in the corridor. If you see her moving it from there, follow her."

"I shall remain vigilant."

"Thank you," Daniel said. "Meanwhile I may have found something upstairs that could complicate our plans. I was just about to take Sam to confirm."

"Do you require assistance?"

"No. We should probably minimize the amount of time we spend together in a group. We don't want anyone wondering what we're up to. Keep an eye out for Wyrrick. If you see him heading for the stairs, try to send up a warning."

Sam tapped her bag. "Two bursts of static on the radio."

"I wish you stealth," Teal'c said.

Sam nodded her thanks and followed Daniel through the crowd to the spiral staircase. "I just stumbled over this while

I was getting the lay of the land," he said. "I was hoping there was some kind of alternate exit, or maybe somewhere we could stash the pedestal so we could come back for it at a less conspicuous time, but instead I found this."

They had arrived at a doorway at the end of the second floor landing. Sam checked to make sure they weren't visible from the ballroom below before she looked at the markings Daniel indicated.

"I'm not a hundred percent sure, but depending on which Slavic language this originally branched off from, I'm fairly certain this says it's an armory."

"Oh, boy," Sam muttered. "Well, he does have a security force to protect his collections. It stands to reason they might need to store weapons on the grounds."

Daniel nodded. "I just thought it would set my mind at ease if we could actually get a look inside. Unfortunately, the door is locked. So I was hoping…"

"What, that I could pick an alien lock?" She bent forward and looked at the keyhole. "There's no guarantee the mechanisms will be anything like what I'm used to." She sighed. "But where's the fun if there's no challenge? Keep an eye out."

Daniel moved a bit further away so he could watch the stairs. Sam got down on one knee in front of the door and examined the locking mechanism. There were only so many ways to craft a lock-and-key mechanism. She had tripped tumblers in Goa'uld motherships and she'd found ways to get around the security in a half dozen dungeons throughout the galaxy. She took off her veil, threaded one of the hooks away from the cloth, and bent it until she had a hook. She turned the other end into a rake, and eased them into the keyhole. The wire was just sturdy enough for her to get a feel for the lock's set-up, but she became less hopeful the more she explored.

"Daniel, I don't think I'm…" The lock suddenly snapped, and she leaned back in case her fumbling had set off some sort of security measure. Nothing happened, so she tentatively twisted the knob and pushed the door. "It's open."

"Well done," Daniel said.

"I don't think I did it."

"As long as it's open, last person to touch it gets the credit."

Sam decided they had spent the past week jumping from one place to the next to find the pedestal, so maybe the universe decided they were owed a little luck. She stood up, twisted the wire back into place, and held her veil rather than putting it back on. She and Daniel stepped into the room, and he swept his palm over a half-globe embedded in the wall. The room slowly filled with light, revealing its contents. Five rows of shelves were loaded with various Goa'uld weaponry, including ribbon devices and pain sticks. Racks of staff weapons stood along the wall like rigid plant stalks growing from the floor.

"Holy Hannah," Sam whispered.

Daniel moved closer to one of the shelves and opened a box. He picked up a small circular object Sam recognized as a tak energy weapon. "I suppose this could just be… excess? In order to get the treasure, Wyrrick decided to take the weapons that were lying around as well?"

Sam shook her head. "He calls this his armory for a reason. This is a deliberate accumulation of weapons."

"So Wyrrick isn't just an eccentric rich man…"

"He's an eccentric rich man who is putting together his own private army."

CHAPTER TWENTY

JACK wondered if whoever claimed history didn't repeat itself ever got the sound kick in the pants they deserved. He stood in his office after dismissing Morello, having been briefed on her conversation with Kali, and he couldn't believe he was in the same position Hammond had been in almost four years earlier. Nirrti had been a guest of their establishment, and she too offered to help them in return for her immediate release. At the time, a child's life had been at stake and Jack hadn't seen the point of debating. His stance was that Cassandra's life overshadowed any benefit they might get from keeping a Goa'uld in a cage.

It should be just as easy now. Kali was offering her help to save every Jaffa in the galaxy. When she was captured, she'd been hiding in the defunct temple of an associate System Lord. She was a homeless wretch without any real power, and she was at best a few years away from being captured and killed anyway. Jack didn't see any downside to agreeing with her terms.

But it wasn't always as simple as yes or no. At the time, Teal'c had been against letting Nirrti go. The life of one person didn't compare to the countless lives at stake with a Goa'uld running free. Would Teal'c feel differently now that his people were the ones under the sword? And if so, could Jack take his vote as unbiased and unaffected by emotion? And as it turned out, Teal'c had been right about Nirrti being a threat. Less than a year later she had turned up again, back to her old tricks, and her genetic meddling had nearly destroyed an entire village of people.

He had General Hammond's number. He could call, run the situation by him, see what advice he had. But no. The second he did that, he would be doing it for every decision he had to make.

Whatever he decided about Kali, he would have to justify it to the people upstairs. He not only had to decide what he thought was right, he had to make a decision he was willing to fight for and defend. When he boiled it down to that, the decision was pretty much made for him. He left his office and discovered Morello was leaning against the wall across from his door. She straightened up when he appeared, but he waved at her to relax.

"Captain. What are you doing loitering out here?"

She clasped her hands behind her back and focused wide, unblinking eyes on him. "I wanted to hear your decision as soon as possible, sir. Not that… I'm rushing you or anything. Oh, God. I didn't mean…"

"Stand down, Morello," Jack said. "I've made my decision. And since you're the one who negotiated it, you should be the one to break the news to her."

Morello wet her lips and swallowed, all but bouncing on the balls of her feet. "The news, sir?"

"Tell Kali we have a deal. If SG-1 gets back with the pedestal, we'll let her go in exchange for shutting down the machine."

She smiled. "Excellent decision, sir!" Her eyes widened. "I mean, I'm sure whatever decision you made would be the right one, even if I didn't happen to agree with it." She furrowed her brow. "Oh, God."

"Relax, Morello." He patted her shoulder gingerly. "Just relax. You might want to take a moment before you go visit Kali. We don't like the Goa'uld to see us giddy."

"Of course not, sir." She took a deep breath and slowly let it out. "Thank you, General."

"Don't thank me. You're the one who did all the heavy lifting."

Morello smiled again and turned, trying to keep a measured walking pace on her way to the elevator. Jack's amusement at her eagerness faded as soon as she was out of sight. All he had done was agree to release a narcissistic maniac in the hopes she would help them prevent a genocide. It may have been the best option, but it would be a long time before he convinced himself it was a good one.

Vala let Wyrrick spirit her away from the party, fervently trying to deflect his wandering hands without appearing violent. As they got farther away from the sounds of the crowd, the more determined his explorations became. They were ostensibly on another tour of the house, this time one that would take her to the 'more private corners' of Wyrrick's little kingdom. Vala hoped it would provide opportunities to get rid of him without causing undue attention to herself, but those hopes were becoming slimmer with each passing second.

She was near panic when she realized they were on a path that would end at his bedroom. She'd certainly done more distasteful things for the purpose of a job, but the thought of going behind closed doors with Wyrrick made her stomach twist. She looked for anything, any possible escape from his pawing mitts, and her chances were dwindling when she spotted what appeared to be a large, complex art piece in one of the rooms down the hall from his bedchambers.

"Ooh, this looks fascinating." She squirmed out of his reach and trotted into the room, forcing him to follow. "What is this?"

"That is my tranquility grotto. You turn on the light and..."

He used a remote control to activate it, and a stream of shimmering light washed over the shape of the statue, then shot up toward the ceiling in a solid stream. It flooded across every available surface until Vala felt submerged by the glow. Far from tranquility, however, she felt a surge of panic. She knew a part of Qetesh had been left behind, some trace element that allowed her to use Goa'uld technology, and she had faith that would be enough to keep her from suffering any ill effects from the light. But she couldn't help but think about the guests, not to mention Tanis.

"This room, um... is... shielded. Correct?"

"Yes." Wyrrick's voice was already distant, his head tilted

back to watch the flow. "The builders insisted upon it, although they… I… took pains to make sure it… wasn't addictive. Why do you… ask?" He chuckled. "Why what? Wait. Did you say something…?"

Vala had seen the light matrix holograms before. Goa'uld used them, but didn't feel the effects of its radiation thanks to their symbiotes. Any human exposed to it for even a short amount of time quickly became addicted to the buzz. Hopefully the room was shielded well enough that she and Tanis wouldn't have to worry about it when they left. It seemed like the sort of thing a host should mention before inviting someone to spend the night.

"I mean honestly," Vala muttered, "who has a light matrix just lying around?"

Wyrrick said, "Honest…"

Vala leaned in close to his face, squinted, and said, "Wyrrick, I believe you are about to be robbed. What do you think you should do about that?"

Wyrrick blinked dumbly, never taking his focus off the light.

"Huh. Okay… Wyrrick, darling… where exactly is your security shut-off?"

"In the bedroom. Nightstand. By the window."

She grinned. "Fantastic. Enjoy the light show." She took the remote from his limp fingers and, after a moment, figured out how to turn it up. The light became thick and nearly solid, and Wyrrick made a guttural sound of approval in his throat. His eyes widened and he swayed on his feet as Vala left the room. She hurried down the hallway to his bedroom, the very place she had moments earlier been fighting tooth and nail to avoid. It was odd how priorities shifted…

She crouched next to the bed and found the security master panel. She turned it on and took a moment to familiarize herself with its functions. Tanis was really more of the tech genius, and Vala couldn't figure out how to pinpoint a single door to disable its locks. She scrolled through the options and discovered a way that she could simply shut down all the locks on every door in the building. Well, that was fine. Never knew when a locked door would stand between victory and defeat. She deactivated the locks and almost immediately a room on the second floor lit up with an unauthorized entrance.

"Not my problem," Vala muttered as she closed the control panel and stood up. She hurried from the room, glancing into the tranquility grotto as she hurried past. Wyrrick hadn't moved from where she'd left him. "Dysmas? Dear? Still… yeah, you're still… okay." She continued down the hallway.

She wasn't sure how wide their window was, but she was fairly certain it would start closing before she was ready.

Teal'c kept to the corners of the ballroom, scanning the crowd with apparent disinterest. He had seen the horned mask Daniel Jackson indicated, and he had been tracking the woman through the crowd. There was something vaguely familiar about her, the way she moved and the square of her shoulders touched on a memory, but he couldn't bring it to the fore. He had a feeling he had seen this woman somewhere before, somewhere outdoors and hot. He had no doubt that if their previous encounter mattered, it would come to him in time. For now he followed Colonel Carter's orders and slipped through the crowd as nonchalantly as possible, keeping the thief at the very edge of his sight line. She made a show of mingling, pausing to eavesdrop on conversations or to examine a snack tray, but Teal'c quickly determined she was making her way toward the treasure rooms.

The big Jaffa was tracking her. Tanis pretended to peruse an offering of sliced meat snacks before waving it off. She couldn't see the Jaffa's emblem because of his mask, but she couldn't shake the feeling she'd seen him before. Given the attention he was affording her, he recognized her as well. She tried to think of all the Jaffa she had lied to, scammed, or otherwise left with a grudge, but none of them matched the hulk eyeing her like she was his prey. She kept her face turned away despite her mask, eager to escape his gaze so she could get the job underway. The quicker she and Vala were away from this party, the better.

She stepped out into the corridor and saw Vala at the other end of the hall. They signaled to each other with quick, furtive motions of their hands.

Someone recognizes me was a sideways cut of her hand, then flashing her fingers in front of her face.

Great going was two raised index fingers with a sarcastic grin.

Tanis gestured something less than kind, then *Where's your date?*

Vala rolled her head back on her shoulders, eyes closed and tongue sticking out the corner of her mouth. Whether that meant dead or, for some reason, asleep at his own party, Tanis didn't care.

Moving now.

Too early!

Too bad!

Vala harrumphed. *Okay. Move it.*

Tanis ran to the treasure room and, after a quick glance into the ballroom, Vala followed her.

Daniel followed Sam downstairs, and they paused at the threshold of the party. "This is supposed to be neutral ground, right? Leave your grievances at the door, we're all just here to have a good time?"

"That was the gist of the invitation, yes."

He nodded and gestured at her collar. Sam grimaced and activated the voice modulator again. Daniel started across the floor and she followed. They had just crossed paths with a redheaded woman with fins glued to the side of her face when Sam was startled by Daniel suddenly turning to face her. He kept his head down and his eyes averted as would befit someone of his supposed station.

"Milady, I do not wish to speak out of turn, but surely this is cause for some alarm."

Sam tried to think of the best response, finally baring her teeth and leaning in close. "We will not speak of it here!"

"But if Wyrrick lured us here under false pretenses, we cannot remain another moment! Your life may be at risk."

The redheaded woman had turned toward them.

"I am certain he has a reasonable explanation for what we saw."

"What exactly did you see?" the other Goa'uld said. She sidled closer, lips lifted in a forced expression of disinterest.

Daniel looked at her and then quickly away. "Lady Morrigan. I was speaking with my mistress."

"In a public forum," Morrigan said, "and on a topic that could affect everyone here. You say Wyrrick's intentions may be less than honorable?"

Sam said, "My lo'taur believes he has leave to speak freely. I shall disabuse him of this notion at once."

Morrigan held up a hand. "Let the man speak. What did you see?"

Daniel saw that they had gathered a small crowd. "I-I am unsure and I do not wish to besmirch a man so clearly revered as Master Wyrrick."

Morrigan looked at Sam. "Your man's loyalty is impressive. Order him to tell us what he knows or I shall teach him a lesson myself."

Sam looked at Daniel. "Tell them."

"A room," Daniel said without hesitation. "At the top of the stairs, there is a room filled with weapons. It makes me question why he gathered us all here, under one roof, under the auspices of peace while he has a stockpile just waiting to be utilized for violent purposes." He grabbed Sam's wrist. "Please, milady, we must leave at once."

Morrigan eyed the rest of the crowd, then looked toward the stairs. "Yes. We should all leave at once. It is only pertinent..."

She stepped away from them. Sam watched as she hurried from the ballroom, most likely seeking another way upstairs.

Sam hooked her arm around Daniel's and pulled him away. "Tell me you didn't do what I think you did."

"I have no idea what Wyrrick originally planned for those weapons, but I think in this case distribution of wealth would be a much better situation. Besides, if everyone starts scrambling for weapons, we'll have enough of a distraction to get away with the pedestal."

Sam didn't like it, but the wheels were already in motion. She could almost see the rumor spreading through the crowd like a game of Telephone. Teal'c made his way through the suddenly-lively crowd. "Colonel Carter, Daniel Jackson. The thief and her accomplice have made their move. Moments ago I witnessed them loading a cart onto their tel'tak. They are currently in the treasure room gathering more spoils. I believe the pedestal was indeed one of the items they removed."

Daniel said, "This could be our only chance to grab it before all hell breaks loose."

Sam nodded. It was better to get out before the fireworks started. "The thieves are still in the Kali treasure room?"

"Indeed," Teal'c said, looking back to make sure they hadn't slipped out in the past few seconds.

"Okay. Come on." She fished into her bag for her zat, pulling it out as they reached the treasure room. She caught a glimpse of two brunette women inside as the door clicked shut, and she stepped back to aim her weapon at the lock. She had gotten familiar enough with the mechanism upstairs to know that two blasts would be enough to twist the tumblers so the door would be extremely difficult to open. She nodded to Daniel and Teal'c and they led the way out the side door.

Teal'c ran to where the tel'tak was cloaked, its side entrance coming into view as if by magic as they rounded the far end. Sam looked back to make sure they weren't being followed. The glass windows of the ballroom were lit with random flashes she identified as staff blasts, and she winced at the havoc they were leaving in their wake. She didn't have room to feel guilty, however, as she dashed inside and hit the control panel to shut the door.

The cart from Kali's treasure room had been left near the back wall of the cockpit, and Daniel had pulled back the tarp to confirm the pedestal was still there. He looked at her and nodded once.

"We got it."

The pressure around Sam's chest suddenly relaxed and she took her first deep breath of the past few days. "Thank God." She looked at Teal'c and said, "Get us out of here. Lucia is relatively close. We can be there in a few hours, drop the ship off there, and then gate back to the SGC with the pedestal."

She walked to the copilot seat as Teal'c lifted off. Below, one of the large glass panes blew out of Wyrrick's front room and shattered on the lawn. Whatever was going on down there, it was no longer SG-1's problem. The pedestal was in their possession, and she had faith that they could figure out how to make it work even if Kali didn't cooperate. She looked back at Daniel, who was slumped against the back wall, and they shared a smile. It had been a long, exhausting road, but they were finally going home victorious.

CHAPTER TWENTY-ONE

JACK came into the gate room with Captain Morello in tow as the iris retracted and his team came through. He knew every team was technically his now, that he was the leader of everyone who walked through the gate, but SG-1 would always be close to his heart. Carter led the way, all of them still dressed for the party and looking none the worse for wear. Daniel and Teal'c had doffed their masks, and Sam had gotten rid of her veil. Jack's attention was more focused on what the men were carrying.

"Let me guess. Wyrrick had swag bags."

"Not that we saw, sir," Sam said. "We had to take something from one of his displays as a souvenir. Know anyone in the market for a golden pedestal?"

Jack grinned. "I think we could find a place for it. I actually have the perfect spot in my sun room. Well done."

Sam nodded in acknowledgement. "Now we just have to convince Kali to help us."

"Oh, didn't I mention when you radioed? Yeah, we sorted that whole thing out while you were rubbing elbows with the rich and snooty."

Daniel said, "You sorted it out."

"Yep."

"Convinced a Goa'uld to stop a plague."

"That's what we did."

"A plague that she herself set in motion."

Jack nodded. "That's the long and short of it. Actually, I can't take all the credit. Or even most of it." He looked at Morello. "I'm thinking of bringing the captain with me next time I have to buy a car. Apparently she is one hell of a negotiator."

"Wow," Daniel said. "Well done, Captain Morello."

Morello smiled, glanced shyly at Daniel and then quickly

looked at the pedestal he was holding. "Well, it wouldn't have meant anything without that."

Jack said, "Yes. And since we all got gold stars for today, what do you say we combine our victories and get this pedestal somewhere it can actually do some good. We're cutting it a little close." He turned to one of the airmen nearby. "Have the prisoner prepared for transport and get a MALP. Wouldn't want to just take her word that she's sending us somewhere safe."

"Yes sir."

Jack motioned for the team to follow him. "In the meantime, you can regale me with the behind-the-scenes of the party. I want to know everything— the fashions, the red carpet report, the whole glitz and glamour of the event..."

Wyrrick was finally dragged from his grotto by a disheveled and panicked Athen. He only vaguely remembered entering the room, and he had no idea what had happened to the lovely woman he'd been trying to impress. Athen had warned him about the risk of becoming addicted to the light, but until now he thought it had been useless worry. Apparently even without the chemical, the light was a dangerous mistress. Once he cleared the cobwebs from his mind he could hear the cacophony from the ballroom. He grabbed the lapel of Athen's coat, holding him awkwardly as they charged down the corridor. "What in blazes is going on?"

"Security systems were compromised, sir. At the same time one of the guests somehow found the armory. They assumed the worst, Master Wyrrick."

"Unfortunately they also assumed accurately," Wyrrick growled through clenched teeth. His reveal had been planned as the party's grand finale. He would spend the day wining and dining everyone only to announce that they could throw their support behind him or face the consequences. His security officers would become the head of his armed forces, and his guests would give him the power necessary to overtake the

Lucian Alliance. He'd been a few hours away from ascending to the heights of power, and it was all ruined by flirtations. It would take all of his considerable skill and charm to worm his way out of this.

He stopped to survey the damage, rage and distress mixing in his mind as he looked at the destruction of his home. Several guests were lying in heaps around the periphery of the room, and the members of the band he had booked were hiding behind their instruments on the stage. He noticed that the floor was littered with gold coins and the occasional dropped tapestry, and he realized the true loss was less noticeable.

"The treasure rooms! They are robbing me blind!"

He shoved Athen ahead of him, weaving through the crowd of furious guests. His original reasoning for the masks was that it would provide anonymity to everyone, making the most powerful Goa'uld in attendance equal with the lowliest Jaffa. Now it simply obscured the identity of those who were robbing him, prevented him from declaring vengeance simply because he couldn't be certain who was who. Those who weren't destroying his home were busy grabbing whatever they could reach and scurrying for the nearest exit.

Amid the chaos, however, he noticed something unusual; the door to one of his treasure rooms was closed. Wyrrick made his way over to it and discovered the lock was welded shut.

"What in blazes…?"

Athen grabbed the nearest armed guest, knocked the man out, then used the staff weapon to blow a hole in the door. Wyrrick rushed inside and stopped when he saw Madame Ai and Miss Oshin crouched against the back wall clutching each other in terror. Both women shrieked at the sight of him, but then Kaori gasped with relief.

"Master Wyrrick! Oh, thank heavens, we're saved!"

Wyrrick narrowed his eyes at the woman who had mysteriously vanished from his side. "Saved… what is the meaning of this? How did you come to be locked in this room?"

Kaori pushed her hair out of her face and straightened her spine. "We were overtaken by these ruffians! We tried to make them stop, but it was as if some madness had overwhelmed their senses. Madame Ai fought valiantly to protect your possessions, but there were too many for even the both of us. We were corralled into this room and they... they sealed us in." She choked back tears and pressed her hand to her lips. "Oh Dysmas. When I think of the damage these hooligans have caused to your beautiful home!"

Wyrrick felt pity for the woman and wrapped her in his arms. "There, there. You did everything you could. It was not your property to defend. Thank you, Miss Oshin, for risking harm to stand up for what is right. But now..." Something crashed out in the main room and Wyrrick winced. "Perhaps now you would consent to remaining in this room just for your own safety?"

Kaori sniffled. "Yes, it sounds quite disastrous out there. Go. We'll be fine here."

Wyrrick looked at Madame Ai. "It is my deepest regret that you were subjected to such animalistic behavior at my party."

"Don't waste time apologizing to me," she said. "Go! Stop these foolish people before they destroy your home!"

Wyrrick nodded. "I will close the door but it won't latch. You might do well to barricade yourselves inside."

"We'll do that," Kaori promised.

Wyrrick nodded and chucked his knuckle against her chin, winked, and ushered Athen back out into the fracas. Wyrrick was a large man, and he was able to forcefully disarm several people simply by grabbing their arms and squeezing until the muscle protested. "This is my home!" he bellowed. "You will not act like animals in my private residence!"

The fighters had broken up into clusters, miniature skirmishes taking place within the larger war, and Wyrrick cringed when he heard something fall to the floor and shatter. Someone grabbed his arm and he brought his fist up in anticipation of striking them before he recognized the chef, Timony. Her uniform was smeared with food and sauces, and there was a glob of something meaty on her forehead that, at first glance, seemed to be a grievous injury.

"Timony! My apologies for these working conditions." Someone swung the business end of a staff weapon at him rather than firing it, and he deflected the blow with his arm. "If you are looking for the chef you've been assisting — "

"The chef?" She laughed. "That foolish girl is long gone. I sent her back to the village to get my supplies." She ignored Wyrrick's perplexed look and carried on with her rant. "This madness will not stand, Master Wyrrick. You have provided a service for our people for a great long while, but subjecting us to this insanity will not stand. We depend upon you to protect us and now…" She swung her arm to indicate the fighting. "You brought the war to our planet, Dysmas Wyrrick. You will be taken to task for this."

Wyrrick didn't have the mental room to process the threat that had just been leveled at him. He pushed Timony out of the way and ignored her cry of protest. If the people of this world were turning against him, there was no need to feign propriety. He stepped over her and fought his way back through the crowd, a surge of panic rising in his chest as he got closer to the treasure rooms. The door with the broken lock was standing open, and he knew what he would find as soon as he stepped through the door.

The larger, bulkier items had been left untouched. But everything that could fit in a pocket or shoulder bag, every item that could conceivably be carried under someone's arm, the prizes that had been scattered across the tables nearest the door, were gone.

He stared in abject disbelief until Athen joined him in the doorway. "Sir!"

"I've been robbed!"

"By several dozen thieves, it would seem. This room is relatively untouched, in fact…"

Wyrrick slammed his fist into the door frame, realizing after his knuckles broke that his sarcophagus and healing devices had probably all been stolen. He cradled his injured hand against his stomach and tried to think of what his next step would be. The house shook violently then, a squall pushed through the broken windows of his front room so strongly that several people were knocked off their feet.

"My al'kesh… no! Not my al'kesh!"

He knocked Athen over in his haste to get to the nearest exit. The antique ship had lifted off its platform, shuddering like a leaf caught between two air currents for a moment before it rolled to the west. Its initial burst of power had caused the gust of wind that nearly toppled his house, and now its engines were struggling to keep it airborne. Wyrrick saw that Athen had joined him with a staff weapon, and he yanked it from his hand. He aimed it at the back of the ship, hoping irrationally he could disable the cargo hatch so its contents would be dumped. Unfortunately it had been years since he'd actually fired a weapon, and his shot went pathetically long. He slammed the butt of the weapon against the ground in impotent rage.

"Get the word out," he growled. "I will have the heads of Ai Okano and Oshin Kaori for my trophy wall. They will be the centerpieces of my new collection."

Something inside the house gave a weary groan, and then there was a chorus of screams as a large portion of the second floor collapsed. Wyrrick let the staff weapon fall to the ground next to him as he watched the ship cut a shaky and inelegant course along the coastline. The al'kesh was an old design, but it was sturdy and he had ensured it was maintained enough to be spaceworthy. Right now they were struggling against the pull of gravity and the weight of too much atmosphere, but that would vanish once they ascended high enough. All they had to do was keep it aloft for the next few minutes and they would be home free.

"Get someone to the DHD," Wyrrick said, his voice weary with defeat. "See if they can figure out the last dialed addresses. Try to track down anyone who is fleeing with my things." He gave a heavy sigh. "On second thought, don't waste their time."

"As you wish, Master Wyrrick."

He looked at the staff he'd dropped, rubbed his face, and then went to see if there were any survivors from his party.

"Well, that could have gone better."

"Could have gone worse," Vala said.

They had flown to the nearest gate planet and dropped the antique ship into a sand dune. The ship handled fantastically in space, but once they broke atmosphere it transformed into a tremulous bucket of metal that threatened to break apart at every shift in trajectory. They had been forced to move quickly after Wyrrick freed them from the display room. She and Tanis had pieced together their story while trying to hack the lock. When they heard Wyrrick outside they had gotten out of the way just before he blasted it open.

After that they had only seconds to load up whatever they could, using tarps and tapestries as makeshift slings. Now that their getaway was complete, they were taking the time to inventory their takings before figuring out what their next step would be. They hadn't gotten everything they wanted, but what they did have would translate into a veritable fortune for thieves like them. It was one of the biggest single paydays either of them had ever had. Vala picked up a chalice, considered it, and put it aside as a possibility.

"We got away with the treasure," Vala continued, "and we have an al'kesh. Antique." She reached up and patted the wall of the cargo hold.

"An al'kesh that barely works."

"Yes, well… whoever we unload it on doesn't have to know that. As long as it flies a little, we can cover the rest with lies."

Tanis nodded. She was sitting next to the door with her

back against the wall, her arms on her knees. "So how is this going to work? You wanted Kali's wealth so you could make up for the lost opportunity you had with Qetesh's riches. But what's my part of the take? We never really discussed what the split would be."

Vala pursed her lips. "Yes. Right…" She crossed her arms and drummed her fingers on her biceps. "To be honest, we didn't really get away with as much as I'd hoped. In fact our take was quite paltry by anyone's standards, I have to say."

"I was noticing that. We lost everything we'd already loaded onto the tel'tak… not to mention the tel'tak itself. Again."

"Right. Sorry…"

"Hmph." Tanis scratched her chin. "Seems like a conundrum."

Vala nodded slowly. Finally she sighed and rolled her eyes. "Oh, put the weapons away, Tanis."

Tanis froze. "Pardon me?"

Vala gestured at the way Tanis was sitting. "What is it, a pistol or a blade? Either way you can just leave it concealed in your boot. I heard you fumbling on the other side of the ship after we landed. Your right hand hasn't been away from your left boot for more than thirty seconds since we started counting this stuff, so I know there's something hidden in there. Keep it where it is."

"It's nothing personal. You are planning to cut me out of this, aren't you?"

"That's where you're wrong." She sighed. "I want you to take all of it."

Tanis furrowed her brow. "We went through all of this because you were on a mission to make up for your missed opportunities."

"Right." Vala tucked her hair behind her ears and looked longingly at the treasure lying spread out between them. "I did horrible things to accumulate Qetesh's wealth. When I think about them… I…" She pressed her lips together and waited until she could speak with confidence. "What am I going to do with all of this, anyway? Fence some of it, run around looking for the best deal, getting caught up in different adventures? Sounds tedious. And I'm sick of you always hanging around. Think it's best if we just part ways for a little while. So you take all of this, and you sell it, and you get a good price, and… you go home."

Tanis tensed. "There's nothing for me at home."

"The Loop of Kon Garat?" Vala said. "Come on, Tanis. You are brilliant, and you're the best pilot I've ever flown with. You have an immense talent, and you need the opportunity to put it to use. You could find a ship, kit together some neat tricks, make it the best thing flying so that it's worthy of having you at the controls. Whoever you crew with is bound to win, then you could write your own ticket. Get out from under your convictions." She poked a finger at Tanis. "A brain like yours doesn't belong in a prison and it certainly doesn't have a place pulling con jobs with me. Not that it ever came in handy. Oh, no, Miss Genius always needs me to come up with — "

Tanis got to her feet. "Are you saying you saved *me* more than I saved you? Because if so, there are quite a few things I could remind you of. Remember that depleted power coil you traded…"

"Oh, please, I had him wrapped around my little finger."

"Is that what you call teetering on the edge of oblivion, because if that is what having a handle on the situation looks like…" Tanis flinched as if she had been hit, then shook her head. "You're trying to pick a fight."

"Trying and succeeding," Vala said. "As always."

Tanis bared her teeth. "You are an insufferable egotist."

"You're an accident waiting to happen. Honestly, have you *heard* of sticking to a plan?"

"You're a petty thief," Tanis snapped.

"Big words from a sloppy brigand."

Tanis balled her hands into fists. "I should never have taken pity on you."

"Taken pity on *me*? If not for me, you'd still be rotting in that cell on some nameless moon. Would you prefer that? Because I would gladly drop you back there."

"You lost my Kull warrior suit of armor!"

"Oh *here* we *go*… did I lose it? Because I don't think you've mentioned it in the past ten minutes! You are far too sentimental!"

"You are far too reckless!"

"Three years stuck on a rock, and you, the big tech genius, couldn't even figure out what a Stargate was for! It would be hilarious if it wasn't so pathetic."

"That streak in your hair makes you look old!"

Vala was brought up short. She reached up and threaded her fingers through her hair. "It does?"

"Well. A little." The fire went out of Tanis. "It's not bad. I just think you would look better without it."

"Hm. Well. Who knows? One of these days I might be up for a change." She tossed her hair over her shoulder. "Are you done picking a fight?"

"I didn't pick…" She let her voice trail off and sighed heavily. "You're not the first person I've partnered with, you know. Corso and Pender? When I was done with them, I made sure they were stuck in a dark deep tank charged with crimes I'd committed. The guys before them? Well. I made sure no one ever decided they had hurt feelings in retrospect and came looking for me. I dissolve partnerships with knifepoints and projectiles and two blasts from a zat'nik'tel."

Vala shuffled her feet. "Yes. Well. I've made it an art of leaving without saying goodbye, so it's very odd to be standing here right now telling you to go. Take it. Let me do something good with the wealth of a System Lord. It won't heal any old scars, but maybe it will be a start of… I don't know. Redemption?"

Tanis laughed. "Redemption. Now who are you trying to con?"

"Oh, the other guy. Always the other guy."

Tanis stared at Vala for a long time, then held out her hand. "When I win the Kon Garat, I'm going to hire a crew, buy my own ship. I'm going to call it the Mal Doran."

Vala flinched. "Ugh, don't do that."

Tanis held out her hand over the pile of goods. "Next time you need a more intelligent trickster to save your butt, come find me."

"Done." Vala gripped Tanis' arm just above the wrist. "And if you ever need your fat pulled out of a fire, I'll be around."

Tanis released Vala's arm and looked greedily at the treasure that was now entirely hers. "So what happens now? You take the al'kesh, or...?"

"You take the al'kesh. You'll need it to carry all your loot. I'll take the Stargate back to Lucia, see if I can hitch a ride with someone. I'm sure there are always people willing to give a lift to a damsel in distress. And if not, I can come up with a story they'll fall for."

"Yeah, you're pretty good at getting where you need to be. Well... we had a good run, you and I."

Vala nodded. "Indeed we did. Caused a little destruction along the way..."

"A sure sign of a successful career."

"I shall sincerely miss you, Tanis Reynard."

"Same to you. Vala Mal Doran... a force to be reckoned with. If only because you can never figure out just what the hell she's going to do next."

Vala preened a bit, then grinned. "Best of luck in the race, Tanis."

"Best of luck wherever you end up."

Vala went up to the cockpit and gathered her things, a few paltry items that she could fit into a shoulder bag. Tanis dumped in a handful of coins from the loot downstairs when she thought Vala wasn't looking, and Vala pretended not to notice. They hugged at the doorway, and for a moment Tanis' arms tightened around Vala's waist. There was a moment when

Vala patted her now-former partner's shoulder and she knew they were having an honestly, human, emotional moment. She didn't like it one bit, so she pulled away and sighed.

"Maybe on your way home you can stop by and see Baleya."

Tanis raised an eyebrow. "Yeah? Think she'd want to see me?"

"Oh, I'd count on it, Tanis Reynard." She winked. "Be safe out there."

"You too."

Vala left the ship and moved a safe distance away, holding up her hand to block the dust kicked up by its engines. Tanis executed a sloppy turn and smiled at Vala through the glass. Vala cupped her hands over her mouth and shouted, "Perhaps I could stick around a bit longer! At least until you find a pilot who can actually fly!"

Tanis couldn't possibly have heard her, but she lifted her hands to execute an obscene gesture nonetheless. She smiled, blew Vala a kiss, and began gaining altitude. Vala watched as the sun glinted off the sleek hull of the ship, keeping her eyes on its journey until it was obscured by clouds and distance.

Left alone on the planet, Vala sighed and walked to the local DHD to dial Lucia.

CHAPTER TWENTY-TWO

MORELLO splashed water on her face, blotted her cheeks and forehead with a paper towel, and then looked at her reflection in the mirror. She took a few steadying breaths, tugged at the collar of her uniform jacket, and finally walked out of the locker room. The pre-mission routine was just that, rote and familiar enough that she could go through it in her sleep. She had been on twenty missions with SG-9 so this morning should be exactly like any other.

She entered the gate room and saw the people she was temporarily assigned with waiting alongside General O'Neill, and her mental pep talk faded to silence. This was no ordinary trip, not by a longshot. She was going on a mission with SG-1. She might as well be walking on stage to sing a duet with Mick Jagger.

Teal'c, one of the first Jaffa to openly defy his god, the man who had done more to defeat the Goa'uld than any other single person, was once again wearing the green uniform of the SGC. Lately when he visited the base he only wore Jaffa robes, a symbol of his dedication to helping his people navigate the rocky seas of freedom after generations of enslavement. He looked comfortable in the BDUs, but she knew he belonged in the robes.

Doctor Daniel Jackson, her idol and real-life Indiana Jones, was speaking quietly to O'Neill. As soon as Kali had provided them with the address of the planet where the Purge was set to begin, Daniel had gone to work comparing Earth's orbit with that of Kali's planet so that he could accurately calculate how long they had before her device activated. Fortunately in the end they had added time, two whole hours, rather than deducting. But still, there was no point in hesitation. Twenty-nine hours were all that stood between the Jaffa and genocide.

Colonel Samantha Carter looked at Morello as she entered and offered a smile. Carter was also something of a mentor to her. A young captain when she started at the SGC, she had risen quickly through the ranks until she was commanding their flagship team. There were rumors all around that she was considering reassignment, and Morello knew that she could have her pick of postings from Atlantis to Area 51. Morello also knew that she would be incredibly lucky to have a career half as impressive as Carter's, and if she did it would be because Carter had paved the way.

"Ready to go?" Carter asked.

"As ready as I'll ever be."

She nodded and looked into the control room. "We're ready for the prisoner."

The technician nodded and picked up the phone, and Morello looked at the gathered team. She was going on a mission with SG-1. *The* SG-1, god killers and world savers. And they were going on a mission with a captive Goa'uld who, if she fulfilled her part of the bargain, they would let go. Part of her still felt like it was bargaining with the devil, but she supposed the ends would justify the means. They had to save the Jaffa, and the ticking clock cut their options way down.

Daniel and Sam checked the components of the pedestal while they were waiting. It had been loaded onto a MALP, which was positioned with its wheels on the ramp. Someone approached Morello, and she resisted the urge to jump when she realized it was General O'Neill.

"You okay?"

"Doing fine, sir."

"You ever hear the story of Colonel Carter's first trip through the gate?"

Carter looked up at the mention of her name.

"No, sir."

"She got so distracted by the fluctuations in the event horizon that I had to push her through."

Carter rolled her eyes. "I would have gone through on my own, sir."

O'Neill said, "Yes, eventually. I'm just letting the captain know that it's okay to be a little... awestruck by things. If you're not taking a few seconds every day to have your mind blown about what you're doing for a living, you don't belong in this business."

"Thank you, General."

A group of airmen entered the room flanking the prisoner. Kali had been allowed to change back into her usual outfit, but she still looked diminished. The erstwhile goddess wore shackles on her wrists and ankles connected by a chain. General O'Neill approached her and, after an incredibly brief staring contest, the Goa'uld looked toward the gate.

"These are the coordinates I gave you?"

"Yep. We sent a UAV through earlier, just to make sure it was as abandoned as you claimed. Your little palace has seen better days."

Kali scoffed. "Haven't we all."

"I don't know. Things around here have been pretty sweet for the past little bit. Ever since you guys got booted to the curb... yeah." He nodded. "The deal is, you send whatever code you need to send to keep this plague from being sent out, and then you take apart the network so we don't have to deal with you ever again. My people confirm you've done that, we'll send you on your merry way."

"We have an accord, General O'Neill."

She was escorted to the ramp, and O'Neill stepped closer to Daniel. "Think we can trust her?"

Daniel shrugged. "Normally I'd say a Goa'uld is a Goa'uld. But Kali kept a strong alliance with Bastet even through the rough periods when turning on her could have been beneficial. She plays the odds. Right now there's nothing to prevent her from helping us."

"Hm. If you say so. Okay, SG-1..." He turned and gestured

to Walter and the Stargate began to dial. "Have fun storming the castle."

"We will, sir."

Morello watched as the general left the room and then caught Daniel's eye. "Did the leader of this base just quote *The Princess Bride*?"

Daniel said, "Yeah… uh. You get used to it. Eventually."

The event horizon formed like a wave crashing on shore, an experience that still made the hairs on the back of her neck stand up. She blinked at it and looked back at Daniel.

"And that?"

"No," Daniel said with a smile. "That, you never get used to."

Teal'c went through first, followed by the contingent of security assigned to watch Kali. They were followed by Daniel using the remote to guide the MALP, leaving Morello and Carter to approach the event horizon together.

Carter lowered her voice. "Do you want me to push you through? It's actually kind of fun."

Morello grinned. "No, ma'am. But thank you."

They passed through and Morello blinked in the sunlight. She took her sunglasses from the pocket of her vest and slid them on.

"Something else you never get used to," Daniel said.

"I thought all of Kali's palaces were dark… oh." Her voice trailed off as her eyes adjusted and she saw the truth. They were inside one of Kali's palaces, but several walls had been reduced to piles of rubble so that the sky was exposed. The MALP was parked on uneven ground formed by fallen rock and debris.

Daniel said, "I guess the Jaffa didn't stop at just ransacking the place."

Kali was staring at the devastation but seemed to physically shake it off. She lifted her shackled hands. "The pedestal was situated just beyond this wall."

Daniel and Teal'c lifted the pieces off the MALP and followed Kali into the side room. There they discovered another table like the one that had started their quest. Kali indicated they should attach the pedestal to the end away from the Stargate. Sam observed and lent a hand when it came time to reconnect the control systems to the main device.

"Captain Morello?" she said. "You're the one who took apart the systems on the other table. How does this look?"

"Oh. Um…" She moved closer and crouched down. Together with Sam she managed to reconnect the systems. There was a sudden frisson of energy as it was tapped back into its power source. "That should do it."

Daniel looked at Kali. "Now what?"

"I send the signal, and it's passed through the network. Once they receive the order, they return to stand-by mode. This time I will send the blackout signal. They will all go dark once and for all."

"Hopefully you won't be offended if we keep an eye on you as you enter the code."

"I would expect nothing less."

She stepped forward and took her position in front of the control panel. She rested her palm on a flat surface until the DHD lit up. She typed in a command, which Daniel and Teal'c both observed. "This will only prevent the next deadline. When that is completed, I will dial again with the complete shutdown." She dialed the gate and they watched as a section of the wall slid out of the way. She rested her hand on a dome that resembled the central piece of the DHD. After a few seconds, the Stargate disengaged and she nodded. "It is done. The rest will be contacted in turn, and the Stargate here will open again when the circuit is complete."

"How long should that take?" Sam asked.

"Not long. Approximately seventeen minutes."

Sam checked her watch and did the mental math Daniel had come up with. Seventeen minutes on this planet roughly translated to twenty-four Earth minutes. "Can you send the kill code while we're waiting?"

"No. The circuit must be completed before a second command is entered."

Daniel sighed. "Okay. Looks like we're sticking around for half an hour. Hope everyone brought a book or something."

While they waited for the cycle to end, Sam and Teal'c did a quick perimeter search of the grounds to make sure the palace really was abandoned. When they returned to the room, Sam noticed that Daniel was watching Captain Morello. The young woman was across the room using her camera to record the carvings that had escaped destruction. Sam sat down next to Daniel and nudged his arm.

"Got a crush?"

"Hm? Oh. No… no, of course not. But she's good. She's very good. She convinced Kali to help us. I mean, that alone is impressive."

Sam nodded slowly. "Yes, it is. It shouldn't be a surprise, though. No one gets this far in the SGC without being in the top percentile." She watched his face. "You're looking for a replacement."

He looked at her, smiled, and shrugged. "It would be nice to know there was someone who could take over if I ever make it to Atlantis. Not to mention the fact I'd feel like I was abandoning you."

"SG-1 could take on a whole new meaning… one member left standing."

"Well, if anyone could make a one-person team work, it's you."

Sam chuckled and bumped his knee with her fist. "I've been thinking along the same lines, actually. The next step. General O'Neill and Teal'c are both moving on, you're trying to get to Atlantis come hell or high water. SG-1 would be an entirely different team anyway, so why be precious about something that's already gone? I guess I'm just exploring my options at the moment."

Daniel nodded. "Same here. I don't want to sound egotistical, I know there have always been people qualified to take my place at the SGC at a moment's notice. I knew they were out there. It's just nice to have it confirmed so completely. As long as Morello is here, I feel confident being... elsewhere. You, though. I think you'll be a little harder to replace."

Sam scoffed. "Please. In a couple of years, Cassie is going to graduate and then I'll be old news. In the meantime, I have an open invitation to Area 51. I might be able to do more good there than out here running from one planet to the next. I could have a lot of fun reverse engineering some of the things we've brought back over the years."

"Just don't make anything to replace iPods. I can't afford to buy all my music again."

She smiled. "I'll do my best." She tilted her head back and squinted into the sky. "Besides, there are a lot of things I've been putting off the past few years. A lot of decisions I put off making..."

Daniel smiled knowingly. "Why do I get the feeling we're not talking about professional considerations anymore?"

She looked away from the sky and smiled at him.

Teal'c approached and said, "It is time."

"Yeah, I think it is." Sam broke the moment she'd been sharing with Daniel and slapped her hands down on her knees. "Let's go"

They stood up and gathered at the pedestal again as the Stargate came to life. Kali watched the display and nodded slowly.

"It is done. The machines have been silenced for this circuit. I will now send the code to deactivate them permanently."

"You'll forgive us if we take a little tour of your planets later to make sure you're telling the truth."

Kali smiled scornfully. "It is your time. Waste it as you wish. But you have my word that once this command is entered, each device on every world will be shut down. The

Jaffa will be safe. And I have your word that you will follow your end of the bargain?"

"We honor our promises," Sam said.

"Very well." Kali activated the Stargate again and, after a moment, she began entering the code.

EPILOGUE

JACK looked up as Teal'c entered his office. The BDUs were gone, replaced by standard Jaffa robes. He leaned back in his seat and dropped his pen, sighing as Teal'c stood in front of him.

"I guess this is goodbye again."

"Indeed. The news of Kali's defeat must be spread among the Jaffa so they know it is once again safe to use their Stargates. I feel I must also do... damage control, should there be any doubt following my subterfuge at Dysmas Wyrrick's party."

"Teal'c, trust me, anyone who knows you would understand exactly what you were doing."

Teal'c inclined his head at the compliment. "Be that as it may, the more I am seen, the stronger the truth shall be."

"Right."

"And what of you, O'Neill? Have your concerns regarding this position abated?"

Jack took a deep breath and looked around the office. "Um. Yes. And no." He drummed his pen on the desk before leaning back in his seat. "I'm starting to wonder if I'm the right guy to be making the decisions around here, to be honest. Someone who won't play favorites."

"Perhaps there are other possibilities for you in another position."

"Yes," Jack said thoughtfully. "Possibilities... Well, that can wait. For now, we need to get you back where you belong."

He stood up and held out his hand. Teal'c gripped it tightly. When he tried to let go, Jack tightened his hold. He narrowed his eyes suspiciously. "You're... coming back, right? Eventually? If just to say an official goodbye? See, we have this whole thing we do where there's cake and... well. You know me and cake."

Teal'c smiled. "I will return, O'Neill."

"Good. Just making sure." He released Teal'c's hand. "I'll

walk you down to the gate room."

"As you wish."

Jack adjusted his jacket and gestured for Teal'c to lead the way out. He patted Teal'c on the shoulder as they passed through the briefing room.

"And, hey, if you're ever in the neighborhood, it doesn't even have to be an official visit. Swing by the cabin. We'll fish, I'll catch us some dinner, we'll watch some hockey... Stanley Cup is right around the corner, ya know..."

Vala didn't believe in miracles or quirks of fate. She thought the universe was a very structured place where bizarre things routinely happened. She believed it was the sort of place that would eventually reward her selfless gesture of giving Tanis the whole treasure, but she didn't expect to step through the gate on Lucia to discover their stolen tel'tak sitting a few yards away.

She approached cautiously, cupped her hands against the front glass to make sure no one was home, then gave the area a quick look to see if someone was lying in wait to catch her in the act. It seemed safe. It seemed utterly and entirely set up for her, so she keyed in her entry code — unchanged, another sign that it was meant to be — and went inside to discover the vast majority of the treasure Tanis had loaded up was still there. Whoever had stolen it from Wyrrick's planet must have flown it here and left it behind when they moved on.

"Well. How do you like that? Everything works out in the end."

She secured the ship before she got into the pilot's seat. She had to adjust its position a bit; whoever had sat there last had been extremely tall. She took off quickly, leaving the planet behind in case anyone else had designs on taking the ship for themselves. Plotting an actual destination could wait for the moment. She tried to think of where she would go next, what rumors she would chase down. She had a few irons in the fire, loads of opportunities to increase her wealth. And just unloading what she had in the cargo hold would take her a few months.

After that, there were really no limits.

Maybe she could swing by and see what the Tau'ri were up to after the war? She had a few Ancient artifacts she thought Daniel Jackson might find interesting. And if he was reluctant, she had some Goa'uld artifacts that could force him to stay by her side. Worst case scenario, she might have a chance to get Tanis' Kull warrior armor back to settle things between them. She hated being in anyone's debt.

Vala rubbed her hands together and began entering coordinates. It was settled: she would get rid of the excess souvenirs from Wyrrick's collection, then she would use the funds to bankroll information that could get her through the Tau'ri's iris. All in all it should take a few months, if that, to get everything prepared. And whatever happened when she got there, she had no doubt it would be an adventure.

She grinned and set out for a reliable fence who could start bankrolling her next quest.

"Get ready, Daniel Jackson. Your life is about to take a turn for the exciting."

ABOUT THE AUTHOR

Geonn Cannon lives in Oklahoma. He is the author of several novels, including the five-part *Riley Parra* series which is currently being produced as a webseries for Tello Films.

He can be found online at geonncannon.com.

STARGATE SG·1.

STARGATE ATLANTIS

Original novels based on the hit TV shows **STARGATE SG-1** and **STARGATE ATLANTIS**

Available as e-books from leading online retailers

Paperback editions available from Amazon and IngramSpark

If you liked this book, please tell your friends and leave a review on a bookstore website. Thanks!